BURY ME
WITH BARBIE

BURY ME WITH BARBIE

By Wyborn Senna

This book is dedicated to Danna Dykstra-Coy, the best next-desk mate I could wish for as well as a kick-ass crime reporter back when *The Tribune* was *The Telegram-Tribune* in San Luis Obispo and Jeff Fairbanks was still with us. It is also dedicated to those who know how many birds are embroidered on the Skipper on Wheels top, what color glitter adorns Barbie doll's 1966 Sears Exclusive Pink Formal, what plastic accessory came with Ken doll's #1416 College Student and what color shoes belong to Francie doll's Check This.

Bent are our minds and all our thoughts on fire, Still striving in the pangs of hot desire, At once like misers wallowing in their store Of full possession, yet desiring more.

Rochester, Poems on Affairs of State, 1697

1

Most Barbie doll collectors have been known to say, "I would kill to have that," but P.J. Croesus meant it literally.

They say it's important to look at the first kill in serial slayings because it typically hits close to home for the murderer—literally or psychologically.

P.J.'s target had been driving her crazy on a message board populated by those as manic as she to score the best vintage Barbie dolls from the Sixties.

Every time P.J. won something vintage on eBay and shared pictures with the group, Gayle Grace would point out that what P.J. had won was far from perfect and that she herself had something better under protective glass in her very own temperature-controlled doll room. This happened for the thirtieth time (by P.J.'s careful count) on the first Saturday in January of 2008 with regard to a flawless Debutante Ball gown she had won, which Gayle claimed had a replacement rosebud because the shade was slightly off.

What kind of idiot did Gayle think P.J. was? Yes, P.J. had auto-corrected the coloring in Photoshop, but a shadow cast across the room ruined what would have been a perfect digital picture. For Gayle to assume the rosebud on the dress wasn't the exact shade it should be was absolutely and definitively the moment P.J. decided to kill her, no matter what.

Getting Gayle's address was no biggie. On the message board, they all swapped home addresses for Christmas cards. Gayle lived in Oswego, New York, and P.J. lived in Southern California. Even that was not off-putting. P.J. knew how to get on a bus, train, or plane. She knew how to rent a car. She knew how to book a hotel room. She even had a half-brother who spent six years in jail who could tell her ways to kill a person that hadn't even come up on the Internet. She had money. She had time. She had opportunity.

She had picked her first victim.

2

P.J. made it to SUNY Oswego and located Sheldon Hall at the corner of Washington and Sheldon. She'd gotten a Christmas card from Gayle two years earlier which displayed the Grace home, bedecked in lights and garlands. On the front of the photo card, Gayle and her husband Mike stood outside in the cold. They rested alongside the family car, which had its license plate in full view. Their arms were raised and waving. To P.J., they could have been any two thickly bundled strangers whose faces were inscrutable in the deep recesses of their parka hoods.

The Graces drove an older white Saturn. After driving around the parking lots flanking Sheldon Hall for a good two minutes, P.J. found it parked at the far right end of the back lot, facing outward toward Takamine Road and Rich Hall. Snow was swirling up and around the Saturn and the cars parked near it. P.J. parked the burgundy Altima she had rented from the East Avenue branch of Enterprise and stepped into the cold, seven spaces away from her target vehicle. The snowfall was so thick and wet she could not see more than twenty feet in front of her. But she trusted in the fact that, as she could see no one, no one could see her. The coat she wore contained what she needed to get her first job done. Her half-brother Darby had walked her through what she needed to do, not twice but thrice.

P.J. went over to the Saturn and kicked away the snow from underneath the front bumper and tires. Then she lay down on the ground in front of the vehicle. She had never felt this cold in her entire life. She had no idea if she was going to be able to feel her fingers, which tingled and felt prickly despite lined leather gloves, if the job took longer than expected. Looking up, she saw the red spark plug wire she needed to locate inside the engine. She pulled the spark plug wire off the spark plug and fumbled inside her coat for her needle-nosed pliers. Next, she spit on the tips of two gloved fingers and rubbed the saliva into the wire above the boot of the spark plug wire. The needle-nosed pliers went inside the boot next. She grabbed hold of the spark plug connector and pushed the boot back over the wire. In her front left-hand pocket, she found the long piece of speaker wire she needed. Wrapping one end of the speaker wire around the spark plug metal, she struggled a bit to toss the other end of the speaker wire toward the rear tires.

Gently easing herself out from under the front bumper, she brushed herself off. She straightened her coat and looked around, refocusing her sights across the street. The façade of Rich Hall rose from the snow and shadows. Packs of padded bodies braced themselves against the wind as they struggled toward dining halls, meetings, and classes.

P.J. picked her way through the deep snowfall and made her way to the back of the car. Once the gas tank was open, she retrieved the end of the wire she had thrown underneath the car and reeled in the length of it. Darby had told her to push at least a couple feet into the tank, but she had more than that to spare. She fed the wire in slowly until it fell in a straight line from the tank to the ground before disappearing beneath the car. She resolved to put her legs in motion and head back to the Altima. She was uncertain she had done everything correctly but wouldn't know how to fix things even if she suspected something wasn't right. Briefly, she looked heavenward and gave a slight nod. God willing, she would have her way.

Luck was with her as she navigated the streets bordering the state university. She easily found Gayle's ranch style home, its long, low profile and large windows crouched in snow banks in a neighborhood bound within a triangle of roads pointing like a planchette at Lake Ontario beyond the Campus Center. Located among cross streets bound by Washington, Swift, and West Seneca, P.J. did not have far to drive.

The home, as predicted, was empty. Both Gayle and her husband Mike had no children and only one pet—an old gray tabby named Frank. Through notes on the message board, P.J. had learned that, in addition to working Monday through Friday, Gayle and Mike liked to stroll around the university's 700-acre campus and they occasionally picnicked at Glimmer Glass Lagoon. Every July, Gayle raved about Harborfest. Every October, it was all about the pumpkins, since Oswego was one of twenty international weigh-in sites for pumpkin growers competing in the Great Pumpkin Commonwealth. But nothing Gayle had mentioned on the boards about Oswego being "cold" prepared her for the gusty winds and frigid temperatures residents endured each winter.

P.J. fought against the wind to get out of the four-door rental. She had parked on the street, where snowplows were making the rounds. Her tire marks would be indiscernible by late afternoon. The snow was still falling without respite, offering a veil of privacy.

The alcove on the Grace porch was well hidden from onlookers as she worked the piece of plastic that was thinner than a credit card on her first lock. Blocked by sheared Arborvitae standing sentry toward the road, P.J. felt as though she had all the time in the world, but she knew she should hurry lest she encounter the unexpected postal worker or UPS man. Gayle bought a lot on eBay, and that stuff had to get to her front door somehow.

The wooden door creaked inward on hinges in need of oil. Warm air rushed out at P.J., who sighed with relief. Her feet were clad in white vinyl go-go boots she'd only worn once before, on Halloween. Stomping her heels, she left a clump or two of snow on the doormat placed directly inside the doorway.

Frank the cat, a friendly soul, approached and sniffed her legs. P.J. smiled despite herself. The canvas duffel bag she had brought along was slack at her side; now to find the doll room. The entry hall led to a living room on the right and a kitchen and bathroom straight ahead. Decorated in Laura Ashley English cabbage roses and ribbons, the place had a traditional, staid appeal. Maple furniture passed down from G.I. Generation parents filled the home, and the carpeting throughout was plush olive.

Skipping the living room and kitchen, P.J. opted to head left. She walked down a hallway that led to two very different rooms, one quite obviously a bedroom and the other undeniably a doll haven.

The doll sanctuary was dark, but there were lamps in all four corners of the room. Still wearing gloves, P.J. flipped the wall switch and surveyed the windowless room. Light controlled, check. Temperature controlled—if Gayle had meant constantly warmer than freezing—check. Dolls in abundance lining the walls in glass-fronted maple curios—oh, holy check of all checks, what a place! Gayle owned every 1600-series outfit shown in Eames. They were not "never-removed-from-box," also known as NRFB, for that honor went to the very few who seldom talked about what they had, and never on the message boards—but this room was awesome in its own right.

Before the big dolls known as American Girls were introduced to the doll world, there were American Girl Barbie dolls, also known as AGs. The outfits here were modeled by the most exquisite array of American Girl Barbie dolls P.J. had ever seen. Her gaze settled first on a high-color, longhaired silver blond with stunning, full ruby lips, dressed in Midnight Blue. The outfit was complete, with long white gloves, deep blue open-toed shoes, and a silver dimple purse. A blond American Girl came next, dressed in the fabulous white and gold lame Holiday Dance. Beside her, a longhaired titian beauty wore the original AG swimsuit. The puffy top featured vertical stripes in a riot of colors, offsetting the suit's solid turquoise jersey trunk. Classic open-toe matching heels completed the look.

On the next shelf, a platinum blond AG in Lunch On The Terrace, a titian AG in Outdoor Art Show, and a cinnamon brownette in Pretty As A Picture formed a stunning trio. They were followed by a standard brownette and a dark brownette, the first dressed in the pastel blue Reception Line and the second in the soft pink Fashion Luncheon.

Gayle indeed owned Debutante Ball, as she had claimed on the Best Barbie Board, and P.J. was quick to note that the rosebud at the waistline on this dress was precisely the same shade as hers, no doubt about it. She felt faint and needed to sit down. A deep, thick-cushioned chair had been squeezed into the corner between two cases. She made her way over to it and collapsed into its plush depth.

The house was utterly still and, transfixed by the beauty around her, she found it hard to breathe. Frank came in and jumped in her lap, staring into her eyes with his imperturbable golden gaze. A moment passed. P.J. stroked the cat with her sodden gloved hands. Then she stood and placed him to the right of her feet on the floor.

There were eight dolls on every shelf. Moving from case to case, she cherry-picked five from every group. Where eight had stood before, she spaced the remaining three out evenly. Fifty dolls and a full duffel bag later, she made her way to the doll sanctuary door, snapping the lights off via the wall switch.

Frank had left the room. P.J. crept down the hallway to the front doorway, stopping only to drop the duffel to the floor. She lifted the bag with her left hand to give her right side a break. At the front door, she indented the lock button near the knob and went out, gently closing Gayle's domain behind her.

A few blocks away and some hours later, the late afternoon winter sun was setting. Gayle and Mike got into their Saturn, discussing the merits of salmon versus pasta for dinner and whether or not they were caught up with must-sees on TiVo.

Mike got in on the driver's side. His wife happily rode shotgun—their normal routine. The key hit the ignition while Mike was mid-sentence, discussing McCain's chances in the 2008 Presidential election. Once the key hit, sparks went off inside the tank and the Grace family car exploded. One door flew off and hit the stop sign at the intersection. The closest car remaining in the parking lot this late in the day was showered with chunks of metal and glass.

Astonished students and administrative personnel came running, coatless and bootless, out of nearby buildings.

Upon arriving at the wreckage, most were initially too stunned to act.

By the time someone realized they should call 911, P.J. was well on her way to the Buffalo Airport to return her rental car to Enterprise's sister agency. Snowfall had turned into sheets of graupel midway through her 113-mile drive on Interstate 90—the bulk of the 147-mile journey—but even hail could not dampen her spirits.

The burgundy Altima, awash in a sea of pelting precipitation, moved effortlessly along the thruway despite the violent storm. Inside the car, P.J. played Seal's *Kiss From a Rose* twenty times before it occurred to her that she might listen to news on the car radio to find out if there had been any accidents up near Lake Ontario. Then she shook her head, realizing she didn't want to spoil her day if the rigged Saturn hadn't exploded.

She could make better use of her time if she unzipped the duffel bag beside her to see what she could of her treasure. While keeping one eye on the road, she managed to get the duffel fully open. The first doll she pulled out, a blond AG in Student Teacher, did the trick of sending her spirits soaring. The doll had all her accessories—the black pointer, the turquoise cardboard Geography textbook, and the aqua and black globe on its white plastic pedestal. They were sealed in a mini baggie tied to the doll's wrist with two-millimeter red silk ribbon.

P.J.'s voice was a bit hoarse but filled with emotion. "Well, girlfriend, it looks like you've got the world in a bag."

Her imitation of Barbie doll was classic Cockney. "Oh, but your bag is ever so much bigger, and you're going to get ever so much more!"

P.J. laughed out loud. Who said a woman in her thirties was too old to play with dolls?

3

Caresse Redd wasn't jealous of her best friend Anjo Josephs, the *San Luis Obispo County Times'* crime reporter, but there were days she wished, as a staff writer herself, she could address more than run-of-the-mill community fare. In addition to holding the most boring writing job at the paper, she was also considered the resident weirdo because she liked dolls—specifically Barbie dolls, and she moonlighted as a staff writer for the international Barbie collectors' magazine. Favorite offbeat topics she'd covered included a series of interviews with a woman who claimed to channel the spirit of Barbie doll's genius Jackie O. designer Charlotte Armstrong and a preppie couple who had rebuilt a life-size version of Barbie doll's New Dream House in Denver. As an at-home hobby, she customized Barbie doll's friends, including her younger sisters Skipper and Kelly, making the dolls over into one-of-a-kind wonders, occasionally re-rooting their hair with saran in a bevy of exotic shades like Fire Mist and Sea Glow.

An example of Caresse's handiwork stood on Anjo's desk. Anjo had requested a one-of-a-kind Ken Cop the year she turned thirty-five. Now he stood, stern-faced, near Anjo's phone, his Monopoly token-sized gun aimed straight at her, daring her to take the next call. Anjo laughed at least once a day when she looked at him.

She was pounding out obits when Anjo's pager went off.

"Where do you have to go?"

She glanced down at it. "An Oceano man pointed a gun at a crew working construction on Highway 1 earlier today."

"Allegedly."

"Allegedly. He lived across the way, and witnesses identified him. The deputies commanded him out of his home. They went in, found the weapon, and arrested him."

"Why was he upset with the construction guys? Was it them or was it what they were doing?"

Anjo shrugged. "Wouldn't say, but I hear talk he's a definite 51-50. I've already been out there once. Looks like I'm headed back."

Caresse grinned. "When are the 51-50s gonna learn it's not okay to brandish firearms in a threatening manner?"

Anjo laughed. "Just keep them away from the silverware, and they're great."

Wishing Anjo could pack her in with her gear, Caresse dragged her feet toward the cafeteria, where Jenna Donaghy, the Arts and Entertainment editor, liked to hold meetings. Caresse felt no better than the *County Times'* equivalent of a floating waitress, helping others but never having a station of her own.

The piece she would have to write was worse than expected. Jenna's brilliant idea was for four staff writers to answer personal ads and go on dates, writing about their experiences, sharing them in the weekend supplement due out the weekend before Valentine's Day.

"I'm going to do it myself," Jenna exclaimed, as a chunk of hair flopped forward onto her face. She blew upwards and smoothed it back, then jumped off the table and repositioned her micro jeans skirt. "I just love romance, all that yummy stuff."

"Fabio," Rhea said, Cheetos falling from her mouth.

Bree giggled. "I can't believe it's not butter."

Caresse got up, signaling that she got the message and knew what to do.

She also knew something else: she didn't want to do it.

She was 37. She was divorced. She was a mom. She was tired.

City Editor Seth Tanner poked his head into the room. Blond and moon-faced, with round-lensed glasses, he grinned and wagged a finger at Caresse, who promptly rose and walked over to him.

"You like Barbie dolls, right?" he asked. He fiddled with his Palm TX, brought up a news story, gave the PDA to her, and studied her expression as she read the condensed newsflash. The online photo showed upstate New York crime scene investigators working around the debris of an extirpated Saturn, one of them holding what looked to be a speaker cover. The headline read, "Oswego Couple Dies In Explosion," with the subheading, "Wife's Barbie Doll Collection Missing."

She scrolled down and read the summary.

An unusual connection has been made between the two beloved SUNY Oswego College employees who died as a result of a rigged car bombing and Barbie dolls. In searching the home of the late Mike and Gayle Grace, who were found dead on the scene in the back parking lot at Sheldon Hall yesterday, Gayle's sister Megan Dailon has informed detectives that the Barbie doll collection Gayle coveted has been marauded.

Dailon affirms her sister's collection was safe as recently as last week, when she dropped by to have dinner with the late couple. "Gayle and I talked about her Barbie dolls all the time," Dailon said. "She loved her collection and took time to look at it daily, because it was her cherished hobby. The placement of each of her dolls on each of her shelves was very important to her. She knew what she had, and she knew what she still wanted to get. We kept an inventory of every doll and outfit. What is left of her collection since the homicides does not even begin to suggest the scope of what she owned. Her best dolls, dressed in the ensembles she cherished most, are now gone. Whoever stole them knew the value of what they took and made only the poorest attempt to make the collection appear undisturbed. There is no doubt in my mind the death of my sister and her husband are directly related to the theft of her Barbie dolls."

She looked up, stunned.

"I know," Seth said, accepting back the PDA. "Totally up your alley."

4

P.J. went to visit her half-brother the following Tuesday. He lived ten miles away in Glendale, in an apartment complex that was built partially beneath the Glendale Freeway near Harvey Drive.

Darby's best friends in the complex were a couple of married drunks who didn't need New Year's Eve to make it a party. The joke was that they both worked in health-care—Bob as a transporter of medical equipment to various hospitals and Bev as a nurse at a local hospital's mater-nity center. A trip down three stairs past the laundry room brought a person to their door and into a world of hard booze and painkillers. If Darby wasn't home, he was likely with Bob and Bev, getting stoned and watching Comedy Central courtesy of Charter Cable.

On this Tuesday evening, however, Darby was home.

He was resting a recent injury to his already ruined back and enjoying Internet porn. When he let P.J. in, he turned to see what was on his monitor before rushing across the room to close a site showing pictures of Swedish girls vomiting into each other's mouths.

P.J. laughed as she flopped onto the aging brown couch and put her feet up on the arm at the far end. "Have you seen the *South Park* 'Logging On' episode? I'm sur-prised you're not looking at Brazilian Fart Porn."

Darby was glad to see his half-sister in a relaxed mood. He straightened his Lakers' cap and sat down across from the couch in an overstuffed brown chair.

"So when'd you make it back?"

"Sunday. Goddamn Amtrak takes four days to go cross-country."

"But the way they've not been checking IDs and keep-ing records, you're home free."

"It worked," she agreed.

Darby went back to the computer desk that faced a porch overlooking a garden bed, the complex garage entrance, and the street below. He Googled "SUNY" plus "Oswego" plus "car" plus "explosion" and came up with the front-page news. Photos of Gayle and Mike, cropped to equal height and width, were embedded in the lede of the article that began in larger font on the left-hand side of the screen. No longer were they two thickly bundled strangers whose faces were hidden in parka hoods. Gayle was a chubby-cheeked brunette with blond highlights in her hair. She wore a strand of pearls, a conservative, high-collared blouse, and simple gold button earrings. Mike's dark hair, gray at the temples and cut short, was parted on the right. His charcoal suit was accessorized with a wide orange and blue striped tie held in place with a diamond tack.

To balance the photos on the left, the right-hand side of the layout was devoted to the investigation. Darby read quietly for a few minutes while P.J. alternated between resting her eyes and gazing at the back of his full head of light brown hair, poorly cut but tucked neatly inside the purple and gold cap. Her half-brother's hair was darker than hers; he had inherited his melanin-rich coloring from his dad's side of the family. Their eyes, however, were their mother's ice-flecked iolite.

When Darby was satisfied, he turned around. "Looks like you listened to the master." He was younger than P.J., but he never lost an opportunity to remind her that when shove came to thrust, he could be smarter, swifter, and shiftier.

"Yep, so what's next?" She smoothed down the front of her pale blue blouse and used the toe of one loafer to peel down the back of her other shoe. It clunked on the floor and the second one followed.

"Are you losing weight?" Darby rubbed the bridge of his nose. She looked great—in fact, quite a bit like the classic Barbie dolls she collected—and he found himself fantasizing for the thousandth time that she would have dated him if they weren't related, but the odds were against him. She was miles above him socially and was married to a successful entrepreneur with two degrees and a great job. She was smart and had her own business. She was beautiful. She was a bitch. She needed him, but she oftentimes found him pathetic.

While Darby considered P.J. that evening, P.J. analyzed Darby in the looks department and gave him a failing grade. "Did anyone ever tell you that you look like the Unabomber?" P.J.'s face was screwed up when she said this, so he couldn't tell whether she was serious or laughing at him. "Finish growing a mustache and grab yourself some old Aviator frame sunglasses and you'll be all set."

The similarities were indeed there, and not just any facial features he might share with Ted Kaczynski. Given the opportunity to blow something up or burn it down, explosions won hand over fist.

"I was thinking about that," Darby said, clearing his throat and sloughing off P.J.'s rude remark. He walked across the room and returned to his chair.

He looked around the high-ceilinged room plastered with metal signs from bottling companies and gas stations. Some were reproductions and some were original. His gaze stopped as he focused on an old Coca-Cola sign above the door. The sign, twenty by twenty-eight inches, had the words "ice cold" on the first line, white letters on green. The middle band read "Coca-Cola" in script, white letters on red. The bottom line told prospective buyers, "sold here," repeating the top line's color scheme. A green glass Coke bottle with a metal cap and a green-on-green diamond-shaped label below the raised glass letters ran the length of the sign on its left-hand side.

Darby lost his train of thought.

P.J. got up and walked to Darby's fridge. There was nothing edible in the stone-age white Frigidaire aside from a half-full jar of Vlasic pickles, a half-gallon of Alta Dena Milk, and a grimy jar of Peter Pan Smooth. A loaf of potato bread, wedged far in the back, was now grayish-green from mold. On the lowest shelf above the empty crisper bin slots, there were dried orange blobs that had fallen from a nearly empty, uncovered bowl of tangerine Jell-O. There wasn't much she could do except continue to supplement Darby on his monthly disability checks of $998 that arrived every month, on or near the sixteenth. The apartment, which he insisted on keeping to himself and not sharing, ate up $650 of that. The rest went to Internet service, cable TV, food, and cigarettes. Sometimes he took an odd job or was of service to friends and came home with a spare bill or two, but it was all P.J. could do to keep from worrying whether or not he could survive without her.

She walked back into the living room, feeling the snagged and tattered holes in the steel gray carpet beneath her toes.

She stared at her half-brother. He had fallen asleep, his Lakers cap now floating up and back around his thick light brown hair like a halo pinned against the back of the chair. Yes, he had their mother's eyes, but his mouth was thinner lipped and his chin was much more prominent. Of the two of them, she had lucked out with the looks.

P.J. took a moment to quietly head upstairs. Darby's mattress lay on the floor, covered by one baby blue blanket, sticky yellowed sheets, and a flat pillow. She stared out the window at the 2 North. Cars were zipping onto the Glendale Freeway, heading up to Montrose and points beyond. Maybe she should work on the next murder by herself. She could think of countless women who deserved to die. For starters, there was Hailey Raphael in Tucson, Time Taylor in Oak Harbor, and Zivia Uzamba in Las Vegas—and those were just the names at the top of her list.

P.J. smoothed back her blond hair and pressed her nose against Darby's cool windowpane. When she grew tired of watching traffic, she headed downstairs, grabbed a piece of paper from the top drawer of Darby's desk and yanked a pencil stub out of a cup. After writing, "Bro, I love you!" in her spidery scrawl, she peeled a scrap of masking tape from the corner of his desk and stuck the note to his monitor.

She stood back to admire it. It was centered perfectly.

Time to retrieve her loafers and put them on.

She left her half-brother, comatose in his favorite ratty chair.

5

The next day at work, Caresse headed to the Best Barbie Board to read more about the death of Gayle Grace. There was no better place online to chat with fellow diehard Barbie doll collectors and fans. A search function allowed her to search for single words or phrases, so she entered the word "Grace" and found what appeared to be the first mention of Gayle's death.

The first note, posted hours after the initial news reports, came from Ilene Lynch, who lived in Oswego and belonged to the same Barbie Club Gayle had helped start five years earlier. Her user name was COLORMAGIC, a nod to the 1966 Barbie dolls with hair that could metamorphose from Golden Blonde to Scarlet Flame or Midnight to

Ruby Red, thanks to innovative color change packets.

The Best Barbie Board website gave members the option to post either a photo of themselves or an avatar. The postage stamp-sized picture Ilene provided was a headshot of her favorite Color Magic, a Midnight beauty, splendid against the lavender backdrop of her original plastic case.

COLORMAGIC: Just heard word of a shocking tragedy. Gayle Grace and her husband are gone. A car bombing, they say. At SUNY Oswego, of all places. They were just leaving work and their Saturn blew up right there in the parking lot. Inside word is, the car was rigged. It doesn't make any sense. I am in shock.

Sabeana Moss, moderator of the BBB and a pretty, thirty-something strawberry blond according to her tiny online photo, was first to reply.

SMOSS: Ilene, I am so sorry to hear Gayle is gone. It doesn't make any sense, does it? If you hear any more from the locals, please keep us posted. And if you talk to Megan, please give her our best.

Ilene had not replied.

Caresse did a search for follow-up conversations, knowing it was long past lunchtime and there should be fewer interruptions, but she couldn't shut out the fact that her boss Seth was red-faced, pacing between the head copy desk and his own. By the time his moon-shaped glasses started to fog, she realized there must be a last-minute change to the afternoon edition in the works.

Anjo explained that sports was set to run a feature that day, singing the praises of an eighteen-year-old seven-footer from Minneapolis who, courtesy of a full basketball scholarship, was ready to make waves at Cal Poly in the fall. Hours earlier, the kid was arrested in Wisconsin for driving the getaway vehicle for his sixteen-year-old accomplice, who entered a bank with a sawed-off shotgun and quietly told a teller to hand over all the money in her drawer.

The young man's high school coach, Mustangs coach Kevin Bromley, and Cal Poly Media Relations Director Brian Thurmond were reeling. The typical comments about him being a nice kid, a quiet kid, a kid with a solid background, did nothing but salt the wounds of those who had held such high hopes for his college career.

"Can't run a fluff piece about how fabulous he is if he's gonna be *in* court instead of *on* the court this fall," Anjo quipped.

Seth slammed down his phone. "Caresse," he screamed. "Go back, locate Skip, and find out if D section has run. We're going to yank it."

Caresse jumped out of her seat and ran toward the back of the building. In her wake, she heard Seth screaming at Bo in Sports to find something on the wire to replace the pulled feature.

The machinery in the pressroom roared like King Kong.

She looked around wildly. Finally, she spotted Skip.

"Stop!" she screamed.

Skip peered at her through his dense goggles and frowned. It did not compute.

"Stop!" she repeated.

Skip was talking to a man whose back was toward her, but she could tell even from his backside, A, he was a stranger to the pressroom, and, B, he was ridiculously handsome. She ran up to Skip and dragged him to the open garage, pulling him down the ramp, away from the noise. Less than a minute later, he flew back inside and threw the switch that halted the run.

Her job had been done, and now she had a chance to scope out the stranger. He was either Andy Childs from Sixwire or his brother, so close was the resemblance.

"Hi," he said.

"Hi," she replied, walking over to him. She was 5'10", and even still, she only came up to his shoulders. His blond hair was lighter than his beard, and he wore a t-shirt over a classic striped button-down with jeans.

The thought of returning to her computer to read more about the Barbie murder was temporarily on the back burner. If she had to go on dates for the Valentine feature anyway, she'd found a great excuse to ask a hottie out.

6

P.J. grabbed one suitcase and her empty duffel and got off the Sunset Limited at the Tucson, Arizona, Amtrak Station on East Toole shortly after noon the last Sunday in January.

She wandered around the station building for a moment to get her bearings. It had been renovated in recent years and had white tile floors in the ticketing and waiting areas that gleamed beneath inset fluorescent lights. Outside the pillared building, on the platform side, the name of the city was spelled out in capital letters.

P.J. sighed with pleasure as the sixty-degree midday winter warmth surrounded her. This was so much better than the journey to Oswego, she could scarcely compare the two. She had decided to alternate her killings between Darby's ideas, which mostly involved complicated wiring, rigging, and explosive devices, and her own hands-on approach.

Hailey Raphael had earned P.J.'s enmity the year before when she shared pictures of her blond freckleless Midge with the Barbie doll board and Hailey accused her of having removed the doll's freckles with nail polish remover.

P.J. remembered the board exchange vividly.

HR: Thanks for sharing your pictures, P.J., but that isn't an authentic freckle-less Midge. If it were, her hair would be longer. Are you sure someone didn't apply a little nail polish remover to her face? ;-)

PJ-RULEZ: Thanks for your note, Hailey. This is an authentic freckle-less Midge. I have had her since childhood. In fact, she was my first and favorite doll, given to me by my Aunt Liz. I am aware some people try to pass off dolls with removed freckles as the real deal, but this is not the case with me.

HR: It's not that I'm calling you a liar, P.J., but something smells fishy. If she was your favorite doll, are you sure the freckles didn't just get rubbed off from constant play? Maybe you were playing next to a bottle of open nail polish remover?

PJ-RULEZ: LOL. Not funny.

HR: And you say you got your Midge from your Aunt Liz? Maybe she removed the freckles?

PJ-RULEZ: Not likely. As I've told everybody here before, my Aunt Liz worked for Mattel in the Sixties and brought home something from the

employee store in El Segundo nearly every week. This Midge was in her box, with stand AND booklet AND wrist tag intact, wearing her two-piece blue swimsuit and white heels.

HR: Hmm. I think your Aunt Liz was having a little fun with you.

After that last note, P.J. was too angry to respond. With her silence, everyone thought she had let it go. What did happen was that Hailey ended up on P.J.'s list, and now she was here to kill her.

Standing outside the station that Sunday, P.J. realized she must have had a scowl on her face because a concerned-looking, clean-cut man about her age approached and asked if she needed help with her bags. She politely declined and tried to smile, admitting to herself that if she hadn't wanted to attract attention, she shouldn't have worn a sheer dress and heels for travel, but she had been in the mood to get out of her jeans and sweatpants ever since bringing home the first duffel-bag load of dolls.

After she said no to the man, he moved a few respectful steps away and lit a Camel he retrieved from a pack deep in his right front pocket. Out of the corner of her eye, she studied him. He was dressed in navy and was compact and cleft-chinned, with a brush cut. Military or just made that way?

Smoke drifted in her direction and she relished it. She still missed smoking, despite having given up Marlboro Lights cold turkey three long years ago. She caught her reflection in a window on the building. Standing in profile, she admired her model-like frame. Her long blond hair was tucked beneath a print Armani silk scarf, clipped in place at both sides and knotted at the nape of her neck. Her stylish sunglasses, handbag, and Manolo heels were the perfect accessories. Barbie doll had nothing on her.

And here she was in Tucson. P.J. had read about the city and knew she was too early for the Tucson Gem and Mineral Show, which would be held in February along with the Tucson Rodeo. She debated visiting the Art Deco Fox Theatre downtown, Reid Park Zoo midtown, or Saguaro National Park in the east. She wanted to head north to check out the boutiques, galleries, and restaurants, but Darby had warned her about being noticed around town, so she surrendered the idea of buying something eclectic and pricey at one of the shops.

A cab that said Allstate on both side doors pulled up to the curb. She nodded her head, and the squat, balding cabbie jumped out. He picked up her suitcase and empty duffel and threw them in the trunk. She got in the back seat of the cab and told him she needed to go to the Ramada on East Tanque Verde.

"Nice place," he said, with a thick accent she couldn't identify. "You bring a swimsuit?"

P.J. studied his ebony eyes in the rear view mirror and read his name off the I.D. tacked to the driver side visor. "Sorry, Avi. It's still a little too cold. I'll wait for summer."

"They got a hot tub," Avi said. "Nice and bubbly."

"I'm good." Her tone was curt.

He took her cue, opting for the most direct route, heading northwest on East Toole toward East Pennington, making a slight right onto North Sixth, and turning right on East Speedway. The twenty-minute drive ended with a turn onto North Wilmot, which quickly became East Tanque Verde. He made a quick spin around the circular entrance drive and was out of the cab to pop the trunk without hesitation.

Before P.J. could open the back door on the right-hand side, Avi quickly opened it for her, gave a slight bow, and took her hand as she got out. She had been pegged as someone with little time for chitchat, so he had rushed there without fanfare.

Somewhat flustered but flattered nonetheless, she waited while he got her suitcase and the empty duffel, which he gave a momentary second glance at. She tipped him five dollars on top of the fare, and he walked her to the large-windowed front lobby. The floors were white linoleum with a high shine, and her heels clicked on her way over to the registration desk. She turned her head to give the cabbie a nod good-bye. He was still sitting out front, waiting, but when she acknowledged him, he broke out in a large grin, started the cab, and drove away.

Checking in was uneventful. She headed up to her room overlooking the courtyard pool. As she sat on the mosaic-print bedspread, a heavy feeling descended on her. She tried to pinpoint the heaviness she felt, but couldn't. Was Tucson, despite its pleasant warmth, just one of those cities at odds with her energy?

She found the remote and turned on the Sanyo TV anchored to the dresser. A quick flip through the basic channels guided her to a world news recap. In Florida, a speeding car flew 200 feet, killing five occupants; in Kandahar, Afghanistan, gunmen kidnapped a burqa-clad American aid worker; in Paris, police questioned a young trader blamed for massive fraud that cost France's Societe Generale bank more than $7 billion; in Los Angeles, a helicopter pilot was killed when his small craft crashed into a freeway and burst into flames; and in Rochester, New York, Arun Gandhi's remarks about Israel and Jews being "the biggest players" in a global culture of violence got him removed as president of the peace center he launched in 1991.

P.J. sighed, stripped off her dress, kicked off her heels, and threw her suitcase on the bed. Clack, clack, both locks popped, and she lifted the soft lid, digging for her blue and white print bikini. Yes, she had brought her swimsuit. No, it was none of the cabbie's business. Slipping into the slinky little flower-patterned suit, she admired her body in the mirror. Then she grabbed two Ramada towels, her sunglasses, and her card key, and headed down to the pool area.

The center courtyard was vacant that Sunday as she stepped into the bubbly hot tub that foamed as though soap had been added. The heat melted her tension as she sank into the churning water up to her chin. She felt as though she could rest in the water forever without getting dizzy from the heat. Looking up at the cloudless blue sky, she felt every last worry dissolve. Tonight was the night. She would head over to Hailey's house, a straight shot up North Sabino Canyon Road to East Ocotillo Drive, and while Hailey's parents were out for their weekly night of bridge from eight to ten p.m.—or thereabouts, as Hailey had shared on the message boards—P.J. would take a sharp tool from Hailey's father's garage workshop (another fact shared: he was a shoemaker before he'd become a machinist and then finally retired, but he'd kept all the tools he had for fixing footwear), and bash in Hailey's skull.

7

As they peeled out of the parking lot in his Sunburst Orange Pearl Dodge Ram truck, Caresse could see Bree, Rhea, and Nibbles standing at the wide picture window, watching. Seth, who had more important things on his mind, had excused her to take off "on assignment." His name was Todd, he was ring-free, he played bass in Skip's garage band, and he was a close friend of Anjo's husband. Once he found out Caresse made the Ken Cop on Anjo's desk, the seal of approval was mutual.

Ten miles up Highway 101 North, they were over the grade and on a hilly stretch of highway that wound through the countryside like a high note by Celine. Comfortably quiet the entire ride, they soaked up each other's vibes while Matchbox Twenty made friends with shadows on the wall, Bruce Springsteen searched for a world with some soul, and Jesus Jones watched the world wake up from history.

Seventeen miles into the drive, while Jason Mraz was falling through the cracks and trying to get back, Todd took exit 218A toward Santa Rosa Road and headed straight on East Front Street.

While she was still marveling over her spontaneity and the possibility that a dating story might not be the worst thing in the world to have to write after all, Todd pulled into Outlaws Bar & Grill, a rustic-looking joint straight from some bad-ass Western. She surmised Outlaws to be one of Todd's regular haunts, judging by how many people he knew. As soon as he picked a booth with cushioned seats and a checkered tablecloth for them, a perky waitress appeared, order pad in hand.

Todd raised an eyebrow at Caresse. "Ribs and fries okay?"

"Mmm," she said.

Pheromones did the two-step on the sawdust-covered floor.

She looked down and was glad she had worn one of her favorite dresses to work that day—a navy knit with bright red flowers splashed across it—and that she had taken the extra time with her makeup and unruly, dark hair. She couldn't guess which spirit guide had prompted her to look her best on a day when she expected to see no one but the news crew and shoppers at Ralphs.

"You guys look good together," the waitress noted.

Todd and Caresse laughed appreciatively.

"Thanks, Manda," he said.

Reluctantly, Manda left the table and Todd focused his full attention on Caresse.

"So if you're the Barbie doll expert Anjo says you are, then I want to hear all about it."

She played with the straw in her ice water and grinned.

"Why Barbie doll and not Ken? What's up with him not being very popular?"

"Ken's included in there, but you know, it's Barbie doll and her friends and family, so—"

"Sympathize with me. I'm the youngest of three boys. No girls in my family, so I didn't really grow up with Barbie doll other than the commercials. She has a family?" As a conversationalist, Todd was trying to make her feel at home on his turf.

"She does."

"Who are the other members of her family?"

"Okay, well, she has a little sister, Skipper, and their sister Stacie came out about twelve years ago. Then they've got another sister Kelly, who's supposed to be a toddler but who's more, like, in kindergarten now, and then there's infant sister Krissy. Of course, they're different sizes. If you take Barbie doll, she's eleven and a half inches tall. Then you've got Skipper at nine inches, Stacie at seven, Kelly at four and a half, and Krissy at less than two."

"They're all the same age?" Busy playing footsy with her under the table, Todd wasn't listening carefully.

A hot flush started to spread across her face. "Well, I hope not. You know, Barbie doll has always been a well-developed teenager. And Skipper is probably—well, Skipper is getting a little older. She's developed somewhat over the years from totally flat-chested into—do you really want to hear about this?"

"Sure." He shrugged. "Why not?"

She scooted her butt around in the booth to get more comfortable and smiled at Manda, who had brought them a basketful of tortilla strips.

"She's gone to being somewhat more endowed. And Stacie and the younger ones will probably always be just scrawny little kids."

Todd bit into a chip. "And why is it so important that she be well-endowed?"

"Barbie doll?"

"Yeah. I mean, was that a conscious effort on the part of the designer?"

"Uh, well, now you have to go back to how Barbie doll was originally designed. This woman, Ruth Handler, watched her daughter play with paper dolls and saw a need to be filled in that paper dolls are all well and good, but they're paper clothes, cardboard dolls. She thought if she could make a 3-D fashion doll, she would have a market there. When it came to designing Barbie doll, she had to wear clothes well. If you design a doll that has a straight, flat figure, clothes are just gonna hang on her. Hence, the shape."

Todd stood up across from Caresse. With barely a moment's hesitation, he came over to her side of the booth and sat down next to her. She didn't miss a beat. She scooched right up against him and let the fire start.

8

The first thing P.J. did when she arrived at Darby's apartment Tuesday afternoon was take the bloody tack hammer and toss it in the building's dumpster. She had rubber-banded it inside two micro-cotton luxury towels and placed it inside a large Hefty bag with used sanitary napkins to disgust and discourage garbage pickers from investigating the trash bag's contents.

Darby had a space for a car, but since he only had a beat-up 150cc classic Vespa-style moped scooter, he parked it parallel to the concrete space bumper and locked it through the front wheel to street-level grill work, which offered a glimpse of dusty scrub between its metal bars. He "sold" his parking space, which was included in the rent, for $100 per month to his neighbor Michael Hornberger, an Adam Sandler look-alike with flaming red hair. Hornberger had no problem paying Darby for the favor. He was just grateful he didn't have to choose whether to park his shiny 2008 black Ford Explorer or his primo silver and blue Harley Fat Boy on the street.

With the $100 he got from Michael every month, Darby rented a storage space in the garage, which was nothing more than a parking slot enclosed between the back wall of the laundry room and the walled-off dumpster. The chain-link gate, which swung wide with a shove, had two combination locks on it.

Darby had given his half-sister full permission to use the storage space for her hauls, which she dared not keep at home. Why he would risk being an accessory to her crimes had more to do with his affection for her than his fear of returning to jail.

Today, P.J. carried the weight of her new Midge dolls and recollections of her trip to Arizona. Darby's scooter was gone, but she suspected he hadn't gone far.

Both combination locks opened to 36-24-36, in homage to Darby's obsession with women. She peered through the chain-link as she spun and unfastened both combination locks. The white Rubbermaid stacking storage bins with opaque drawers lined both sides of the stall as well the back wall, so it resembled a walk-in closet. Only the concrete floor, dust, and several spiders detracted from the organized tableaux.

P.J. closed the chain-link gate behind her and went to her American Girl stash in the first two storage bins to her immediate left. The drawers in each bin were wide and deep enough to lay dolls flat so their heads were toward the back of each drawer. When she wanted to pull out drawers to examine their contents, she was able to completely remove them. She kept a metal folding chair tucked between two bins that she could unfold and sit on, placing each drawer on her lap, one at a time.

When she had originally put them into storage, P.J. had forgotten to double-check if all the American Girl Barbie dolls were on their correct bendable leg bodies. She badly wanted to check them now. She selected the top drawer in the first bin first, talking to each of the dolls as she examined their bodies.

While P.J. hadn't been alive in 1965-66 when Barbie doll 1070 had been issued, she knew the range of American Girl Barbie dolls in existence thoroughly. An AG face could be high color or low color. Her hair color could be any shade ranging from platinum blond to dark brunette. Lip colors ranged from pink to raspberry. Hairstyles ranged from a middle-parted chin-length bob to a center-parted, soft-textured longer bob.

P.J. gazed at the eight dolls spanning the width of the first drawer. To see them again was to be struck anew with appreciation for their 1600-series outfits, which were more elegant in nature than any clothing for Barbie doll made before that time. Many of the 1600 fashions issued during a short two-year period came with exquisite accessories and closed-toed pumps that looked better, in her opinion, that Barbie doll's open-toe slides.

Knit Separates 1602 was worn by a high color blond longhaired American Girl. Instead of wearing the slim blue knit skirt shown in the Mattel catalogs, she wore gold knit slacks with navy shoes and a multi-stripe knit blouse. The skirt, baggied like the accessories for Student Teacher, was put in a Ziploc and tied to the doll's wrist with a two-millimeter navy silk ribbon. The doll itself had an extra full, long factory cut for a high-color blond.

P.J. checked for leg damage, stains, tears, and chew marks in the doll's leg vinyl. Finding none, she bent the doll's knees. The left leg clicked three times, the right one only twice.

"What's wrong with your right leg?" she asked as herself.

This was followed by a response in Cockney. "Oh, but yours don't click at all!"

P.J. laughed at this as hard as she did at Kathy Griffin's jokes about Clay Aiken. Ah, working class Londoner Barbie doll was hysterical.

She put down the blond doll and examined the next one. This lemon-lipped honey blond was perfectly suited to her elegant Black Magic strapless dress with matching tulle evening cape, and her legs clicked three times.

Next up was an ash blond with faded peach lips wearing Junior Designer. The adhesive-backed cutouts on the dress were not aligned precisely, but she looked good despite one non-clicking leg.

The blond Student Teacher she had checked out on her departure from Oswego was still intact with her baggie of accessories. Her legs were in perfect working order.

The fifth doll in the box had serious leg defects, with a split behind one knee and a slight ankle tear. The brunette wore On The Avenue, a lovely gold and white knit suit gathered at the waistline by a flashy gold belt. While the doll's face was flawless, P.J. thought she might put the outfit on another doll at some point and redress the brunette in a gown to hide her flawed gams.

Dolls six and seven in the first box were a platinum blond dressed in Lunch on The Terrace and a silver ash blond wearing Riding In The Park. Both wore hats—the first, a wide-brimmed affair in gingham and polka dots, and the second, a brown riding cap. After checking their legs, she removed their hats to make sure their hairdos were rooted well.

Last in box number one was a titian doll wearing her original American Girl swimsuit. Her legs were as flawless as the rest of her pristine face and body.

P.J. was quicker at examining the second box, which contained a brunette with thick hair dressed in Garden Tea Party, a high-color brownette with raspberry lips wearing Junior Prom, a highly-prized silver blond dressed in Midnight Blue, a pale blond looking chic in Aboard Ship, a silver brunette looking sexy in Sleeping Pretty, an ash blond looking fabulous in Coffee's On, an ash brunette looking stylish in Club Meeting, and a yellow blond ready for bed in Sleepytime Gal. Some had perfect legs, but others needed to have their outfits swapped out to hide problem areas.

P.J. pulled paper and a pencil out of her purse and began making notes.

A pink-lipped platinum blond American Girl Barbie doll was first in the line-up in drawer three. She wore Barbie Skin Diver, and her bright orange sweatshirt offset her tresses vividly. With her unoxidized hair nearly white in appearance and silky to the touch, the doll reminded P.J. of her own mother Angela, who called to mind Grace Kelly--if Grace had been a chain smoker with a deep, resounding cough.

Tenderly, P.J. stroked the doll and realized it had been a while since she and her mother had talked. It had been New Year's when P.J. had vowed she would come visit her in France before much more time passed. In reality, she probably would not see her at all. She had an aversion to her stepfather Dirk, who was Darby's dad, because she knew for a fact Dirk was cheating on her mom. She had overheard a phone call late one night during the last trip she'd made to see them before they decided to retire abroad. She wondered if Dirk knew *she* knew about his philandering and if this had lent impetus for them to end up an ocean apart.

P.J. assumed Dirk's need to run around was just a variation on his family's curse. Darby would run around if he had half the schmooze and smoothness of his dad, who could have doubled for the charming Charlton Heston. Alas, Darby was a step down in looks, two steps down in personality, three steps down in demeanor, totally hopeless when it came to small talk, and absolutely angry at the world. If he could find a plain Jane who liked to play Russian Roulette on a rainy Saturday afternoon or an emo Emily he could share a tome on nuclear war and the inevitability of World War III with, he'd be all set, but P.J. doubted he'd ever find such a dark Debbie in Los Angeles County.

P.J.'s own father, Steve Croesus, had left home when she was only five years old. Angela had been harping on him for not making more money and not handing her the good life, which to Angela meant a better house, better jewelry, and better vacations. It was as simple as him not coming home one night after he got off work at the restaurant he helped his best friend manage.

Ironically, the place was called Sea You Soon, and Steve always smelled like breaded fish, tartar sauce, and perhaps more exotic seafood P.J. wouldn't be able to pronounce let alone want to taste. But she loved his scruffy face and his wide smile, and she missed him, wherever he was, to this day.

Dirk entered the scene weeks later, introduced to Angela by a mutual friend. Within a month, he moved in. Three months later, Angela was pregnant with Darby. At the five-month mark, Dirk and Angela planned to wed, pending finalization of her divorce "due to desertion."

P.J. laid the platinum American Girl Barbie doll back in the drawer after making sure her legs clicked properly. A coral-lipped brownette side-part AG rested beside her, dressed in Saturday Matinee, a fur-collared gold and brown tweed suit.

Toy industry legend had it that Mattel manufactured fewer side-part American Girl Barbie dolls due to their more complicated hairstyle. Not only was her hair parted on the left, there was the slightest wave to it, and factory workers had needed to add a turquoise ribbon hair band to each one.

This side-part had perfect legs, but a quick check beneath her chic tweed hat revealed a missing plug near the part and a professionally repaired neck split. P.J. sighed and noted both flaws in writing.

Next came a geranium-lipped cinnamon high-color AG wearing Disc Date. A rhinestone button second from the bottom on the fuchsia skirt was missing, but the white lace blouse was still crisp and vibrant. She had pinpricks near her ankles, but because the floor-length covered them, she wouldn't need to be redressed.

The white plastic helmet to Miss Astronaut popped off to reveal a silver ash blond high-color side-part AG with a tan skin tone. Her flag, space suit, and boots were mint. P.J. elected not to remove her outfit to see her legs. Instead, she gently bent them to hear the requisite three clicks.

A beautiful pale blond, low-color side-part wearing Poodle Parade had her accessories—tote bag, trophy, and dog show award—baggied and tied to her wrist with an olive ribbon.

"Darling, are you a side-part too?" P.J. already knew she was, but she was reveling in the fact she had picked up more than a few of these harder to find AG Barbie dolls.

"Let me see your eyes," she said.

P.J. removed the doll's sunglasses to view her perfectly painted blue irises. A faint rub on one eyelid required documentation, even though it was barely discernible.

"You know I really don't need to be wearing a scarf when I'm wearing a hair band," Miss Poodle Parade complained, her Cockney accent stronger with her umbrage.

P.J. removed the pink scarf.

"I can fix that for you, darling," she said, untying the baggie from her wrist and opening it. She flattened the scarf, which had been knotted beneath the doll's chin, and slipped it inside the Ziploc. The turquoise hair band clashed with the olive sheath and diamond-patterned knit coat, but P.J. could always redress her another time.

"Much better," Miss Poodle Parade said, sounding as chipper as Mary Poppins.

P.J. laid her back down after inspecting her legs.

"Are you talking to yourself?"

The voice seemed to come from nowhere.

It took P.J. a moment to register that it was not part of her reverie.

She looked up and saw a carrot-topped man in a red and white football jersey staring at her through the chain-link of the gated stall.

9

Apparently nonplussed by the fact Caresse was nearly sitting in his lap, Todd continued to talk. "All right. 'Cause the reason I brought that up was, I was listening to Sammy Stoudt's show the other day on KVEC, and he had a show on sexism in the restaurant industry, about the way women are made to look in some restaurants, and one of his callers said, 'well, you know, you should have a Barbie doll expert on.'"

"No kidding." Caresse was genuinely interested. KVEC was right in San Luis, and if she remembered correctly, her pal Marilyn in Classified Ads was Sammy's good friend.

Todd continued, "Because he saw one being connected to the other, right? That here we have a doll that's not like Raggedy Ann or anything. This is a good-looking, California, full-bosomed babe."

"Right."

"And is that the image women have to ascribe to as they're growing up now?"

"No, they don't, but the whole thing is that when you're a girl and you're playing with dolls, you don't want to play with an ugly doll. So if you're going to make her pretty, why not make her the ultimate of what's conventionally considered beautiful?"

Todd studied Caresse's face. "You've got the most amazing green eyes I've ever seen. Would it be all right if I kissed you before I went back to my side of the table?"

Manda the waitress had terrible timing. She was hovering, holding two plates of ribs, a copy of *USA Today* tucked beneath her left arm.

"Were you guys talking about Barbie dolls?"

She placed the ribs on the table and unfolded the newspaper.

Caresse's gaze went straight to the bold headline, "Sister Claims Gayle Murdered For Barbie Dolls," and her hand was out to take the paper before it was even offered. Immersing herself in the story, she finally looked up to see Todd dabbing rib juice from his beard. She hadn't seen him return to his side of the table and had forgotten about the proffered kiss. Entranced by the bounty before him, Todd was fully absorbed in his meal, so she continued reading.

The byline read, "Megan Dailon Says Valuable Collection Ravaged."

As recorded in the first news report she read, which was subsequently corroborated by Ilene on the BBB, Megan Dailon had lost her sister Gayle and her brother-in-law Mike Grace in a "suspicious" car explosion.

This story, however, offered additional details about Gayle's collection.

"We updated my sister's inventory list only six months ago," Dailon told a reporter for USA Today. "She had a choice vintage collection, but she was particularly attached to her American Girl Barbie dolls and outfits from the mid to late Sixties. The robber chose to take at least one example of each rare outfit and the best of Gayle's dolls, leaving those that were less mint or wearing duplicate or more common outfits rearranged uniformly, three to a shelf. I will have to go over the list, but I estimate that over four dozen dolls that were here are now gone."

Dailon is certain there is a connection between the robbery and the deaths of her sister and brother-in-law.

At this time, law enforcement will not commit to robbery as a motive for the homicides, but Dailon insists otherwise.

"Gayle and Mike didn't have any enemies," she said. "There was no reason on earth for anyone to want them dead."

Caresse looked up from the newspaper, her mind buzzing.

The killer had a penchant for American Girl Barbie dolls.

Juicy guy, juicier story.

10

P.J. stared at the man wearing the Reebok San Francisco 49ers jersey.

He looked down at his shirt. "It's a replica," he explained, waiting for her reply.

She froze. On her lap was box number three, containing the requisite eight dolls. She had only checked the first five before the interruption.

When the man realized she wasn't going to say anything, he opened the gate and approached her, offering his hand. "You must be Darby's sister. I'm Michael."

P.J. began to get up, but the box in her lap shifted and threatened to spill. Michael caught it and helped her keep it upright, whereupon she abruptly tugged it away from him and went to slide it back into the Rubbermaid unit.

"Your brother lets me use his parking space," he told her.

She finally spoke. "Michael Hornberger. You're the one with the new Explorer and the Fat Boy. Why does a guy with money live in this dump?"

Michael grinned shyly. "Me? I get restless and like to move every few years." He looked around. "So you like dolls?"

P.J. disregarded his question.

"Did you get the money from your parents?" It was a rude question, but she had no trouble asking it.

"No. I write for TV," he said.

"Anything I would know?"

"I doubt it," he said.

"Try me."

"Have you heard of *Monk?*"

"Oh, sure," P.J. said. She folded her hands and began wringing them.

"I must be bothering you."

Michael started to back away, hoping she would stop him.

P.J. held up her left hand and flashed her diamond ring at him, wishing the substantial Marquis cut could blind him.

"I get it," he said.

Number 52 turned and left the stall, closing the gate behind him.

As he walked away, she noticed that the back of his jersey read "Willis."

11

The crime scene in Oswego, New York, had been broken down into two locations—the Grace vehicle parked at SUNY Oswego and the Grace home, mere blocks away.

When police arrived and cordoned off the parking lot facing Takamine Road and Rich Hall, the only two cars present were the remains of the Graces' white Saturn and, ten spaces away, a putty-colored Mitsubishi Diamante that had been dinged, dented, and marred by flying debris. Beyond the perimeter, administrative personnel and students stood in the snow, most without coats, hats, and boots, trying to piece together what had taken place.

After photos had been taken, emergency personnel arrived and extricated Mike from the driver's side of the Saturn. Since the passenger door had flown off and hit the stop sign on the corner, it was easier to remove Gayle.

"That's Mike and Gayle!" a woman shouted from beyond the perimeter. Through the shattered car window, the woman saw fragments of the dark blue pinstripe suit and crimson and dark blue tie he had worn that day, now charred to his skin. The diamond tack he stuck in his tie had been blasted off and was now embedded in the crumpled and fragmented car hood.

Mike's ear and cheekbone were partially intact, but graying dark hair hung like a washrag from his skull. Gayle's face was entirely gone, but fragments of the pale yellow, high-collared blouse and white Playtex bra she'd worn that day were stuck to her shoulder blades. Some of her blond-streaked hair was stuck to the headrest, and a gold button earring she'd worn blinked in the harsh sunlight, yards away.

The thick, wet snowfall had slowed, but gathering evidence was still difficult.

Martin Phillips was concentrating on photographing, then watching forensics bag the remnants of speaker wire. The speaker wire nearest the fragmented engine led to the discovery that the frayed end was still partially wrapped around one of the spark plugs.

The car was rigged, Phillips thought. His mind went through the steps the perpetrator would have taken to make it work. *Crude, but effective.*

Powell Griffin was busy following a trail of spike-booted footprints leading to and from the Grace vehicle from seven spaces away. Impressions in snow were hard to photograph because of lack of contrast, but Griff knew the procedure. First, he sprayed the boot-prints with orange spray paint, holding the can three feet away from each impression so the aerosol didn't cause damage. By directing the spray at a forty-five-degree angle, the spray paint marked only the highest impression points. Then, since the highlighted impressions were liable to absorb heat from the sun, they were shielded with canvas tent screens until they could be adequately photographed.

When he had finished protecting the prints, Griff walked over to Phillips. He had something on his mind, and Phillips knew him well enough not to ask what he was thinking until Griff thoroughly formulated what he wanted to say and was ready to share it.

Phillips joggled his body back and forth in the cold, keeping his feet stationary so as not to mar the scene.

"Have you ever seen a woman in this town wear spike-heeled boots?" Griff asked finally.

"I'd have to ask my wife," Phillips replied. "But I'd guess no. It's too slippery. You'd fall down as soon as you hit the ice."

Griff looked past the crime scene tape at the gathered crowd. Nearly all looked frozen, nearly all wore parkas and heavy hiking boots, and nearly all were undoubtedly locals or relatives of locals who had dressed them or advised them on what they'd need to survive upstate New York winter weather.

"Do we have any dental stone?" he asked.

"Always. Bags of it."

Griff did the math in his head. He had over a dozen clear prints of both the right and left boots.

Dental stone with a compressive strength of at least eight-thousand psi was used for impressions in soil, snow, or sand. Phillips went to the forensics van and brought back an armload of premixed, re-sealable plastic bags, setting them at Griff's feet in a trackless spot. Then he went and retrieved four gallon-sized jugs of water, bringing them back and setting them down beside the bags of dental stone.

Griff picked a bag up and grabbed a jug. He poured sufficient water into the bag, sealed it, and shook it up. "I feel good about those prints," he said.

"You think a woman could have done this?"

"Think Mike was having an affair and this was the other woman getting back at him when he tried to cut things off?"

"Don't know yet," Phillips said. "But we'll figure it out."

He watched as Griff massaged the first bag of dental stone until it was the consistency of watered-down Bisquick.

"There are two good car tire impressions, left front, left rear, where the boot-prints start and return. Let's get those two, while the wind is cooperating."

Phillips nodded and headed off.

The man on the second floor of Sheldon Hall did not want to go outside. Other than the car that had been blown to bits, his was the only car left in the Takamine Road lot. If he went out now, there would be questions, and he wasn't sure he wanted to get involved.

He had been gazing out at the parking lot when the blond woman was standing near the Grace car. The gas tank was on the right side of the Saturn, and it was parked in the right corner of the lot, so his view was partially obscured. After watching her a while, he decided she must be putting gas in the tank. He went back to reading his hardback copy of *A Winter Haunting*.

Movement caught his peripheral vision again, however, and he turned and looked out a second time. The woman stepped away from the car and looked heavenward. Then she gave a slight nod before scurrying, slipping and sliding in her white vinyl boots, over to an Altima parked three spots away from his Diamante. She was driving a rental car. Enterprise had slapped a substantial sticker advertising its website on the car's rear bumper.

The man knew he had information that would likely mean something to those investigating the crime. He also knew he was not quick to get involved in situations that might prove troublesome.

Until he was ready to come forward—if and when he was *ever* ready—what he witnessed would be filed away and forgotten. The only problem he really had now was how to kill sufficient time until forensics cleared out of the parking lot and he was free to get in his Diamante and head home.

He looked down at the book he was carrying and realized he had over 120 pages left to read. Glad he had brought a good novel with him that day, he moseyed off in search of a coffee vending machine and a more comfortable place to sit than the window nook he'd been resting in.

12

P.J. dreamt of the Tucson murder that night at home in her California King bed.

Her bedroom was replete with a fireplace, walk-in closet, and mirrored walls. Her white cockapoo Chao was a shade darker than the extravagant goose-down comforter adorned with hand-embroidered flowers that gently draped over the cedar hope chest at the foot of the bed.

Hailey Raphael had gone down easily.

P.J. had arrived in Hailey's neighborhood in a rented green Sebring delivered to her by Enterprise at the hotel twenty minutes before Hailey's parents left their sloped driveway. The Raphaels had a double garage with an inside door leading into their opulent abode. The exterior garage entrance on the left-hand side was down a narrow walkway. Wearing dark clothing and thin leather gloves, P.J. moved carefully over the pale gravel and tried the knob. It was unlocked.

Once inside, it took a moment for her eyes to focus. The door leading into the hallway from the garage was half-open, and a light in the laundry room was on. She found a workbench near the half-open door that offered a surfeit of tools, and the best of the lot was incontrovertibly a minacious-looking tack hammer. P.J. picked it up and valuated its weight and ease of use, judging it perfect for the job at hand. She dropped it into her empty duffel and glanced toward the half-open door leading into the hallway that led to the laundry room.

Clothes were neatly folded atop the dryer, which rumbled quietly while it dried its current load. Using the running dryer as cover, P.J moved swiftly into the laundry room and found a wide-based, lidded hamper behind the door. Testing it to see if it would hold her weight, she finally stood on it and saw that, with the high doors and ceilings, she was obscured at full height behind the door, which opened inward. Taking some spare change out of her jacket pocket, she leaned around the back of the door and began pinging it at the top of the washer, which was open but empty. As each coin hit, it clinked against the top, fell into the washer, and brattled on the bottom. After pitching the tenth coin, P.J. heard a sharp slam and footsteps in a room beyond.

P.J. had seen photos of Hailey, thanks to PictureTrail links posted on the Best Barbie Board. They revealed a young woman who looked as fresh-faced as sweet young Laura Ingalls from *Little House On The Prairie*. In one, she held a sandy-haired Midge doll close to her face. In another, she was dressed in lavender, one of three bridesmaids at an outdoor wedding. In a third, she was lying beside a pool in a chaste one-piece swimsuit. The fact that she taught second grade only added to her rep as a darling. But knowing what kind of virulent messages she could and did leave on the boards suggested to P.J. that Hailey was anything but seraphic and nothing like her best friend Beth.

When Hailey pushed ever so slightly on the half-closed laundry room door, P.J. jumped forward, grabbed her, and struck her skull with the lancinating end of the tack hammer.

A single utterance escaped Hailey lips that sounded like "bahhh." Disoriented, she stumbled in an effort to leave, but it was too late. Her long, light brown hair was already becoming matted with blood from the first strike when P.J. landed a second wide-arced blow behind Hailey's left ear, exuviating a spray of blood all the way up to the ceiling.

Hailey stared blankly as she fell down on the laundry room floor, trying to place her attacker. Once down, P.J. kicked her repeatedly in the upper torso and head.

Soon Hailey was little more than a rag doll. The room had been renovated from white to dark red. P.J. pried the tack hammer out of Hailey's final, expressly deep head wound. She put the bloodied tack hammer in a plastic bag and selected two plush towels from the folded stack atop the dryer to wrap the bag with before sliding two jumbo rubber bands around the bundle.

She stepped over the glassy-eyed woman at her feet and took her shoes off at the entrance to the laundry room before proceeding through the house to find where Hailey kept her dolls.

The Raphael home was uncluttered and neat. Whatever wasn't beige ranged from dark brown to red to burnt orange in an autumnal palette that suggested the hand of an interior decorator. As P.J. passed through the living room, kitchen, and foyer, she noticed the Dora Tse Pé pottery as well as Apache, Paiute, and Hopi baskets. A print of Carl Redin's *Enchanted Mesa* hung above the living room fireplace. *Last Gleam* by Maynard Dixon exploded in the foyer. *White Faces* by Gerard Curtis Delano lined the hallway leading to a triad of bedrooms.

P.J. stared at *White Faces*, wondering how the cowboy managed to keep the cattle clustered around him. If she were one of those mooing McBurgers, she would surely find a way to hightail it to greener pastures.

She struck gold when she entered the first room off the hallway on the right. An assault of calico drapery and bedding reinforced the image P.J. had of Hailey being born for prudish prairie life. A personal computer sat on the desk, along with student papers exhibiting youngsters' evolving penmanship as they practiced writing the alphabet.

A curtained window in the room faced the backyard, where there was a large kidney-shaped pool and lounge chairs. It was the same pool seen in the photo Hailey shared online with friends. With hands still gloved, P.J. opened the window and a light breeze blew in, slamming the bedroom door with a loud bang.

Whaa whaa whaa whaa whaa whaa whaa whaa...

P.J. jolted awake and put her hand against her racing heart. The alarm clock beside the bed was flashing "8:00," which looked like BOO, BOO, BOO, BOO in the darkened room.

She was home.

She had slept through the night.

The door had never slammed at the Raphael house in Tucson. The light breeze, instead, had been refreshing as P.J., who had been sweating copiously, started to calm down and assess Hailey's collection.

Midge and bubble-cut Barbie dolls, most of them dressed in 900-series outfits, lined plywood shelves along two walls. There were plenty of unparalleled Midge dolls, including an assortment without freckles, some with side-glance eyes, some with teeth, and some high-color. There were at least a dozen *bendable* leg Midge dolls with bobbed hairdos. There were five never-removed-from-package Wigs Wardrobe Midge ensembles. There were three straight leg Midge dolls that wore two-piece swimsuits appropriate for their differing hair colors.

"Midge Hadley, you're coming with me," P.J. said, sweeping the shelves of all the Midge dolls, leaving the bubble-cuts behind.

"What about Barbie doll?" Midge cried out in a high-pitched, silly voice.

"Believe me, I'll have plenty of them by the time I'm done, and I've got to leave some dolls behind, or it will be obvious someone was here for you."

"But she's our best friend," Midge wailed, sounding like she'd inhaled helium.

P.J. threw loudmouthed Midge in the duffel, zipping it when it was packed full.

Six Midge dolls were left behind, but they were in duplicate 900-series dresses and inferior to the ones she culled.

She blended the shelves so the dolls were evenly spread out, with a Midge in the middle of each lineup on the upper three shelves on both four-shelved walls.

Less than fifteen minutes later, she was back in the rented Sebring parked on East Ocotillo, flying down dusty North Sabino Canyon Road, on her way back to the hotel to pack for home.

13

The last Thursday in January, Caresse noticed a change in mood as soon as she logged in at the Best Barbie Board on her home computer. Collectors were buzzing, but not about Gayle Grace, who was yesterday's news. Surprisingly, Gayle had been one-upped by a MMS— Murder More Sensational. Hailey Raphael, a collector from Tucson who virtually lived on the BBB, had been found dead Sunday night by her parents, who had just returned home from their weekly game of bridge with friends.

This time, no car explosions were involved. Hailey's skull had been bashed in with a tack hammer, according to Hailey's friend Beth, who lived in Phoenix.

Beth's postage stamp-sized avatar was of a saguaro cactus instead of her face, so unless they'd seen the selfies she'd posted online, they didn't know what she looked like. What BBB members did know, however, was that she was generally helpful and kind.

DESERTLIFE: Hi, everyone. As you know by now, we've lost my dear friend Hailey Raphael. News reports that she was found bludgeoned to death are accurate. Or, to put it more graphically, her head was bashed in with a tack hammer taken from her parents' garage. That's all I know at this point. I've read a lot of gossip here about Hailey's "many" boyfriends. The insinuations that she was skillful at playing them off each other--well, you can just drive that truck in a different direction. Those of you who are so quick to jump to the con-

clusion she was killed by an unsavory suitor who couldn't handle her game-playing anymore didn't know her very well. No offense, but I know who she was dating, who she was no longer dating, and everything was fine in that department. Yes, we wrote to each other every day, so I know what I'm talking about. Now on to what you all really want to know. Gayle's sister Megan was first to introduce the doll theft angle, and that hasn't been ruled out as a motive in Hailey's case. Investigators want to see Hailey's room to determine if any dolls are missing. This is all happening tomorrow morning, super early, so I'll let you know what's up as soon as I'm back online. Ciao for now, and quit your gossip! Hailey was awesome, and I'm going to miss her more than I can say.

As far as Caresse remembered, Hailey's collection focused on Midge rather than American Girls, the dolls of choice in the first homicide/theft. Maybe this *was* a crime of passion, as the violent MO suggested. She would just have to wait and see what Beth had to share after she met with detectives in Tucson.

With the beginnings of a headache, she turned her thoughts to her next assignment for *Barbie International* magazine—an interview with collector Nancy Roth. After that, she needed to go on her next date for the *San Luis Obispo County Times* feature.

While on the phone with Date Number Two, Caresse's radio was blaring Maroon 5, with Adam Levine singing about having no choice 'cause they wouldn't say good-bye anymore.

Her date's name was Bill, and they'd arranged to meet at Brubeck's downtown at seven-thirty. Bill, Brubeck's, two

Bs, easy to remember. No need to change out of her jeans. She was set to go.

She dialed Nancy's number in Walnut Creek, located outside east Oakland in San Francisco's East Bay, next door to Concord. Nancy had left a message earlier in the day that she would be able to email pictures of her vinyl goodies, sufficiently nixing the extra hundred she would have made if Nancy had shipped her some stuff and Caresse got photo credit.

She sat on her couch with her back toward her window and glanced over at the PC facing the mirrored wall. The phone, plugged in behind the couch now, was placed on the deep, inset ledge beneath the window where her wilting plants and narrow wicker basket, stuffed to the brim with unpaid bills, rested.

Now Hinder was on the radio, singing about how hard it was to be faithful when their girl had the lips of an angel. She turned down the volume and slid the tempered glass pane window shut. The tree-lined street below was devoid of traffic, with most people home, preparing and eating dinner. She wondered what her son Chaz would be having that night and hoped her ex, Brian, would serve some green vegetables or a salad with the inevitable frozen dinner or fried chicken.

A small black suction cup fitted to the top of the phone receiver, and it had a cord that jacked into her small micro-cassette recorder. Instead of pacing while she did interviews, she pressed the suction cup against the receiver until the tip of her finger was white, allowing it to become the focal point of her stress. She'd once made the mistake early on of not doing this, and the cup popped off during her interview with a company that made Barbie doll party and paper goods. She'd missed recording more than half the interview, and it showed in the results. The article only contained three quotes. The saving grace was being able to utilize photos from a press kit they'd sent her. Artwork carried the piece. She had no other choice save calling them back, and she wasn't about to do that. The woman she'd interviewed hadn't seemed that interested in talking to her to begin with.

"How do you like this for an opening?" she asked, once she had Nancy on the line.

"Let's hear it," Nancy said. Her voice was husky. Caresse concluded she was either a muscle-bound bodybuilder or had a bad cold.

"Vinyl collector Nancy Roth owns so many Barbie doll cases, trunks, travel pals, and hat boxes, her initials should be changed to SPP, one of the manufacturers of Barbie doll's vinyl products."

Nancy laughed hard and coughed. She rustled around and then blew her nose.

"Sorry," she said.

"Bad cold?"

"The worst. Probably caught it at work. My boss is really sick right now."

"What do you do?"

"I'm a paralegal. I have to lug home 500 pounds of paperwork each weekend."

"Even more sorry."

Nancy laughed. "It pays for the vinyl."

"So let's get on with it." Caresse pressed the cup against the receiver with all the strength her index finger possessed. "How does your husband deal with your collecting obsession?"

"Oh, Ward? Ward is great."

"Ward? As in Cleaver?"

"That's about as far as the connection goes. My Ward is short, fat, Jewish, and sells used cars."

"Okay." She could feel Nancy warming up to the idea of chatting and *she* knew how it would go. Talk about trunks and she'd start to hear a lilt in Nancy's voice. Talk about trunk artwork, and she'd hit Nancy's sweet spot dead center.

14

After Michael the *Monk* writer left the parking garage that day, P.J. was rattled. Nevertheless, she stayed to inspect the rest of her American Girls and put away her new Midge dolls. When Darby still hadn't arrived via scooter by the time she was done, she went into his apartment and retrieved an old blue sheet she found near his bed.

She left a note near his computer saying she'd be back on Thursday and then went outside to tack up the sheet on the inside of the gate to the storage stall.

As promised, she returned that last day in January with two Starbucks and a new set of twin bed sheets from a local department store. She explained what had happened with Michael and that she had hung the sheet to impede looky-loos and avoid future chats with nosy neighbors.

That morning, P.J. had emailed a picture from home that she wanted Darby to see. It was another Christmas photo card, this one from Time Taylor, who lived up in Oak Harbor, Washington. Time was online at least ten hours a day and posted responses to newbies' queries on the Best Barbie Board as if she was the world's top doll expert.

Her BBB avatar showed a grossly overweight woman with stringy blond hair dressed in baggy clothes. Her one close BBB pal Sally was the only one to back Time up in any online argument, and many assumed they were more than friends.

"She has the biggest part down solid," P.J. said, as she showed Darby Time's Flikr photo albums. "She weighs what? 320? 340?"

He clicked through photos that showed the inside and outside her home, her poodles, the Burger King where she worked, and some fellow tubbies in over-sized shirts and baggy jeans. "Yikes."

"Not passing judgment," P.J. said. She leaned over Darby's shoulder as he sat there, so close he could smell her Oscar de la Renta perfume. It was sweet and heady.

"Why do women smell so much better than men?" he asked. He turned to look at her and caught a glimpse of her arching an eyebrow, batting her eyelashes, gently mocking.

"Pheromones? Hormones? Who knows? Just pay attention. I want to get into her home, but she's having construction done. They're adding an enclosed porch, so the back is blocked off. She's been complaining online that the only way into her home until March is going to be via the front door, and she hates having to lug her groceries all the way up the front walk when she's used to pulling into the driveway, pulling around back, and being right at her rear door."

"I see," Darby said.

"So the problem is, the front door has one of those locked screens, and it's impossible to slide a card into one because there's a metal lip where you would slide it."

"So pick it," he said. "I've shown you how."

She sighed. "I'm not comfortable with that. Sometimes I can get it, sometimes I can't, and it takes me too long."

Darby clicked through Flickr until he found an album dedicated solely to exterior shots of Time's home.

P.J. was snide. "She's a parentless pothead, for Christ's sake. Her alcoholic mother and deranged father were both gone for different reasons six months after her eighteenth birthday three years ago, but Daddy did one thing right. After Mom died of liver cancer, he wrote a will giving his only daughter the house her mother had loved, as well as piles of dirty money stashed in every room, left over from two decades of drug deals. Daddy went to prison, got in a fight, and ended up dead. The will he had written after her mother's death, before he died, was valid. She got the house, complete with cubby-holed cash. Now she spends all her time eating and complaining about her life to e-quaintances online."

"What does she have to complain about?"

"Most days she consciously tries to forget about her preposterously abusive childhood—ignored, neglected, and battered by her mother, and virtually abandoned by her daddy, who liked the weather in South America so much better than rainy Washington State."

"She shared this on a public message board?" Darby, always the private soul who wouldn't even keep a journal for fear someone would find it and read it, was appalled.

"Some women use the board for therapy. Some are so lonely, their only friends are chat board people they'll never meet."

"Why is she named Time, anyway?" he asked.

P.J. rolled her eyes. "Oh, it's the stupidest story. I guess when her mom and dad were discussing names, her mom's water broke, and her mom said, 'It's time,' and her dad said, 'Time? Time Taylor? I love that for a name!' So it stuck."

"Should have been Time-To-Get-Some-Exercise Taylor," Darby said maliciously.

"Ooh. You can be as mean as I am."

"And why'd she piss you off?"

"That fat old sow," P.J. muttered so low Darby almost didn't hear her.

It was hard for her to remember the chat board exchange and not punch a wall.

TT: P.J., thanks for sharing pictures of your new number three ponytail, but she isn't worth $1,175. For one thing, she doesn't have her gold hoops, and for another thing, her eyeliner is brown.

PJ-RULEZ: Thanks for your opinion, Time, but I prefer brown eyeliner over blue, even if the blue is rarer.

TT: You still got ripped off. I wouldn't have paid more than $300 for that piece of shit.

PJ-RULEZ: You're kidding, right?

TT: God, look at her! It's so obvious she has new bands and a new bottom hard curl. Why would you pay for something that needed to be restored?

PJ-RULEZ: You know, I shouldn't have bothered telling you all what I paid for her, but you all saw the auction on eBay so you would have known what I paid anyway. But even without your input, I would buy her all over again for every penny I spent because I love her.

TT: Hmm. Maybe you'd like some things from my collection for three times what I paid for them too?

P.J. grimaced and struggled to control herself.

"Did you say something, P.J.?"

"No," she said. "You wouldn't understand."

"It's a doll thing?" He turned to look at her and saw her eyes were wet. He wanted to show concern and make her feel better.

He got up from his desk chair and went over and held her. She was trembling.

"It's a doll thing?" he repeated softly.

P.J. pushed her half-brother away. "Yes."

Darby studied her and realized she was going to be okay once she was on her way to Washington. He sat back down at the computer and went through Time's Flickr albums until he located the photo he was hoping to find of the front step area.

"Perfect," he said. "You see how she's got about an eight by eight raised concrete entrance outside her front doorway that's kind of arched over?"

P.J. didn't answer. When he turned around, she raised up from the couch where she had gone to lay down. "What?"

"I think I solved your problem. Her front archway looks like stucco to me, which is just what we want. I'll explain what you'll need to do and we can even practice here if you want before you leave. But I promise, you're gonna love it."

"But what about getting inside if the screen door is locked?"

"You're gonna have to go over there in the middle of the night your first night in town and fill the keyhole in the screen doorknob with Loc-Tite. The next day, when she leaves for work, she won't be able to get her key in the knob to flip the inside lock behind her. She'll opt to leave the screen door open and lock the inner door instead, which you can card open."

At that moment, the sun broke through the cloudy sky outside the apartment and shafts of sunlight poured through the vertical blinds facing Chevy Chase Drive.

Mother Nature herself sanctioned the solution.

15

The headache that might have ruined Caresse's evening departed as she threw herself fully into the interview. Better than two Tylenol, Barbie talk was once again cheering her up.

She continued to bear down on small black suction cup fitted to the top of the phone receiver, afraid to lessen the pressure lest she lose the call and ruin the rapport that was building. "So Ward is supportive?"

"Not only that. He takes pictures of my pieces, and if I'm not happy with them, he retakes them until I *am* happy. We want to do a vinyl guide book, so good pics are essential."

"Sounds great. Whom do you buy from?"

"I've bought a lot of vinyl from Debbye Bascom. She always has lots of lovely things for sale. She's the only dealer who's ever had a nice vinyl collection and advertises it in her subscription. Every time her list comes out, about ten to twenty items are choice."

"Did you have Barbie dolls when you were younger?"

Nancy grew quiet. "No. My mom didn't encourage it. She's not a doll person. I wanted them, but I kind of dropped the issue. I got other toys instead."

Caresse leaned back into the couch. In the background, Marc Cohn sang about a pretty little thing waiting for the King down in the jungle room. Nancy was just about ready to fully open up. In a way, asking leading questions was akin to therapy.

Nancy explained that she had more than made up for her mother's unwillingness to give her dolls. In 1992, she was stricken with Barbie doll fever. Her friend Margaret, in San Francisco, started collecting Barbie dolls first. Nancy was visiting her in the Bay Area when they went to a flea market, where Margaret spotted some Barbie dolls.

"And then I realized," she said, "all these things are still around! After my first blond bubble cut, I began stockpiling dolls and clothes as fast as I could get my hands on them. I bought a case and I thought, 'you know, I really like the graphics, the artwork.' Then I started going to shows and began realizing there was such a variety. Every time I thought, 'Oh, I've gotten all the cases,' I'd go, 'No, I haven't. There's another one, and another one!' Trunks, cases, hat boxes, and travel pals—what can I say? They're intriguing and fun."

Caresse smiled, thinking Nancy should leave the legal world for a job in PR or advertising.

"I can store my dolls and clothes in them," she enthused. "And I view them as a real sampling of our culture at the time, what with the way the dolls are dressed and the artwork is done."

"Tell me about some of your favorite cases," she prompted.

Nancy first described a case she called "The Equestrienne." It was a beige case featuring artwork of Barbie doll and Skipper wearing riding outfits. Then she described a case that was dubbed "The Picnic." It showed artwork of Barbie doll, Ken, and Skipper.

"They're sitting down, having a picnic, and they have a watermelon. There's a butterfly in the scene and a blue jay in the trees," she explained.

In addition to Nancy's fondness for the lavish artwork, she was fascinated with different color combinations. "There's a case which shows Barbie doll dressed in Red Flare," she said. "This case is intriguing because on some cases they used Red Flare in red, like it really is, and they put it on a blue, black, or white background. Then, for some reason, they made the case again and used a yellow version of Red Flare, putting the Barbie doll graphics in yellow on a blue, black, or red background. Six cases with two variations of Red Flare! Who decided to sit down and say, 'Let's just put this in yellow here, on red'? Did they leave it up to the artists? Was it because one day they didn't have enough dye?"

Caresse laughed. Nancy was running at full steam now. "Of course, you have vinyl friends?"

"I have many friends who are equally into vinyl collecting," she stressed, pausing to blow her nose again. "We have a great system so we're not competitive. We like to know what we're each specifically looking for. At shows, we'll say, 'I've got my heart set on finding this,' and then we work it out. We don't just run in and snatch it. Whoever wants something that day gets it."

"And what would you like to add to your collection that you're missing?"

Nancy sounded a bit vague as her mind wandered to her wish list. "There's a Skipper Purse Pal I want. It's done in the shape of a purse you'd carry in the Sixties. I also want the case that features the head of a side-part American Girl. The case was originally sold together with a brunette Swirl. There's a window in the case, and you can see the doll."

"Got kids to pass your collection on to?"

"No," she said, "but my three-year-old niece is a budding Barbie doll collector. On her third birthday, she had a Barbie doll party. I'm training her to follow in my footsteps."

"Sounds good," Caresse said, glancing at the wall clock near the computer monitor. She had half an hour to get to 726 Higuera Street for her work-related date. It occurred to her to ask Nancy if she'd heard about Barbie doll collector Gayle Grace being murdered in upstate New York or Midge fanatic Hailey Raphael being bludgeoned to death in Tucson, but she was out of time. She released the pressure from the receiver cup, disconnected the recorder, wished Nancy a speedy recovery from her cold, and said good-bye.

16

After Hailey's parents were led away from the crime scene on East Ocotillo Drive, forensic technicians in Tucson staked out the Raphael property from the road, down the side of the garage, across the backyard, and back to the front curb.

Bagging anything found on or near the lawn, driveway, and sidewalk, the force worked tirelessly, tweezing anything that might be important. Cigarette butts, strands of hair, bits of paper—all of it was collected in an attempt to determine who had killed the young schoolteacher who loved nothing more than eating popcorn while watching Westerns and volunteering her time on weekends to Meals on Wheels.

Everything outside the house that could be considered potential evidence was photographed and marked on a sketch. Collected, initialed, sealed, and dated bags went to the van. Two cotton-gloved investigators focused their attention on the left-side garage entrance, where the body-width walkway created cramped working quarters. Alek Bryce headed down the narrow path first. He stopped near the garage door and squatted down in the pale gravel. Scanning the area, he stopped and used his forceps to pin a long, vibrant strand of hair lying in pebbles.

"Get Sketch and Viper," he said to his partner Eitan. "Got a blond beauty here."

The first team of investigators combed the workbench inside the garage. An empty spot on the pegboard filled with hanging tools was photographed and sketched.

The entire garage was scanned visually with a laser for latent prints. Since the bench was dark, white powder was applied to the surface for contrast. Then, using a short-hair brush, a technician removed excess powder, avoiding over-brushing lest the prints lose clarity. Transparent tape was used to lift latent prints, which were then placed on dark backing cards for contrast.

The garage floor was dusty, and examination yielded several footprints. Lighting was focused on each section of the floor. Examination-quality, thirty-five millimeter photos using a manual focus camera were taken. Using a tripod, it was necessary to focus directly over the impressions so the film plane was parallel. As recommended by the FBI, the f-stop was set at f/16 or f/22 for greater depth of field, and an electronic flash with a long extension cord was attached to the camera. As warranted in every photograph, a thin ruler or measured piece of cord was included in each shot to show scale. Additionally, labels were placed in pictures to correlate impressions with crime scene notes. Ambient light was blocked with a sunscreen to maximize light from the flash. By focusing on the bottom of each impression instead of the scale in each photo, clarity was assured.

Inside the home, a second photographer was shooting prints on the hallway carpeting, positioning the camera flash at a ten to fifteen degree angle to the impressions to enhance their detail. By shooting several exposures, it was possible to bracket toward overexposure to obtain maximum details. It was then necessary to move the flash, adding a few additional angles, moving the light and adjusting the sunscreen in a progressive path toward the laundry room.

Iden "Sketch" Wayne stood in the entrance to the laundry room and graphed out the small area. Clothes remained neatly folded atop the dryer, which had long since gone quiet. Through the cracks between the door hinges, Wayne noticed the lidded hamper, marred by smudges and blood spray.

The murder victim, Hailey Raphael, lay in a semi-fetal position on her right side, facing him. He glanced quickly, then sketched roughly, capturing her as best he could. He had an embarrassing habit others knew nothing about to prevent himself from getting sick. By squinting so he only saw through a watery, blurred field of vision, he could accomplish the necessary strokes on his pad without becoming overwhelmed by the blood.

Down went impressions of the fresh, young face. Down went the splayed hair. Down went the crushed skull. Down went the ravaged chest. Down went the battered arms and legs. Down went the bloodied clothing. Down went the bare feet. Wayne exhaled and stepped along the baseboards, moving toward the top of Hailey's bloodied head. He continued along the wall to the washing machine, which still had its lid up.

Bryce stood in the doorway, watching his colleague. "Anything in the machine?"

Wayne leaned forward.

There were ten pennies inside the empty washer.

17

P.J. damaged the screen lock before the sun came up Monday and stayed parked, down the street from Time's home, in a rented Toyota Avalon Touring Sedan. She was not far from the Candlelight Suites, where she had taken a spacious room complete with a kitchen and desk area, where she could work on her laptop.

The rain-soaked neighborhood was intersected by Northeast Oleary, and from there, it was just a short drive to Northeast Sixth. The evening before, she had driven out to the Oak Harbor shore and watched the water lap up on the grainy land. The sand was soft from recent storms and her heels dug into the wetness, leaving a deep set of tracks behind her. The wind whipped her lustrous hair, and she pulled her jacket tight. Farther down the rocky coast, a weathered man fed seagulls from a loaf of bread. With feeble hands, he broke off chunks and tossed them as high as he could into the air.

P.J. decided to walk the other way and eventually found a swing set and play area for children. She sat in a small swing and kicked off, pumping higher and higher as her momentum increased. Her handbag on the ground grew smaller with each arc. Finally, one loafer fell off and she had to stop and hop through wet sand to retrieve it.

Now, as she rested in the white four-door amidst pillows and blankets she had borrowed from the hotel room closet, she felt relaxed enough to nap. She set her small two-hour timer to its maximum setting and allowed herself to doze.

Two hours later, the beeping alarm brought her out of a deep sleep. She dreamt she had discovered a trunk buried along the Oak Harbor shoreline and had pried it open to discover prototype dolls and outfits. Her unconscious mind has invented a Miss Barbie doll with rooted hair, a Skipper wearing a smaller version of Barbie doll's Outdoor Life, and a three-doll wedding set including Barbie doll, Skipper, and Tutti, with Barbie doll as the bride and Skipper dressed in a larger version of her younger sister's Flower Girl outfit.

"That was the best dream ever," she said aloud, reaching for her now-cold drive-thru coffee in the holder in front of her. She retied her hair back and sat up straight, re-zipping her hooded sweatshirt.

A few minutes later, as she sipped the cold java, she saw Time Taylor. The woman emerged from her home and nudged two poodles back from the door's threshold.

"Visual confirmation on the dogs," P.J. said aloud. She felt around in the pockets of her hoodie until she uncovered the cold slices of bacon wrapped in Denny's napkins.

Time's stringy blond hair hung around her face as she tried to insert her key in the screen door keyhole without success. She stopped, wiped her chubby hands on her baggy pants, and tried again without success. Finally she straightened up and leaned in to lock the regular door, slamming the screen with a frustrated sigh before heading down the walkway to her car. She started her Ford Taurus and was off in a cloud of exhaust, careening around the corner onto Oleary as if she were in hot pursuit of the very next breakfast BK would serve that morning.

P.J. drank the rest of her cold coffee before she grabbed the canvas tote and empty duffel out of the back seat. Walking slowly up the street, she stopped once to look around before approaching Time's front door. Then she carded it open and let herself in.

18

The first Monday in February, Caresse and her four-year-old son Chaz discovered a storefront a few doors down from the Salvation Army store on Islay that bore the sign "Monya's Antiques." Caresse said they had to go inside, suggesting there might be toys. She was hoping they might have some old dolls to grab cheap.

Quickly, she made herself at home amidst some of the heftier items in the collectibles paradise while Chaz wandered off. The shop owner, Monya, was a woman who spoke in absolutes whenever she felt expansive. She was half Ukrainian, half L'Oreal Preference Fade Defying Color & Shine System Permanent Intense Red Copper RR-07. She had passed heavy forty pounds ago, and today she wore a red and orange silk muumuu and too much Emeraude. Her lips were painted orange to match her tangerine talons.

Despite being off any scale measuring visual refulgence, she had a firm handshake and a beguiling smile. There was no question she could sell Cubic Zirconia to a fine gems expert. Caresse took an instant liking to her but nevertheless wanted to assess her knowledge. She waited patiently while a woman in gray sold Monya some cut glass her grandmother had left her. Monya gave the lady half the resale value in cash, and the woman left the shop, arms empty, smiling at Caresse as she passed by.

Chaz had discovered an open box of old wooden trains and track pieces in the corner of the shop, where a bit of space had been allotted for set-up and play, so he was fully occupied. Caresse approached the main counter while rearranging her bra strap so it was once again hidden by the loose neckline on her beige shirt.

There was nothing quite like coming right out with it. "Got any old Barbie dolls?"

A skinny guy with jet-black hair and *Blues Brothers* shades skulked in from the back room and caught Monya's eye. He pointed to the staircase. She nodded slightly and he slunk away, up the stairs and out of sight.

"Barbie dolls, Barbie dolls," Monya murmured as she walked over to a curio cabinet and took a doll down from a high glass shelf. She walked back over to Caresse and put the doll on the counter. "How can you not fall in love?" she asked.

The doll presented to her wore an elaborate red-sequined gown, a lavish cape, and a heart-shaped head-piece with a red feather sprouting from it.

Chaz approached the counter, holding one of the small wooden trains from the box.

"That's a Barbie doll?" he asked.

"The Queen of Hearts by Bob Mackie," Monya replied. "A very expensive, highly-collectible Barbie doll."

Caresse studied the creation. She was impressive. The doll's dress was so sparkly, reflection from the sequins caught in the mirrored items throughout the shop and bounced off the overhead lighting.

Chaz beamed at Monya. "I like your hair."

"Why, thank you!"

"It reminds me of fire."

The kid in the dark glasses slipped back down the stairs, nodded to Monya once, and left.

Monya smiled benignly. "He always steps in to check my records."

Caresse was surprised. "He's an accountant?"

Monya frowned. "Records. LPs. Vinyl."

Caresse hunkered on the edge of a chair dressed in dusty tapestry upholstery depicting hunters on horseback.

Chaz peered into one of Monya's glass cases. "Hey, Mom, your magazines."

He pointed at a vintage stack of *Barbie International* issues from the late eighties.

Monya looked where Chaz was pointing.

"*Your* magazines?" Her curiosity was piqued.

"I write for *Barbie International*."

"Well, why didn't you say so?" Like the Wizard of Oz emerging from behind the curtain, Monya came around the counter and took an upholstered chair near the one Caresse occupied. Monya was about to tell a story swiftly and tell it well.

Once upon a time, back in the mid-Eighties before Barbie doll turned thirty, a little-known woman who worked for the American Cancer Society decided a monthly Barbie doll magazine would sell to baby boomers who treasured her. The woman put together a now-archaic desktop publishing system, found a printer, learned everything she could about distribution, and was soon clearing $20,000 profit each month from sales of *Barbie Doll Digest*.

When Sierra met her husband, she was already known on the Barbie doll circuit as a real go-getter. She had majored in journalism and thought she should write about Barbie doll, combining two loves. She wrote to Annie, the woman who launched the first Barbie doll magazine, and started contributing articles to her publication. But soon, Sierra had more plentiful and better ideas than Annie had. Additionally, she was in Southern California where Mattel was, while Annie was stuck on the East coast.

Everyone told Sierra she should give Annie a run for her money. When Sierra got married and her husband wanted to finance her dream, it was all over for Annie. About half of Annie's subscribers decided if they could only afford one Barbie doll magazine, they'd rather buy Sierra's. Sierra was more creative and had better stories.

"Annie was pissed, but what could she do? It's a free country." Monya threw up her hands and then let them flop onto her lap.

"How do you know all this?" Caresse asked.

"Annie is my sister."

"Wow."

"She's still back east," Monya said, anticipating Caresse's next question. "Have you ever met Sierra?"

"No. We email, and we've talked on the phone once or twice. I send my features and photos to her, and that's about it. I get checks when issues come out, and I have to file a freelance tax thingie each spring. She's got a lot to do to publish every month."

"Did you hear about the Gayle Grace murder?"

Caresse held her breath. Finally, someone might offer some tidbits that hadn't been published.

"Annie told me some woman in upstate New York was murdered, and her American Girl Barbie doll collection was raided. As far as they can tell, the dolls were taken the same day the couple was killed."

Chills ran down Caresse's spine. Instead of letting Monya know she had heard about the homicides, she decided to let her talk to determine whether or not the old woman had information she hadn't run across.

"Both Gayle and her husband died in an explosion," Monya continued. "Investigators talked to Gayle's sister Megan, who originally helped Gayle inventory her dolls. They went through the Graces' home, and guess what? Many of the dolls on the list were missing."

Caresse wanted to hear Monya's suppositions. "But why kill them? If you just want someone's dolls, you take the dolls when they're not home, right?"

"You've got to consider the killer had a grudge against Gayle and wanted her dead. Taking her dolls was important, but killing her was meaningful too."

Chaz approached slowly, dragging a box of trains and track pieces with him.

"Mom, I want this."

Caresse stood up and smiled.

"How much for the whole box?" she asked Monya.

Monya placed her right, liver-spotted, many-ringed hand on Caresse's shoulder. They had bonded. "The whole box, ten bucks."

"Such a deal," she said, returning the woman's warm smile.

She turned to Chaz. "You're gonna have to help me carry it back to the car."

Chaz considered this, realizing they left the Honda clear over by Mitchell Park prior to their inner-city trek. "It's worth it," he said finally. "And Mom, I'm gonna leave this stuff at your place. Dad says we've got too much clutter."

She raised an eyebrow. "He does, does he?"

"He should see *this* place," Monya said, and the three of them laughed.

They left the shop with Chaz on the left, his small hands beneath the bottom of the box on his side, and Caresse on the right, doing the same. They walked semi-sideways in tandem for a while until Caresse almost tripped. Then she told her son to hang on to her belt loop while she balanced the box on her head all the way back to their car.

19

The poodles greeted P.J., their tiny black-nailed feet slipping and sliding on the smooth cerulean tile floor in the entryway.

P.J. took the napkined bacon out of her pocket and addressed them by name.

"Hi, Pooh. Hi, Schmoo." Their ridiculous monikers made her smile. The treats were a hit. She had made friends.

Everything in the living room was pastel. Light peach, lemon yellow, and touches of sky blue gave the place a lighthearted feel. The poodle babies followed her into the room, watching her with curiosity in their eyes. She headed up the plush peach-carpeted staircase. The bathroom was at the top landing, a study was set up in the room to the left, and the master bedroom was to the right. She opted to go into the study and was rewarded by the sight of cardboard boxes stacked high beside a curio cabinet packed with Barbie dolls. The curio was lit, but P.J. could barely tell because sunshine creeping in beneath the half-drawn blinds muted it.

"What, does she leave the light on all the time?" she asked.

Pooh—or perhaps Schmoo—yipped in response.

P.J. chuckled and opened the cabinet with her thin-gloved hands. Number one and two ponytails—the mother lode in Barbie doll collecting—were both there and in mint condition. A group of number threes was dressed in mint examples of some of Barbie doll's earliest outfits including Commuter Set, Gay Parisienne, Plantation Belle, Roman Holiday, and Easter Parade. P.J. had never seen an Easter Parade coat that wasn't a reproduction. The black faille was soft and spotless, and the matching hat, a simple bow of silk organza, seemed as fresh as it must have in 1959.

The dolls and outfits moved forward through Barbie doll's history as one gazed down the length of the cabinet. At the bottom, Twist 'n Turn Barbie dolls were dressed in outfits as diverse as Dreamy Blues, Bright 'n Brocade, and Fab City. Each outfit was complete, from Trailblazer's goggles to Dreamy Pink's slippers.

A bevy of AG and bubble cut Barbie dolls filled the middle shelves, and some of her favorite 1600-series ensembles were here. Of course, she had them all, thanks to Gayle, but there was no harm in taking a few duplicates. In addition to a blond bubble wearing Here Comes The Bride and a dark brownette AG wearing London Tour, there was an exquisite raspberry-lipped, longhaired silver brunette AG dressed in White Magic.

P.J. filled her duffel bag rapidly, squeezing in her last two picks—a low-color, coral-lipped silver-ash blond side-part AG dressed in Theatre Date and a choice 1966 high-color, long-haired ash blond AG wearing Country Club Dance—before zipping the bag closed. After hoisting it, P.J. added the second tote to her load and went back downstairs.

It dawned on her she must be getting stronger. Despite the weight she carried, she had not needed to stop and rest mid-retreat. Kneeling beside the poodles, she pet them good-bye. Then she rose and slipped out the front door, shutting it gently behind her.

It was time to kick Darby's plan into effect.

She examined the arch extending over the entrance porch.

The ever-resourceful Darby had a friend who did the chrome work on motorcycles. Knowing they used cyanide to etch the metal, he had no problem paying his friend a visit and boosting a bucket before he left. Then, at the hardware store, he bought plaster of Paris and glue, followed by a trip to the grocery store, where he stocked up on more toilet paper, rubber gloves, aluminum foil, and two large pots.

The following day, he went to a hobby store and bought sand-colored spray paint and itty-bitty engines used for shooting off model rockets. At home, he laid everything out on a sheet of cardboard roughly half a foot wide. He glued the engines with primer wire sticking out everywhere until the cardboard was covered with nearly two hundred of them.

P.J. watched as he took thin speaker wire and glued that to the cardboard too. Ultimately, a wire led to each igniter.

Darby went into the kitchen and poured the cyanide into the pot on the stove, mixing it with glue as he heated it. When it was ready, he slathered it onto aluminum foil and let it dry.

Next, he filled a vat with toilet paper, water, and glue to create papier-mâché.

"Did you bring the mixer?" he asked.

As though she were in the presence of a scientist dancing on the edge of madness, P.J. did not speak as she went to the box she'd brought over and removed the electric mixer from home.

"Bring it to me," he said.

She did so, helping him adjust the settings once he had it plugged in and running.

"Just let it run," he said, returning to where the aluminum foil had been spread out. The cyanide-glue mixture was dry, so he put on rubber gloves and started breaking it into pieces like malleable peanut brittle. When he was done, he glued a crystallized hunk of cyanide to each rocket.

Darby turned off the mixer and moved the vat of papier-mâché to the floor, where he spread out fresh aluminum foil. After pouring it out, he went to the table with the plaster of Paris. He coated the wires with a powdery layer to protect them and then applied the papier-mâché to the cardboard.

A chunk of sand-colored stucco "borrowed" from a home farther up Chevy Chase Drive that looked close to the stucco Time's archway was made of served as a model for their next step. The stucco had been filled with plaster of Paris so when the two parts separated, they had a model of the opposite of the finish.

Applying the model to the papier-mâché with the inverse side created a stucco effect. By morning, it would be dry and then it could be spray-painted the proper sand color.

P.J. was determined to follow through on Darby's hard work and bring things to fruition in a way he would sanction. He had explained that radio control airplanes came with servos and that the wires would run down to a little remote control, and that she would have the switch.

As she appraised the archway, she realized just where he would hang the strip of stucco—off to the side, in the wall of the arch, where trailing wires could hide behind the potted plants on the porch.

After gluing it into place with the pungent glue Darby provided, she ran the wires behind the plants and down off the porch, placing the big battery behind the shrubs. Then, afraid to linger, she grabbed her bags and hastened back to her rental car.

If what she posted on the Barbie doll board held true, Time would be home at noon to check on her babies. She didn't like to leave them alone for more than a morning or afternoon, and certainly not a whole day.

Exhausted, P.J. rested in the car while waiting for her victim to arrive, setting her alarm for eleven-thirty in case she nodded off. At one point, the gray skies began to lull her, but she shook herself awake. Eleven-thirty came, and she shut the alarm off, regaining her excitement for what lie ahead.

She didn't have to wait long. At eleven forty-five, Time pulled up in her Taurus and jumped out, running to the front door. When she stopped on the welcome mat to dig for the house keys at the bottom of her large bag, P.J. pushed the switch.

With a whooshing, the archway exploded in a spray of plaster and smoke.

It wasn't as loud as P.J. expected, but it was messy.

Inside the car, P.J. shivered with delight.

She remembered Darby's assurances. "The blocks of cyanide will be pushed into her skin. She'll look like hamburger meat, and her guts will liquefy. It'll take about thirty seconds to a minute for the cyanide to enter her bloodstream. It's definitely faster than having her ingest it. I mean, it'll be right in her system in no time flat."

The neighborhood remained quiet, save for a flock of birds emerging from a nearby pine tree, flying up, over the homes and away.

P.J. allowed a minute to pass. When all remained quiet, she started her engine and slowly drove up the street, daring one peek at Time's home as she passed. She could see the woman lying slumped beneath the archway, with one raw arm outstretched across the porch.

Turning onto Oleary, P.J. began to relax. She reflected that what Cowley said of books might be true of Barbie dolls: "Because the soul of Man is not by its own Nature or observation furnished with sufficient Materials to work upon, (they) are essential to solitude, for it is only by a continual recourse to them that the soul can be replenished with fresh supplies, otherwise the solitary would grow indigent, and be ready to starve without them."

Even more apropos, referring to the pursuit of knowledge, when Confucius said he not only forgot food and sorrows but did not even perceive old age coming on, P.J. could readily apply that sentiment to her aim of getting all the dolls she needed, wrapping armfuls around her svelte self, squeezing the bundle tight, grinning the most satisfied of all smiles, lips tinged with blood.

20

FREDERICKS – Paul Francis Fredericks, 90, of San Luis Obispo, died Monday at a San Luis Obispo Hospital. Arrangements are pending at Los Osos Valley Mortuary.

Caresse hurried through the *County Times'* death notices she needed to write in order to make time to log in at the Best Barbie Board. She had half an hour before she had to run to the Starbucks downtown for Date Number Three.

A quick glance around the newsroom told her this was a good time to surf. Seth, Anjo, and even Jenna and her three stooges were AWOL. Laura was at the switchboard up front, putting calls through to advertising, laughing as late morning sunlight streamed through the windowed lobby, touching upon a sparkly gewgaw in her hair. Over in Classified, Marilyn Garrett was online, playing Scrabble.

Beth had posted a message only three minutes earlier, sharing information about her morning visit to the Raphael residence.

DESERTLIFE: Hi, everyone. Thanks for knocking off the idle speculations about Hailey's love life if just for the simple reason she's no longer around to defend herself. As promised, I met with the Tucson police this morning—way earlier than anyone should have to get up—and they allowed me to go into Hailey's room. Boy, was it weird to be in there with them, with them watching and waiting to see what I'd say. On first glance, Hailey's room seemed pretty much the way it always did—clean, neat, organized. And to look at her doll shelves, an outsider would think nothing was amiss.

This is what I saw when I went in. I looked at both sets of shelves, four on her west wall and four on her north. Her dolls used to be lined up almost as though they were holding hands, with no real space between them, and she used to have fewer Barbie dolls than Midge, who was her favorite.

What I saw on her shelves shocked me. The dolls were spaced evenly, inches apart from each

other, and there were only six Midge dolls left, placed dead center on six of the eight shelves, the bottom-most shelves remaining Midge-less. All of her best Midge dolls were taken, along with some NRFB Wigs Wardrobes. The thief did not touch Hailey's bubble cuts. I don't know why.

It's still debatable whether or not the Tucson Police believe Hailey was murdered for doll-related reasons, but they were appreciative of my time. We'll see what happens from here on out.

So that's it, guys. I am seriously tired (not to mention depressed), so I'll check back in later to hear what you all have to say.

Peace out, Beth

Caresse remembered what Megan Dailon had said.

The robber chose to take at least one example of each rare outfit and the best of Gayle's dolls, leaving those that were less mint or wearing duplicate or more common outfits rearranged uniformly, three to a shelf.

Beth's description of Hailey's shelves was similar.

The dolls were spaced evenly, inches apart from each other, and there were only six Midge dolls left, placed dead center on six of the eight shelves.

The killer had stopped long enough to rearrange the dolls on both victims' display shelves after swiping the ones that met his or her fancy.

It was the same person.

Caresse shook herself out of her reverie and glanced at her watch.

No matter how much she didn't want anything Venti with a guy named Jerry, she was committed to her next date at Starbucks.

21

As soon as she returned home, P.J. took care of some work, stored her Oak Harbor dolls at Darby's, and was back on the road again, this time Greyhounding her way from L.A.'s Union Station all the way to Las Vegas.

As the people piled up for a weekday excursion, she realized the bus would be packed because rooms in Sin City were cheaper midweek, particularly in the winter. This was the on-a-budget crowd who couldn't or wouldn't fly or drive or enjoy a two-day stay at the Wynn. Greyhound security was lax to nonexistent, and identity checks were nil. The only way to trace P.J.'s whereabouts would be to know what her alias was (Devvon West) and to know who retrieved mail from the P.O. Box in Glendale where her bus tickets were mailed (Darby). Darby and "Devvon" had set up the P.O. Box together late the previous year with fake IDs, posing as a married couple that wanted the P.O. Box for anonymity regarding mail order transactions.

Buses heading to Vegas arrived at a depot hidden by most of the Union Station terminal, which primarily served Amtrak and offered stop and start points for Los Angeles underground rapid transit. The benches in the depot sat beneath roof overhangs where those who smoked stood or sat on benches and blew smoke rings over the heads of mothers with babies, the elderly, the disabled, and the disenfranchised.

When P.J.'s Greyhound pulled in, her group moved forward en masse and waited for the attendant to open the belly of the bus so they could throw their beat-up suitcases into the mosh pit of belongings. P.J. was one of the first to board. She chose a seat in back, next to the right side window. She was carrying a handful of fashion magazines in her over-sized satchel. The drugs she would use to murder Zivia Uzamba were stowed with her clothing and toiletries in the bus cavity.

P.J. had once offered Zivia $4,500 for a Japanese side-part Barbie doll with silvery brunette hair she was determined to add to her collection. When Zivia refused to sell the doll, P.J. bumped the offer to $4,750, then $5,000, and finally $5,200. Zivia continued to say no, and P.J. became enraged. Zivia had money, like she did, and this wasn't about cash value. It was a power struggle for one woman to keep what was hers, and determination on the other woman's part to take what was withheld, if all reasonable offers were refused.

Why P.J. fell in love with that particular doll was hard to say. She had seen other Japanese side-parts and found them attractive, but there was something about how Zivia's doll's full bangs complemented her extra full, slightly waved bob. When combined with her brilliant turquoise shadow, flawless strawberry-colored lips, and the fact there was no discoloration to the tip of her nose whatsoever, the doll was a must-have.

There were many more rarities in Zivia's collection that P.J. hungered for, including Japanese Francies, Skippers, and Midge dolls. Zivia also hoarded several outfits manufactured exclusively for the Japanese market that P.J. was anxious to acquire.

A tall man with disheveled hair and a prominent nose took the seat next to P.J., smiling as he sat down and made himself comfortable. He had a copy of Al Gore's *The Assault On Reason* with him. A book light clipped to the book's binding illuminated the pages. He also had a copy of the day's *L.A. Times* and a black briefcase, which he slid under the seat ahead of him—a difficult feat since the space was so narrow.

"A little crowded," he commented.

P.J. judged him to be a youthful forty-five, with barely a hint of gray in his dark hair and a small thatch of laugh lines near his eyes. He looked distinguished and out of place among the bus crowd.

He seemed to read her mind. "Beats driving," he said. "Can't read or get work done when you drive, and Amtrak doesn't go to Vegas from here."

"I know," P.J. said. "But you could fly."

She played with her bracelet nervously, afraid this man would want to talk the entire trip. She would parse down her sentences until she barely said a word and then tune him out entirely.

"Hate to fly," he said, sounding earnest. "Something about being on the ground makes me feel a lot safer."

He glanced down at the bracelet she was fingering.

"Barbie doll," he said.

P.J. gasped.

"What, you're surprised?" He stifled a laugh. "You got a sister who's as into it as mine is, you know a Barbie doll bracelet when you see one."

P.J. looked down at her wrist and cursed herself for wearing it. The gold-plated work of art by Patricia Field featured a Barbie doll silhouette charm that fell onto the back of her hand, glinting off her tanned skin. More than the shoe or the star or the handbag charms, the classic profile of the ponytail Barbie doll charm was a dead giveaway.

She opened her satchel and pulled out her stack of *Elle, Glamour, Harper's Bazaar*, and *Vogue*. She snuggled down in her seat—a near impossibility since they seemed to have no cushioning whatsoever—and opened the top magazine which featured a sexy Kate Bosworth on the cover, wearing dark peach silk.

She flipped it open and began to read about Kate's feelings about her ex and first love, Orlando Bloom, and her current involvement with model/musician James Rousseau. Meanwhile, the man beside her buried himself in world news. She glanced over and saw that he was reading a story about a teenage boy in West Baghdad who was arrested for the attempted rape of a schoolmate. The boy knew that because she was a Sunni, no one would protect her.

The man noticed P.J. looking at the *L.A. Times* story.

"It's the Sunni minority versus the Shia majority," he sighed. "The Sunni have got to be feeling extremely pregnable ever since Saddam Hussein was overthrown."

P.J. looked at him blankly. *Who was pregnant?*

He chuckled sympathetically. "You don't keep up with what's happening in Iraq, do you?"

In that instant, P.J. felt a flash of anger combined with a healthy dollop of defensiveness. World news was always part of the viewing fare at home, but she more or less tuned it out, using it as background noise for her own, more important thoughts.

With his right side virtually pressed against her left shoulder, the man turned slightly and extended his left hand toward her.

"Craig Krieger," he said.

P.J. swallowed hard. "Devvon West."

22

The San Luis Obispo Starbucks was in the Downtown Centre on the corner of Marsh and Morro. On the four-radio-song drive over, Gavin DeGraw shared that part of where he was going was knowing where he was coming from, Hoobastank wished they could take it all away, Paula Cole didn't want to wait, and the nights were still so lonely for Train.

Caresse's date, Jerry, was her age nearly to the day. They'd both had birthdays in January, hers on New Year's and his on the ninth. He resembled her cousin and raised an impulse to give him a noogie, messing up the gel job he'd done on his auburn hair.

The ninja barista behind the counter, a blond in her twenties, worked quietly and efficiently, mastering chocolate, caramel, and peppermint combinations as she went.

Her workmate, a definite rock star barista, greeted old friends and newbies like old pals recovered after an exhaustive search combing Hollywood nightclubs and bars.

"Caresse!" he screamed after scribbling her name on a Venti cup. "Venti. Venti—what'd you say you wanted? Where you been?"

"Here," she replied.

Jerry had already placed his order for a Toffee Nut Latte.

Rock Star laughed like Caresse was funnier than *Frisky Dingo.*

"Venti house," she mumbled. It was an unimaginative selection, and she knew she was in for it.

"House? House?" She thought he was going to cry and ruin his manscara. His guyliner was muddy brown, matching his java-colored eyes. "Damn, gir, you're making me miss the days of Chanticos. You look like a Chantico woman."

Caresse hadn't heard anyone call anyone "gir" since she'd tried watching *Noah's Arc* on Logo. And did her butt really look that big? She was, in fact, a Chantico girl, discovering them the very week they debuted in late 2005. That drinking a Chantico was roughly like downing six ounces of brownie batter made her wonder how fat Rock Star really thought she was. Didn't her over-sized sweater at least hide her slight tummy?

"Black is all I drink now," she told Jerry. "It's kind of a long story."

And it looked like it was going to be another long date.

But could it be as bad as date number two?

On that disastrous outing, she had forgotten it was Farmers' Market night so parking on Higuera was out. She'd headed down Broad all the way to Peach, listening to 3 Doors sing about how a hundred days had made them older. By the time she'd had parked, Tracy Chapman had a feeling she could be someone, be someone, be someone.

After locking the Honda, she ran down Chorro past Mill, Palm, and Monterey, thanking the stars she wasn't one of those chicks who needed to wear high, strappy sandals to impress on a blind date. Sneakers, jeans, and a gorgeous heliotrope top worked just fine. The sexy shoes would wait until she found out whether she was even attracted to the guy.

The smoke from the outdoor grills cooking ribs slathered in barbecue sauce wafted toward her as she hung a right onto Higuera. She was nearly at Garden Street when Downtown Brown the bear nearly collided with her. For a few seconds, she was up close and personal with the city mascot's flat blue and white eyes. Downtown stepped left as she stepped left and then stepped right as she stepped right. Onlookers paused to watch the mysterious dance between the adult in the furry costume and the harried-looking brunette in her mid-thirties, trying to get past him to get to Brubeck's. Finally, Downtown stood still and she offered him profuse thanks as she ran off.

Bill looked to be in his forties, with dark-hair, Tommy Lee Jones eyes, and a gaunt frame.

"Hi," she said, offering her hand, sliding into the chair across from him.

Bill stood up halfway and sat when she sat, pulling in his chair.

"Caresse," he said.

"Caresse?" she quipped. "I barely know you." This was an old joke of hers that she pulled out when meeting others for the first time to see if they laughed. He didn't. She covered. "Sorry about being late. Farmers' Market."

"And you've lived here how long?" he asked. The implication was that if she had lived there even a few weeks, she would have to have had the brain of a tree frog not to know downtown San Luis Obispo was virtually inaccessible on a Thursday night.

"Since my son was eight months old."

"You have a son?" He sounded like she had a communicable disease.

She had smiled. It could only get worse. And it had.

Bill stared at the TV that hung over the bar where two ESPN commentators were discussing the game in progress. The TV had closed captioning on, with the sound muted to allow for the live jazz band to command center stage. The quartet was playing *A Love Supreme,* and while they weren't Coltrane, Tyner, Garrison, and Jones, they were damn good.

She'd ordered grilled fish with a side of pasta and a glass of white wine, and Bill said, "Make that two."

He had spent the meal talking about what turned out to be his main interests—death and dying, and lingerie. To top off the evening, he pulled a copy of Elisabeth Kübler-Ross' groundbreaking 1969 tome and handed it to her after inscribing the front page.

She'd accepted the paperback and stuck it in her small black purse.

"Don't you want to read what I wrote?" He sounded surprised.

"No," she replied. The date had gone through its own five stages of grief—denial that this was actually her date, anger that he wasn't kinder, bargaining that at least she got a meal out of it, depression that the wine wasn't better, and acceptance that she would never have to see Bill again.

Staring at Jerry over her coffee now, with so little to say, she was ready to part ways as soon as she took her last sip.

After saying good-bye, she went into the Downtown Centre's Barnes & Noble and headed upstairs to the magazine section. They would have the February *Barbie International* in stock before she would get her copy in the mail at home, and she wanted to see her latest article.

Upstairs, to the left, there was a coffee bar and several tables where people were reading. Straight ahead was the children's section, decorated with colorful cartoon animal cutouts. To the right, there was mainstream fiction and her favorite section, the collectibles, craft, and hobby books.

She seldom had the honor of having artwork connected with one of her features on the cover, but the front of the February issue of *Barbie International* was an exception. It displayed work from one of 130 artists and designers from the German-speaking world, including Austria and Switzerland, who accepted the invitation to represent Barbie doll as an aesthetic cult object for an exhibition held in the Workman Archive exhibit space at the Martin Gropius Bau in Berlin. A box of slides had been shipped to her upon request from Mattel Germany based near Frankfurt, and in turn, she selected a dozen favorites and sent them to Sierra Walsh with her story. World-famous artists whose mediums ranged from interior design, sculpture, painting, graphic design, photography, video, industrial design, furniture design, jewelry, fashion, and hair design, worked alongside unrecognized artists to create everything from a lamp that included Barbie doll as part of its base and a chandelier that blended Barbie dolls into its crystal and candles framework to a human-sized King Kong sculpture holding a Barbie doll in the palm of its hand and paper-money-clad ballerinas posed atop bars of gold.

Barbie doll in Cosmos by Ricardo Wende featured dozens of modern blond Barbie dolls attached to a flat surface. Vidal Sassoon created a trio of blonds with wild, carefree hairstyles. Escada created a sequined gown for a blond with a towering up-do. Jorg Bollin painted Barbie doll gold and stood her upright in a velvet-lined box. Anything deemed provocative or obscene was excluded. Since children were bound to attend the showing, the artist Stilleto's streetwalker Barbie doll was nixed. It seemed humorous to exclude a scantily-clad doll from Mattel's imaginary red light district, but they had no problem approving Frank Lindow's four-shelf display containing numerous jars of pickled beets, pickled sausage and—you guessed it—pickled Barbie dolls, chopped to fit an assortment of jars.

A woman with chestnut hair was watching her from the end of the magazine aisle. Caresse looked up and smiled.

The woman took her smile as an invitation to approach. "Is that a good magazine?"

It seemed a silly question. If she had even glanced through a copy, she'd know how good it was. "It's gotta be. I'm a staff writer."

Caresse was about to experience one of her first-ever fan moments as the woman grabbed her. "You do? I still have all my dolls," she gushed.

She tactfully sidestepped the issue of the woman's age. "What era?"

"Oh, the Sixties."

"Yeah, the Sixties rocked."

"Are there certain things people should look for when starting to collect?"

She thought for a moment. "Yeah. The first thing you don't want to go and do—unless of course you have the resources and the room to do it—is go out and clean out a toy store, you know, because that's a little crazy. You may make mistakes at first, buying things that don't really appeal to you. The first thing is, ask yourself, do I like this doll, and what do I like about her more than the ten different dolls beside her? I mean, if you like her, there's a good chance that other people like her and that she's a winner. Try and stay away from the real cheap, standard bathing suit models. If you're looking to explore this to make money, look at the price tag. There truly is a correlation between dolls that are more expensive at the outset increasing in value over the long run. Play dolls generally don't appreciate that much, so if you're looking at it as an investment, don't get into them. Once you're dealing with the pricier dolls, buy what you like, and you can't go too far wrong."

The woman looked overwhelmed. "What do you like?" she finally asked.

"Oh, I'm a sucker for the repros that have been coming out, particularly those that are more recent, in the retro packaging. I don't have them all. I don't seem to need them. I get one or two a year and put them in back-to-back eleven-by-fourteen-inch shadow boxes, with their retro dioramas as backdrops. Then I hang them on the wall, up close to the ceiling, where they're out of the way. My apartment's kind of short on space."

"Do you still have your childhood dolls?"

She thought about the collection she'd inherited from her sister Cami when she passed down her dolls from 1966 through 1969 to her. The Seventies, when Caresse cut her first Barbie doll teeth, were a letdown by comparison.

"Nope. I played with them virtually every day, and they were thrashed. Not what you might consider lightly thrashed, but nearly destroyed from constant play. I was relentless and would play for hours at a time, and they didn't look good enough to display. They originally belonged to my oldest sister. I asked her if she wanted them back. She thought about it and finally said yes, rather than see me pass them on to a dealer who might try to revive them. She said something to the effect that keeping them in their original albeit rough condition would preserve their childhood mojo. She predicted I'd want them back someday and said she'd hang onto them. I just couldn't imagine having them around. Picture the heartbreak of looking at a Skipper you wanted to glam up, so you drew big black circles with a magic marker around her eyes, hoping to create a little Amy Winehouse magic, and you've got the full horror of what we might call my idea of maximum play value."

The woman was goggle-eyed. She took the copy of *Barbie International* Caresse had in her hands and started to walk away.

"I'm gonna get this," she said, when she was too far away for Caresse to grab it back.

"Great."

She watched as the woman started making her way down the main staircase. Only her head and shoulders were visible when she glanced back and flashed a quick smile. The woman hadn't introduced herself, but it didn't matter. Caresse was willing to chat about Barbie doll with anyone, anytime, for any reason. She reached into the rack and pulled out another copy of the February issue, riffling through it to make sure there wasn't anything wrong with it, like a center-spine glue blob.

A quick glance at her watch told her it was time to get back to work, where Marilyn would be waiting for her latest date report.

23

After Xpress Rent A Car of Las Vegas delivered a plum-colored Geo Metro to P.J. at The Luxor, signing her at the daily rate of $39.99, she returned to her room and called her half-brother to tell him she was never going to travel by Greyhound again.

The bus had been uncomfortable, the ride had taken all day, and because she did not have the luxury of sitting by herself, far from those who liked to strike up conversations, she had placed herself in jeopardy of later identification. She recounted her meeting with Craig Krieger and allowed Darby to berate her for wearing her Barbie doll bracelet.

"So he has a sister," he said. "Did he tell you what her name is?"

"No, but Krieger rings a bell for some reason," P.J. said, falling onto the queen-sized bed and staring at the slanted wall which, to outsiders, created the illusion of a giant Egyptian pyramid.

The beauty of the hotel distracted her, and she found herself mesmerized, staring down at the atrium fifteen floors below before she had even gone into her room. She had heard Criss Angel lived in a penthouse directly beneath the pyramid tip, which shone the brightest beam of light in the world directly up into the heavens every night.

"You've got to see this place, Darby," P.J. said, getting back up and stripping off her jeans, shirt, and sweatshirt single-handedly while talking. "If you were in a plane over L.A., you'd be able to see Criss Angel's light at flight level."

"Great," he said. "Let me hop on a plane, and you go up to the rooftop and see if you can send me signals from three hundred miles away."

P.J. pouted. "It's less than three hundred miles from home. It just seems farther when you take the fucking bus."

"So, do you want me to check your database?"

Over the past decade, P.J. had methodically amassed a list of a quarter million Barbie doll collectors and the cities they lived in.

"Sure," she said, "and call me back."

"Are you gonna do it tonight?"

P.J. sighed, falling back onto the bed in just her underwear and socks. "To be honest, this is the first time I've checked into a hotel that made me just want to relax. There's a whole vibe here, and I'm not just talking about the Egyptian ambiance. It is so cool. You've got to come stay here sometime so you know what I mean."

"What? And forgo my VIP suite at Circus Circus?"

"Ha ha," P.J. said sarcastically, but she was smiling. "Tomorrow night. Tomorrow night, I'll do it."

"Are you gonna call your husband?"

"Sure. I talk to him every night," she lied.

Darby laughed at how sad his half-sister's marriage was. The union worked, but mostly, he thought, because she and Heath rarely saw each other.

"That reminds me," he said.

P.J. had the TV remote in her non-phone hand and was surfing for a good movie.

"What?"

"I think I met someone."

P.J. paused on the channel that aired information about The Luxor. A room service menu appeared onscreen and tantalized her with Italian food, steak, and fine wine. Of course, if she were feeling brave and didn't feel like dining in, she could always head down to the foyer level and play nickel slots until one of the waitresses making the rounds had her breathing a 4.0.

"You think you met someone," she parroted, just to let him know she'd heard him.

"A girl."

"No duh, a girl. If you became a switch hitter all of a sudden, I'd run down to Carrot Top's show tonight and do a strip tease for him onstage."

"I didn't know you liked Carrot Top," he said.

"I don't." All of sudden, P.J. wanted to get off the phone. She didn't want to hear what Darby had to say about any prospective girlfriend.

"She likes Barbie dolls," he said.

"How do you know that?"

"She's the same as you and all your friends. You're addicted to Barbie doll jewelry. She was wearing a gold Quentin Tarantino Barbie doll cameo bracelet with crystals and pearls the day I met her."

"*Tarina* Tarantino," P.J. said hotly.

"I know it's not Quentin. I was just being funny. Of course, you could make it a Quentin bracelet if you hung little daggers and vials of pills and beer cans and cool cars off it."

"Well, where'd you meet her and what's her name?"

"Jordanne," he said.

"Jordin, like Jordin Sparks?" P.J. was an avid *American Idol* fan.

"Not Jordin Sparks."

"I know it's not Jordin Sparks, but her name is Jordin like Jordin Sparks?"

"Jord*anne*," Darby clarified.

He explained that Jordanne was the sister of a friend he knew at the Glendale Market where he went—not often enough—to shop for groceries. His fridge, it turned out, was much fuller these days, thanks to his desire to go hang out with her. She had graduated from Glendale High School in 2007 and was almost nineteen. Her new job as a cashier at the market where her brother had worked as a stock boy for as long as Darby could remember had begun two weeks earlier, and she was nearly done with training. He had begun smoking again so he didn't feel awkward joining her on her cigarette breaks outside, in back, by the loading docks.

"You know that song *Tiny Dancer* by Elton John?" he asked.

"Who doesn't?" P.J. wasn't even trying to keep the animosity out of her voice now.

"She's tiny, like a tiny dancer," he enthused. "She's blond like you and..." he trailed off realizing P.J. didn't want to hear about her at all.

"Thanks for wrecking my night," P.J. said.

It was Darby's turn to get a bit cross. "How could I possibly do that?"

"Well, how do I know you're gonna be around for me if you go getting yourself involved with little Miss What's Her—"

"Jordanne," he said. "Listen, P.J., I started this project with you and I'll finish it, whether it's ten more outings or twenty or thirty or forty."

"Outings," she scoffed.

"Well, you think of a better term when you're talking on the phone—which isn't exactly private, no matter how much you think it may be. You know, anybody could—"

"Okay," P.J. relented, picking up the TV remote she had dropped on the bed.

She resumed channel surfing. This woman was roughly half Darby's age. He would get what he needed from her physically, find out they had nothing in common, and then he'd dump her. She just needed to wait it out.

But as inexplicably mad as P.J. felt when she threw one of her shoes against the wall after hanging up, she would have been far angrier if she knew Darby had already gone into P.J.'s storage and taken a blond American Girl Barbie doll and given it to his new sweetheart, rationalizing that P.J. would never miss it.

24

Back at the *County Times*, Caresse found time to log on to the Best Barbie Board. First, she did a message search for "Grace" and came up with the latest news.

BBB Moderator Sabeana Moss had posted that services for Gayle and her husband Mike had been held on Lake Ontario, with scattering of ashes at sea.

In response, Gayle's sister Megan had posted a note beside a new profile photo of herself and Gayle playing with dolls when young.

MEGAND: Thank you for mentioning that, Sabeana, and thank you all so much for the cards and flowers. The Barbie community is a true brother and sisterhood, as evidenced by your outpouring of warmth and consideration. Now, with Time Taylor gone as well, we need to stick together more than ever.

Caresse bolted upright. She knew who Time was. She had lived on the BBB as the self-appointed authority-in-residence, answering questions from newbies oftentimes only minutes after they had posted their requests for help. She had one friend who always backed her whose name was Sally, and if anyone had issued the alert, it would have been her.

A search for "Sally" turned up the only Sally on the board, and it was indeed Time's friend. Her user name was CASEY_LUV, because she was particularly fond of Casey, a good friend of Barbie doll's "MODern" cousin Francie. A full body shot of a 1967 Twist Casey, wearing her gold mesh-topped swimsuit and single gold-tone triangle dangle earring, served as Sally's avatar.

CASEY_LUV: I have bad news for everyone. There is no easy way to put this so I'll just come right out with it. Our friend Time has been killed, I think by the same maniac who murdered Gayle and Hailey. A UPS deliveryman found her Monday afternoon, and I guess after he saw her bloodied body sprawled on her doorstep, he dropped her package (don't know what it was—the police have it—but she was expecting a new Twiggy dressed in Snake Charmers from Janet Lambee) and ran back to his truck to call 911. I told the Oak Harbor Police that Time might have been murdered for doll-related reasons. I don't know if they took me seriously, but they sure gave each other a weird look. If they do take me up on it, I will go through her stuff like Beth went through Hailey's and let you know what I find. When I called them back this morning, they indicated concern that cash and drugs had been on the scene before Time's father went to jail and said detectives were following up leads involving revenge or the quest for hidden money or illegal substances Time's father had bragged the cops hadn't found at the time of his arrest. Time and I went through the whole house a long time ago. There's nothing. I really am thinking it's all about her dolls.

While attempting to get more information, Sabeana had replied with as much tact as possible.

SMOSS: Dearest Sally, all of us here are so sorry for your loss. You said Time was found dead and mentioned she was bloodied, but how did she

die? Was she bludgeoned to death like Hailey? And when will you know if you can go into her home and see if any dolls are missing?

Sally's reply had not been posted yet.

Caresse knew that Time's collection not only included some of the best examples of the earliest Barbie dolls and outfits but superlative examples of later dolls as well.

If the killer had struck again, this time they were not focusing on any one Barbie doll, friend, or era.

The killer was totally unpredictable in his or her collection preferences.

But perhaps, Caresse thought, *that's because the killer is rapacious.*

25

Military explosive ordnance disposal personnel from Naval Air Station Whidbey Island arrived at Time Taylor's home on Northeast Sixth in Oak Harbor after it had been assessed she died in a explosion involving a toxic substance. Neither the local police nor the toxicology expert they brought in from the University of Washington had ever been called to a crime scene of this precise nature before. It was eye opening, unsettling, and abhorrent.

It was critical for personnel operating in and around the contaminated entryway to remain cognizant of the dangers presented by skin contact with any toxic substances. They were less concerned with inhaling airborne contaminants since they were standing outside in the light but chilly breeze.

Investigators treated the victim as a Jane Doe, pending confirmation that she was the woman who lived there. Prior to the collection of evidence, the photographer, sketch preparer, and evidence recorder took stock of the crime scene.

Evidence recovery personnel and specialists in and around the porch area wore safety glasses, gloves, and protective clothing as they worked. Methodically, technicians began bagging bits of plaster of Paris and glue, cardboard, toilet paper, aluminum foil, tiny rocket engine fragments, and primer wire. The adhesive and plaster used could be compared with suspected sources by color and chemical composition. Because it was impossible to submit the wall of the archway itself, samples of the stucco were removed with sharp, clean instruments, and transferred to leak-proof plastic bottles. Hanks of Time's wispy blond hair were carefully collected with clean forceps to prevent damaging the root tissue. Each hank of hair was then packaged separately in an envelope with sealed corners. Tissue, bones, and teeth were collected with gloved hands and clean forceps. Tissue samples were placed in clean, airtight containers without formalin or formaldehyde. Teeth and bone samples were wrapped in clean paper.

Time's bracelet-style Seiko wristwatch was recovered and bagged. It had stopped running when hit by flying debris at eleven forty-seven a.m.

When technicians finished lifting prints from the screen door, they discovered the lock had been filled with glue. Using a thin tool, they filed and scraped the keyhole, depositing shavings of hardened glue in a bag they marked into evidence.

Investigators followed the trailing wires that fell behind the potted plants and discovered the large battery hidden in the shrubbery.

"Remote control," Detective Mel Brinkman surmised. "The killer had the igniter. That explains those little rocket engines."

"So something poisonous hit her from all sides," his partner Keenan Francis guessed.

"She had open wounds from the detonated rockets, and the poison they carried entered her bloodstream," Brinkman replied.

Francis got the picture. "Like chemical darts." He paused and thought before he spoke again. "Isn't that a rather convoluted way to kill someone?"

"Creative," Brinkman replied. "Insanely creative."

Time's Taurus was parked in front of her house.

The UPS man who had called 911 sat on the curb by his truck, too weak to stand. The package he had been attempting to deliver remained on the lawn near the front walkway. Investigator Adam Puchalski sat down next to him and attempted to get him to talk, but the man was too shaken to speak.

"You were on the porch," Puchalski said. "I'm gonna need to see the bottom of your shoes."

Without answering, the man lifted his left foot. Puchalski bent over and looked. Embedded in the tread of the man's running shoes were bits of skin, plaster, glue, and toilet paper. Gently, Puchalski untied the man's left shoe, took it, and debated removing the evidence from the grooves with forceps. He realized he should get photographs first, so he told the man he would be back. He stood up slowly, casting a glance backward, and headed off to find a photographer.

The UPS man, whose name was Don Chambers, had been on the job for twelve years. Until that Monday arrived, he had been quite content with his line of work.

Now, as he sat on the curb, missing a shoe, he wondered if he would ever be able to get the vision of the large blond woman, zombified into a bloated creature with craters of skin missing over her entire body, from his mind. Her eyes had been opened, but not by choice. She was missing her eyelids, eyebrows, and forehead. She had lost so much blood she was in a thick, slick, dark pool.

Raw meat, he thought. *She looked like something ready to be hacked up by a butcher.*

Working on the assumption that the vic was indeed Time Taylor, investigator Editha Moran did the necessary background check and learned her father had been killed in prison and her mother died of liver cancer. She also confirmed Time had been arrested once for possession of marijuana, owned the home she lived in, lived alone with two poodles, and drove the Taurus that was present at the scene.

Another investigator, Patty Graybill, began to canvass the neighborhood. She went door to door, asking anyone who answered if they had seen anyone suspicious in the neighborhood that morning.

Outside, in the arched entryway, technicians removed Time's tattered baggy pants, shirt, and Birkenstock sandals. The sandals and clothing would be bagged, and she would be transported nude to the coroner's office, where her official cause of death would be determined.

Inside, detectives found two crumbs of bacon the poodles had missed in the front hallway. They combed through the pastel living room with meticulous precision and then headed up the plush peach-carpeted staircase. After analyzing the bathroom, they moved to the study and discovered the smashed curio cabinet. Shards of glass covered the floor, flung as far as the stacked cardboard boxes across the room.

Two clear impressions of footprints remained in the carpet, directly in front of the cabinet. They would need a photographer as well as someone to dust the smashed cabinet for latent prints.

Time's friend from work, Sally, pulled up a distance away from the crime scene vehicles and patrol cars. She ran up to the house and Brinkman and Francis approached to block her path.

"Sorry, Miss," Francis said to the heavyset brunette. "You can't go any closer."

"Do you know who lives in this house?" Brinkman asked.

Despite the chill in the air, he was sweating profusely. He removed his shades to wipe his eyes.

"Time. Time Taylor—my friend from work. We work at Burger King right around the corner. When she didn't come back, I thought I'd run over here and—"

"See if anything was wrong," Francis finished for her.

"Why did she come home?" Brinkman asked.

"Oh, she does that every day," Sally said. "To check on the dogs. Is she okay?"

"Does Miss Taylor have any relatives in the area?" Francis asked, already knowing the answer.

"No," Sally said, looking at the ground. "We're her family. Her friends."

"We may need to talk to you further," Brinkman said, pulling out his pad and pen. "Can I get your contact information?"

"Sure," Sally's voice quavered. "But why? Is anything wrong?"

Francis put his arm around her, offering comfort.

Sally was crying now, sensing the gravity of the situation. "She was my best friend."

"Do you know why anyone would want to hurt her?" Francis probed gently.

Sally looked up. Her face was blank.

"Money? There was supposed to be some money her father hid in the house before he was sent away, but we looked and I swear, we never found it."

"Anything else? Does she have anything of value anyone would want?"

"Just her dolls," Sally said. "I would have to look and see if they're all there."

Francis and Brinkman exchanged a quick glance. They had heard about the cases in Oswego and Tuscon and braced themselves to make the leap that anything was possible.

26

Zivia Uzamba lived in the Canyon Gate community outlined by West Charleston Boulevard to the north, South Buffalo Drive to the east, West Sahara Avenue to the south, and South Fort Apache Road, which buffered Canyon Gate Country Club, to the west.

P.J. MapQuested the route to Zivia's home on Via Olivero and made a beeline to her neighborhood her second night in town, close to midnight. The city was awash with visitors mesmerized by flashing neon signs and stellar attractions. She blended in with the heavy traffic effortlessly.

This month, the Divine Miss M would replace Celine Dion at the Palace. This week, Wayne Brady would make people laugh at The Venetian, Boz Scaggs would take fans on a trip back to the Seventies at the Las Vegas Hilton, and Bryan Adams would pack The Joint at Hard Rock.

Zivia's husband, a bodyguard for Lil Beef, had been arrested before the 2007 BET Hip-Hop Awards by federal authorities charging him with possession of six unregistered machine guns. That night, T.I. was arrested on similar charges. Since Lil Beef and his entourage were fringe players, T.I. had stolen most of the media thunder.

Federal agents had been having a field day all week, setting up illegal gun sales in various parking lots at downtown Atlanta shopping centers, doing what they could to nail as many of the bad boys as they could.

In honor of Lil Beef, his entire entourage was encouraged to subsist entirely on hamburgers and steak and call themselves anti-vegetarians. Rick Uzamba vowed to continue the all-beef regimen after he posted a four million dollar bond, largely consisting of equity on his $8.5 million Las Vegas residence. He was escorted home, committed to house arrest for a year.

Zivia complained on the Best Barbie Board that Rick was driving her crazy, eating massive amounts of ground beef mixed with a little bit of pasta and sauce and then falling asleep in his music room with his headphones on and a white paper napkin shoved in the neckline of one of his many Lil Beef Tour t-shirts. This happened nearly every night, she said, so P.J. wasn't worried that on a Wednesday night he would deviate much from his given routine.

It would be important for P.J. to take care of Rick first, to get him out of the way. She had no idea which room either he or Zivia would be in. The estate was massive, consisting of nine bedrooms, six bathrooms, a kitchen, living room, screening room, bowling alley, music room, doll room, and den.

Wherever Rick was, it was likely Zivia would not be with him. If Rick had a drink, P.J. was prepared to spike it courtesy of her baggie full of Midazolam, which Darby had scored for her in the form of Dormicum tablets.

She had four strips of fifteen-milligram tablets that were blue ovals marked Roche on one side. They were now in the left breast pocket of the plaid flannel button-down shirt she wore as a light jacket.

Just in case he didn't have a drink nearby as he ate and listened to music, P.J. also had a handful of ten-milliliter sealed glass vials of Dormicum that she poured into two separate hypodermic needles and put in her right breast pocket, needles upward. Darby had her practice administering water via hypodermic into oranges, and by the time his trash was full of bloated Sunkists, she felt competent to stick someone without hesitation.

As a backup to the drugs, P.J. brought sharp wire with her. If it came to strangling either of them, the wire would be her choice because it lacked bulk. As far as tracing it as a weapon, the wire was not specific enough to provide leads, but to be safe Darby had secured it from a friend of a friend living in Boston.

P.J. parked down the street and walked toward the house, which did not have a security gate at the foot of the driveway. Walking along the hedges toward the back of the house, she saw a series of sliding glass doors leading into expansive rooms filled with marble support columns, Travertine floors interspersed with stretches of rose-colored carpeting, and wide, open windows. As was often the case when the front of a house was shut tight, the back area, which included tiered Cocobolo decks, a hot tub, a pool, gardens, umbrellaed tables and lounge chairs, was open and inviting because shrubbery lent the illusion of privacy and security.

Standing in the shadows of the hedges in her over-sized men's sneakers (if the shoe doesn't fit, you must acquit), P.J. saw that Zivia was in an upstairs bathroom.

The window was open and she heard the sound of running water. Logically, the bedrooms were all upstairs, and it was unlikely she would return downstairs anytime soon. On the BBB, Zivia had shared how much she enjoyed lengthy showers and hot baths surfeited with salts, in a calming environment of lambent Blackberry Blossom Aromatherapy candles and John Ondrasik's soothing music.

On the backside of the house, one room away from the sliding glass door leading into the corner room, P.J. saw flickering lights sparking off the windowpane. Creeping along the length of the backyard, she realized it was reflection off the big screen TV Rick was watching. The huge window helped her judge the room's layout and her prospective entry point. His back would be toward the door to the room as he relaxed in his recliner, headphones off and lying near a speaker. It was not music he was listening to tonight. Rather, he had the speakers cranked to level ten so he could enjoy *Sin City* on DVD.

Rick had a folding table set up alongside but slightly behind his chair, blanketed with dishes and a tall, iced drink. So much for Rick's pact to keep the Lil Beef pledge to only eat steak and BK burgers (hold the pickles, hold the lettuce, hold the mayo, hold the bun). Traces of ravioli, gnocchi, and clams swimming in red sauce remained in dishes pushed to the edge of the table, in danger of spilling onto the carpet.

On the floor stood a bottle of Captain Morgan's spiced rum, which he reached for now, tipping the bottle into his glass, refilling it to within an inch of the rim.

Rick himself was an African-American Hulk, so strangling him was out of the question. Within seconds of having the wire around his neck, he looked strong enough to reach back and flip her over his head, sending her crashing to the floor. At 5'8" and 120 pounds, she didn't stand a chance.

That his folding table was positioned slightly behind one armrest so he had to reach back to get what he wanted was a plus. She evaluated she could hide behind his massive chair and doctor his drink without being seen.

Rick sat there, his massive arms bulging on the armrests, and chuckled. On the flat screen that filled much of the west wall, Dwight dunked Jackie Boy's head in the toilet and told him never to bother Shellie again.

P.J. had seen *Sin City* at the local AMC in 2005 and thought it must be only halfway over. She hypothesized that she had about an hour before he would bother to get up, unless he had an incommodious bladder.

As if on cue, Rick reached back for the remote on the table. He wiped some sauce off of it with the tip of his napkin bib before freezing the movie on a headshot of Benecio del Toro. Then he got up, ran a hand through his Adam Duritz dreads, stretched his arms, and palpated the Jesus pieces hanging from his neck.

P.J. was transfixed by his jewelry. All of it looked like it was 24-karat gold, all of it looked like it was encrusted with real diamonds, and all of it looked heavy. Dare she deviate from her routine and grab some bling?

She looked at her empty duffel, felt the tablets and syringes in both breast pockets, and checked for her car keys in her jeans pocket while thinking how fun it would be to risk selling some gold on the street for quick cash. Of course, Darby would be dead set against it, but she was still so irritated he was dating the blond cashier bimbo she didn't really care at this point. In fact, she felt like being contumacious to spite him.

Rick went to the east wall of the room and pushed on a door that led into a bathroom. Because the window that faced the backyard was open, she heard him take a leak and flush the toilet. Vagariously, an old motto of her husband's, "if it's yellow, let it mellow; if it's brown, flush it down," glided through her thoughts.

When Rick returned to his chair, plopped himself down, and pressed "play" on the remote to resume the movie, P.J. began to move stealthily toward the corner of the house, where a screened sliding glass door was ajar.

The screen was not latched. Gently, carefully, she slid it across its track and stepped inside onto a linoleum area measuring six by four feet. It was a suitable area to wipe one's shoes when coming in from out back, using light from the backyard lampposts in the evenings to see in the dimly lit room.

She bent down to remove the size-nine Nike Huarache 08 BBall iD men's basketball shoes and three pairs of athletic socks that padded her slim feet to help keep them on. Beyond the blank wall to her left, she could hear the movie. Shellie was pleading Dwight not to follow her.

P.J. had plenty of time.

The wall to the right was filled with empty shelving. Straight ahead, there was a wall filled with Lil Beef On Tour photos, a shrine to the man and his music.

That was all to be expected, given whose home she was in. Nothing out of the ordinary here, except for one thing that left her stupefied.

She was standing in a room that had no door.

27

For Caresse, going to the Madonna Plaza for her next *County Times* date beat the stuffing out of trying to find a parking space downtown, midday, evening, anytime.

The shopping center was across the street from the famous Madonna Inn, a San Luis Obispo landmark right off the 101, equidistant between San Francisco and Los Angeles. Head 200 miles south and you'd be in the land of fast cars and movie stars. Head 200 miles north, and you'd be gazing at the Golden Gate Bridge.

The shopping center itself boasted Mervyns, McDonald's, Big 5 Sporting Goods, Payless Shoe Source, SuperCuts, See's Candies, Sears, Blockbuster, and a Wells Fargo branch office. Adjacent to the stores sat Taco Bell and Applebee's. Fortunately for her, it was the latter she was heading to for dinner at seven p.m. that first Wednesday in February.

His name was Carl, and he was eight years older than she was, with dark hair and a mustache. Squeezed into the cramped restaurant foyer, he took her hand in both of his when she asked if he'd been waiting long. She looked into his eyes and felt a professional vibe, like she was meeting him for business. He said he worked for a real estate appraisal company in SLO, but he dreamt of making a living as a guitarist.

She was not fully present; her mind was on Chaz. It was her night to have him for a sleepover, and she had dropped him off at her friend's house reluctantly. She was only halfway through the number of dates she thought she needed for a good story. Aiming for six encounters, she was booked through Saturday and would write her article Sunday.

Tonight, she was probably looking better than she felt. She had bothered to wear a dress, a blue and white floral affair with a wide skirt and capped sleeves. Applebee's was packed and the Cal Poly crowd was having a good time. She loved the noisy atmosphere, colorful decor, and heaping plates of food. She hoped the surroundings would compensate for her lack of enthusiasm.

They ordered an appetizer plate that included mozzarella sticks, Buffalo wings, and potato skins, followed by heart-clogging helpings of Shrimp Alfredo. Since she was subdued, Carl stepped it up a bit and asked her about herself. She told him she was a mom, a *County Times* writer, and a Barbie doll magazine staff writer. Astonishingly, he picked Barbie doll as the topic *du jour*.

"How the heck did you get interested in Barbie dolls?"

Caresse smiled and repositioned herself closer to the table. There was nothing offensive in asking a collector about their passion; it was non-controversial hobby talk. Like Todd, he was likely choosing that subject because he knew she would feel at home discussing it. Unlike Todd, however, there was no subtext to the chitchat, no smoldering chemistry, no hint of romance.

They sat on high stools at a round-topped table piled high with their feast.

"I was in New York in '89 at a wedding when I saw the very first Barbie doll book I'd ever seen. It was the history of Barbie doll's first thirty years, and designers had created costumes for her. As I flipped through the pages and saw everything I'd inherited from my older sister, I said, 'hey, I still like this stuff.' I was only nineteen and had stored my childhood playthings by then. I went back to my undergrad college in New York and found myself buying them again. It was rather humiliating. I hid them in my desk because I didn't know anyone else in college who bought dolls. I didn't *think* there was necessarily anything wrong with me, but I felt the compulsion to keep buying the doll I loved as a child."

She stopped, took a breath, and picked up a chicken wing dripping with hot sauce.

"Had you ever collected anything else before?"

"Never."

"So you don't collect anything and all of a sudden, Barbie dolls? When you were a child, were you into Barbie dolls a lot?"

She washed her bite of wing down with ice water. "Very much so. It's hard to say Barbie dolls meant more to me than to any other little girl. It wasn't so much a matter of just dressing her up and admiring the way she looked. I got into creating situations and dramas, creating stories and falling into a world where everything was an adventure."

Carl wiped his mustache and smiled. "Yeah. And since you've gotten involved in collecting, I'm going to assume you've found other people who share your passion?"

"Oh, sure."

"How widespread is this?"

She thought about his question. "I would think there are probably half a million adult collectors in the United States and abroad, and what I think is primarily responsible for all of us networking the way we have is *Barbie International* Magazine. When it came out, it was well publicized, 'cause it came out in her thirtieth anniversary year and the *L.A. Times* covered its debut. Once I got my hands on it, I knew I could pair my love of writing with my love for Barbie dolls. I became a staff writer, and I was on my way. Basically, what that magazine provides is a way for people to connect regarding attending conventions, starting Barbie doll clubs, or just making Barbie doll friends. We've even got a Central Coast Barbie Club that meets once in a while."

As long as he asked questions, she would talk. There was no way she was leaving before she finished her last forkful of creamy Alfredo.

"Is it a strong chapter?"

"Well, twenty-five members. I think that's just about all we would want so we can meet comfortably at homes." She paused, took a breath. "Are you really interested in this?"

"Sure, why not?"

She frowned, realizing she should probably think of some questions involving real estate appraisals, but she had never owned a home and didn't know squat about property values and assessments. He seemed to sense as much and continued to talk about Barbie dolls.

"Is she still as popular today? Are kids still getting Barbie dolls?"

The waitress came over and refilled their coffee cups, not interrupting, but making eye contact to see if they were doing all right. Caresse nodded and Carl gave her a broad grin.

"More than ever. World awareness is estimated at 95 percent. Most girls back in the Sixties had maybe one or two or three Barbie dolls. The average girl today has about ten or eleven."

"That many?"

"Yeah."

"How many do you have?"

"Only a couple dozen. I'm space-challenged, so I just get ones that really speak to me." That was her standard answer. The deeper side note, which she wasn't going to delve into with him because exploring metaphysics could keep them there till closing, was that anyone, once they realized God truly resided within them, became much less selfish, self-destructive, and materialistic, and the number of dolls in a collection really didn't matter at all. And if she brought up the fact she believed a divine spirit, spark, or soul existed within everyone and that all souls were one, that each was a spark from the original soul and that that soul was wholly inherent in all souls, he might just leave the restaurant and stick her with the bill. She wasn't conflicted about feeling one with God and liking dolls. Dolls were part of this dimension. She didn't need them or necessarily even want them; she just liked them, like she enjoyed the pictures on her walls and the interesting pottery in her cupboards. She didn't envy those who had more; material goods would always be transient.

"How much are Barbie dolls worth as collectors' items?" Carl was perking up. "If I wanted to buy one, am I talking a couple bucks, a couple hundred bucks?"

Caresse shifted on her stool, straightened the hemline of her dress, and picked up her fork to stab the lone potato skin remaining on the appetizer platter.

"Are you talking about buying something that's old?"

"Yeah."

"Well, if you were to find an absolutely gorgeous number one in the box with the stand, you'd probably have to pay about $4,000 for her. About ten years ago, you'd have paid twice that."

Carl almost dropped the ketchup bottle. "$4,000?"

"Yeah."

"$4,000?"

"Yeah."

"It's a *doll*."

"It's a doll, but the number one—especially the number one brunette—is just that scarce, as are some of the earlier outfits."

"And what makes them so expensive is demand?" Carl put the lid back on the ketchup bottle and finished the last mozzarella stick. His pasta bowl had been scraped clean.

"Right. Common outfits, even from the Sixties, can go for twenty, thirty bucks if they're still relatively plentiful. Better outfits, if they were more expensive at the time, are harder to find now and are pricier. Even rare accessories can command a bundle."

"What were some of her more popular accessories?"

She was certain he was just messing with her now. He couldn't possibly care about Barbie doll's trappings. Nevertheless, she obliged him. "If you go back to the Sixties, she had everything from purses and princess phones to pots and pans. She had a Dream House, an Austin Healy, and a Little Theatre. Everyone talks about the stuff she has now, but she had even cooler stuff back then. A lot of accessories that are hard to find today include key chains, pearl necklaces, bracelets, and earrings. And you know what I'd like to do? If I could find a garbage dump that just had vacuum cleaner bags from the Sixties—"

"Yeah?"

"I'd like to go in there with a protective suit on, gather up all the old vacuum cleaner bags, open them, and find out what people Hoovered up."

Carl looked thoughtful. "It's probably there."

"Yeah," she agreed. "It's all there."

28

As soon as P.J. recovered from the shock of being in a door-less room, she studied the walls. Near the floor on the wall of photos, she noticed a sliding track and realized it was a false wall. She approached it and started rolling it back from the corner of the room where a narrow piece of metal extended, serving as a handle.

What she found behind the wall astounded her. She was in a six by twelve foot enclosure with a door leading out into the hallway. Before her, stacked randomly on shelves, were firearms, including a scoped rifle, two shotguns, three pistols, a chain gun, armfuls of submachine guns, an assortment of silencers and ammunition, and classic machine guns her half-brother Darby would later identify as an M1941 Johnson, an M2 Browning, a Colt CMG-1, and a SIG MG 710-3.

P.J. looked down. Her gloved hands were shaking, and so were her knees. Sweat began to trickle from her underarms, down to her ribcage. She walked over to a large metal box and cracked it open. It was stuffed with hundred-dollar bills.

I'll be back here later, she told herself. *I have work to do.*

She focused her thoughts and went, one barefoot step at a time, to the door. Watching where she walked, a random thought passed through her mind. She needed to repaint her toenails, preferably in vermilion.

Turning the door handle, she stole a look into the empty, rose-colored hallway. It was dimly lit by a series of sconces. Step, step, step, and step.

She was at the doorway to Rick's music room, her duffel left behind in the hidden room. She had what she needed in her pockets. Pressing the door inward, it opened with nary a creak. Down on her hands and knees now, she moved across the rug and positioned herself behind the wide chair.

Rick reached for another sip of his drink and took another forkful of ravioli, guffawing at the movie even though it hadn't reached a particularly humorous scene.

You find something, Murphy? ...Looks to be our poor dead cop's badge ...It's all bent up ...Oh, bloody hell... It's the bullet ...You son of a bitch! ...Bastard! ... They weren't cops... They were mercenaries... And if they were hired by who I think they were, the bad times haven't even started yet.

P.J. realized Rick's drink was beyond her reach, even though the table was to the side and back a bit. She could try to reach it, but if he was not absolutely in the moment with the movie, he might catch her movement out of the corner of his eye, turn, and find her there.

And everything seemed to be going so well... Remember, we don't have to deliver every last inch of the man, Brian... You got a good point there, Ronnie... Hand me a knife... Should take a nap while I'm doing all this waiting... I'm at the bone, all right? ...Here we go.

P.J. took one of the needles out of her pocket and tapped it. A drop of cloudy liquid fell from its tip like a single tear.

Have you ever seen anything so pretty in your whole life? We're in back of you... And if anyone happens by, use your imagination. Okay?

Slowly, she rose behind the chair and looked down at Rick's thick black hair. It had a beautiful shine to it.

Silently, she reached over and cupped his chin in her left hand. He gave a jolt. Surprised, he glanced up, perhaps expecting to find his wife looking for a quick kiss. With her right hand, P.J. jabbed the needle into the right side of his neck, plugging the full dose of Dormicum into his bloodstream.

No air to breathe... Only the horrid oily tar taste creeping up my nostrils... Let it in. Let it fill your lungs... They were counting on you, and you blew it... Skinny, steely fingers at my wrist... Miho, you're an angel. You're a saint... You're Mother Theresa. You're Elvis... You're a god.

Rick shot out of his chair, clawing at the long needle. The empty hypodermic glistened in the glow of the TV screen.

He did not scream nor did he shout. He stared at P.J. and tried to place the blond, ponytailed young woman in the plaid flannel shirt. If he only thought hard enough, he could figure out where he knew her from, find her somewhere in his past. He could not. He did not. His mouth gaped wide and he stumbled, hitting the small table his food was on, sending it crashing to the rug in a flurry of plates, congealed sauce, and splashed soda. He kicked the Captain Morgan bottle and went down on one knee as he pulled the needle out of his neck. His eyes bulged, his face awash with sweat.

Finally, he was on his back, his eyes glassy, his breathing ragged. He struggled against going under, but P.J. knew he wouldn't be able to continue the fight. The drugs would win. He would go under.

She stood there, waiting as the minutes passed. It took eleven minutes, and then he lay still. She suspected he was dead, but she was fearful of taking his pulse. She had administered enough Dormicum to wipe out Jim Jones and his entire posse of Kool-Aid kids. She kicked him with her bare foot. Rick was limp, out of it. She gingerly lifted the edge of his Lil Beef Tour t-shirt and stared at his hairy belly. Then she took the second hypodermic full of Dormicum and pushed it into the fat near his navel. This would double the dose of poison in his system.

P.J. took the spare vials from her breast pocket and filled both hypodermics in case she'd need them for Zivia.

She left Rick, dead on the floor of his music room, and made her way upstairs.

29

Caresse was in no mood for Thursday's lunch date with an older guy named Al who wanted to take her to Fat Cats in Port San Luis. That was where the boating crowd hung out and she knew that, with a jacket, they could enjoy the fresh air and views, but her heart wasn't in it. She was getting itchy to write her article and be done with the spate of dating. Todd aside, she was striking out at every turn and wasn't having much fun.

Shortly before seven a.m. Friday, she woke up in a blanket fort she'd created with her son. Somehow they'd never made it to bed and had fallen asleep amidst the pillows and blankets on the floor.

She had scheduled her next date at Sunshine Doughnuts on Higuera Street at eight and had to be at the *County Times* between eight-thirty and nine. She dropped Chaz off for the day and by the time Newton Faulkner finished singing about the place he goes when he's alone and

The Counting Crows were done paving paradise, she pulled into the Sunshine Doughnuts parking lot.

Zac was inside, wearing the black button-down shirt he told Caresse to look for. With hair graying at the temples and hazel eyes, he was boyishly handsome. It was only when he stood up that she realized he was six inches shorter than she was and cringed. She'd always felt self-conscious around guys shorter than 5'6". Nothing against them, but they made her feel huge. And judging by the napkins laden with buttermilk and lemon doughnuts piled on the laminate table, she was about to feel huger.

Zac was an electrical contractor, a stretch for her conversationally, but she found out he had two kids, ages eleven and nine, so they talked about parenthood for a while. Within a half hour, they were both glad the date had been just a before-work doughnut stop. Outside, they shook hands, wished each other well, and never promised to call each other.

She got to her desk and checked in at the Best Barbie Board first thing. Sally had written to let everyone know the Oak Harbor detectives had finally asked her to accompany them through Time's house so she could assess what—if anything—was missing. She also addressed the subject of how Time died.

CASEY_LUV: Dear Sabeana, you asked how Time died. Well, it's a bit complicated, but her death is listed as poisoning. No, not your old-school arsenic in the tea. This poison was delivered via—oh, God, how do I explain it? Only some Hannibal Lecter with a MacGyver brain could think of it. Stuff flew at her and stuck in her skin and it had the poison on it, so the poison got in her system. Sorry I don't have a better way of putting it.

Anyway, on to what is missing. And yes, Time's dolls have been cherry-picked. Time had a curio cabinet displaying dolls from Barbie's earliest years to about the standard 1972 vintage cut-off point. Earlier dolls were chosen over later ones: her number one and two ponytails were, of course, stolen, as were half a dozen number threes. About half her TNTs are gone, as are half her American Girls and bubble cuts. Time didn't keep a list like Gayle and Megan did. But the whole cabinet arrangement looks different, spread out. The unit is mostly glass, and I noticed immediately how much light was passing through it, whereas before, it was dense with dolls. Sorry I can't be more helpful, but you've gotten the gist of it.

The detectives made note of what I said. We'll see what happens from here on out. RIP, Time. I will miss you most of all.

Caresse found it strange the killer would want Time's bubble cuts in light of the fact he/she didn't take any of Hailey's, but nothing about this murderer *wasn't* strange.

Sabeana Moss once again followed up with a reply on the group's behalf.

SMOSS: Dearest Sally, thank you for sharing that news. I am so sorry about what happened to Time. My heart goes out to you. It is heartbreaking to know we've lost her, and the BBB will feel her absence for years to come. It sounds like the killer has not slowed down. Though it's been said here before, everyone, please be careful. The cops need to catch this person and do it soon.

Caresse thought, *Amen to that.*

30

The shower was still running in the upstairs bathroom at the west end of the house.

P.J. walked past room after room of exquisitely appointed furnishings and decor, knowing that if her home was fabulous, this home was positively ferosh. She passed the doll room, pausing momentarily to catch her breath before heading to the bathroom, where Zivia was now singing.

I need love, love's divine, please forgive me now I see that I've been blind, give me love, love is what I need to help me know my name.

P.J. listened to Zivia's voice through the thick shower curtain. She had good pitch and a sweet quality to her voice, plaintive, without any vibrato. Placed in small glass holders around the room, candles flickered and created a holy atmosphere.

Oh I don't bend, don't break, show me how to live and promise me you won't forsake, 'cause love can help me know my name.

Zivia stopped singing. P.J. heard a hollow thud and knew Zivia had dropped a bar of soap. She heard the woman grunt as she picked it up. The rest of the shower went by silently, the water sounding like rain battering a windowpane as it pounded the bottom of the tub. P.J. readied the first needle, flicking it with her gloved index finger.

The sole of Zivia's pivoting foot squeaked on the porcelain as she made her first tentative step out of the shower and onto a plush gamboge scatter rug. Her black hair was a mass of splendiferous ringlets dripping onto her flawless ebony shoulders and ample breasts. She was reaching for a towel on the bar nearest her when she saw P.J. standing there. Her hand stopped and rested on the towel bar.

She had one leg in the tub and one leg out when P.J. rushed at her and pushed her down, causing her to hit the small of her back on the tub's edge.

Zivia shouted in pain and then called for her husband.

P.J. jabbed the needle into her upper arm and held on to her. Zivia screamed and fought, then faded into unconsciousness.

Now it would be easier. P.J. grasped Zivia by the ankles and pulled her away from the tub, across the scatter rugs, toward the sink and vanity. Bending over the woman's naked body, P.J. shoved the second hypodermic into the soft skin above Zivia's left breast, beneath her collarbone, almost catching her in the armpit.

Now it was done. She debated whether to throw a towel over Zivia's face and torso before recalling what psychologists might say about the action. She certainly had no need to distance herself from her victim, so she left Zivia as she was, naked, in the soldier position on the floor.

As a final gesture, P.J. blew out the candles and closed the bathroom door behind her before heading down the hallway to the doll room.

The room was fuchsia with white painted stripes running horizontally around the room near the wall plates. Lexan-covered cases were stacked checkerboard-style along every wall, each lit from the interior with tiny white lights that resembled dripping strands of illuminated pearls. The bottom-most row caught P.J.'s eye first.

Starting at the left-hand side, the first three dolls, all Japanese side-part American Girls, had silver ash blond, frosted blond, and midnight tresses. Sold only in Japan, these beauties were made of a pinker vinyl and had straight standard Barbie doll legs. The trio was dressed in complementary kimonos sold only in Japan; one was silver and featured a labyrinth pattern, the second was a silver cherry blossom print, and the third was charcoal gray and silver.

Standing beside the threesome was the doll P.J. craved—the Japanese side-part Barbie doll with silvery brunette hair Zivia refused to sell. She was dressed in a gown exclusive to the Japanese market, a pink satin masterpiece with a beaded bodice. P.J. clasped her gloved hands to her mouth and let out a squeal. There would be no attempt to fan out any remaining dolls evenly among the shelves when she was done. She wanted as many as she could take. Hell, she wanted them all.

She ran downstairs, past the music room where Rick remained motionless on the floor, and glanced at the big screen where Bruce Willis and Jessica Alba were deep in conversation.

Stay away, Nancy. They'll kill you if you don't stay away. Don't visit me, don't write me, don't even say my name... If you won't let me visit, I'll still write to you, Hartigan. I'll sign my letters "Cordelia." It's a name of a really cool detective in books I read. I'll write to you every week. For forever... Sure, kid. Now run on home. It's not safe for you here.

P.J. ran into the hidden storage room and scooped up a hammer, four olive green duffel bags stamped "Army" that were lying in the corner, and her own camel-colored duffel.

Hurrying back upstairs, she ran to the bathroom. Zivia was lying in the same position, and her open eyes were dull. P.J. was certain she was dead but dared to check her pulse.

Nothing.

P.J. returned to the doll room and smashed the bottom cases. She snatched the Japanese American Girls, taking special care in handling the one she had been so desperate to claim for herself.

Next in the lineup came scores of Japanese Francies. The ones in Zivia's collection were all brunettes. Some had pink lips, blue eyes, and brown eyebrows. Others had red lips, blue eyes, and darker brown eyebrows. A third variety had rose lips with dark brown eyes and brows. It was the brown-eyed ones that captivated P.J. the most. Barbie doll's teenage cousin had never looked so good.

Blond, brunette, and titian Skippers came next. They each had huge dark brown eyes, very dark brows, and pale lips. All wore kimonos in an array of colors and patterns.

Next to them stood a handful of Japanese Midge dolls that Hailey Raphael would have loved to own. These dolls struck P.J. as similar to Fashion Queens; both had lash ridges and molded hair with blue plastic hair bands. The Midge dolls in Zivia's collection wore a series of dresses sold only in Japan, including floral-print pak sheaths in yellow and blue, a unique version of Suburban Shopper in a bold floral print, and Friday Night Date in a bright yellow and orange floral pattern, utilizing the same white petticoat as the U.S. version.

The rest of the Japanese-exclusive outfits were modeled by swirl Barbie dolls, which P.J. liked every bit as much as American Girls. A bevy of babes with brunette, titian, platinum blond, ash blond, and standard blond swirl ponytails, wore outfits as diverse as a pink version of Sleeping Pretty, Cinderella featuring a gold fringe-trimmed veil, Candy Striper Volunteer with a pink gingham and floral pinafore, and Theatre Date done in the reverse brocade of Evening Splendor.

After that came row upon row of bubble cuts and early ponytails wearing outfits like Gold 'N Glamour, Evening Gala, Sunday Visit, and International Fair.

Into the duffels they went, all of them, without exception.

When P.J. had over 200 dolls packed in the four Army duffels, she assessed the situation and realized she would need to make two trips. She picked up two packed Army duffels and her empty, bland duffel and headed downstairs. She walked slower than she needed to, admiring the opulence of the home as she departed.

She stopped again at the music room to see if *Sin City* had ended. Not quite, but close. Alex Bledel, who played Becky in the movie, was talking on the phone.

Oh, Mom. Don't go on like that. It's not the city. I could've gotten in a car accident anywhere. Yeah, just a fracture. The doctor said it's a clean break. Should be right as rain in no time.

P.J. went into the music room and carefully removed the iced-out jewelry from around Rick's neck. There was a crucifix measuring approximately four inches long and a half-inch thick, encrusted with diamonds on both sides. There was also a hefty chrome medallion featuring Jesus' face, with diamonds scattered throughout his crown of thorns. A skeleton with a kama weapon, a skull with diamond eyes, and a Last Supper pendant rounded out the mix. After collecting the pieces and stuffing them into a duffel bag, P.J. went into the storage room.

She loaded her camel duffel full of guns for Darby and then went into the room where her socks and sneakers were. The dyshidrosis on her feet was worsening. She had had the condition since she was in college, and it tended to flare up when she was under stress. Standing near the sliding glass door, using light from the lampposts outside, she took off her gloves and scratched her bare feet. The ugly blisters were beginning to flare up on her index fingers as well. She popped one of the blisters on her finger and then scratched the inside of her right foot vigorously, putting her gloves back on when she was done.

Once her gloves, socks, and sneakers were back on, she removed the contents of her breast pockets and tucked them into the camel duffel, looking twice at the four strips of 15-milligram Dormicum tablets she hadn't used. She supposed they might come in handy sometime, but for this occasion, liquid dosages administered by needle had worked brilliantly.

Running back to the hidden storage room, she grabbed the metal box filled with hundred-dollar bills and carried it over to the camel duffel filled with guns. The box wouldn't fit, but with careful placement, the money could be stuffed into crannies and still zip properly.

P.J. went out the same way she had entered, through the sliding glass door. She hurried across the lawn and up the side of the house, where the shrubbery was thick.

She was almost home free, but not quite. As she was just about to cross the driveway, she was forced to pull back into the shadows of a large bush. A red Mercedes was pulling into the driveway, its CD player blaring Lil Beef music at full volume.

"Hey!" the driver shouted.

There was a second man in the car, just as muscular, just as menacing.

P.J. felt faint. She had nowhere to go, so she squatted in the darkness and held her breath.

31

There was sufficient buzz in the national news about the Oswego and Tucson murders to warrant Caresse's Barbie interview with Sammy Stoudt on KVEC.

Before lunchtime on Friday, she headed over to the small radio station on Zaca Lane on foot, since it was a mere fifth of a mile from work. No one told her who had arranged it. Todd? Marilyn? Another friend? Didn't much matter, as long as she was spreading Barbie love far and wide.

She stepped into the pleasant lobby at half past eleven and took a seat across from the receptionist. A bowl of Valentine conversation heart candies sat in a covered dish on the woman's desk. Caresse trained her eyes on the glass, trying to read the little sayings as she waited. Music was playing, and it was her kind: Top Forty. As she listened to Corinne Bailey sing about sipping tea in a bar by the roadside and Nickelback croon about wanting a bathroom they could play baseball in, Caresse decided the pink heart in the dish facing her read "WANT U" and the mint green one read "U R MINE." While Daughtry was striving to see beyond the scars and make it to the dawn and Keith Urban was hoping to die in his lover's arms in a cabin by a meadow where the wild bees swarm, she felt certain the white heart in the dish read "EZ 2 LUV" and the yellow heart read "PURR FECT."

She had gotten two more phone messages from Rob Weber, one to say he still hoped to meet her, and a second one letting her know he had met a girl named Caresse when he was young. The first message sounded sincere and straightforward, but she doubted the second one. How many people in the world were named Caresse? And if it was a line, could he possibly be less inventive?

Sammy Stoudt, as fast on his feet as he was quick-witted, stormed into the lobby and zeroed in on her. He was a burly man, dressed in a flannel shirt and khakis, with a full lumberjack beard. "Caresse!" he boomed in his deep, made-for-broadcast voice.

She jumped up. "That's me."

He appraised her, from her windblown brown hair and haphazard clothing to her tennis shoes. He was likely thinking, *Thank God this isn't television.*

"Come on back," he said, and she meekly followed him into the recording studio.

"Is there a way to get an audio recording of the show?" she asked, doubtful.

"Of course," he said, surprising her. "It's a no-pay gig, but we've got some class. You'll get a nice cassette for posterity to share with your grandchildren."

Caresse wasn't thinking about any grandchildren that might or might not be in her future. She was thinking it would be nice to share with friends who missed the broadcast.

Sammy expertly positioned the mic and motioned for her to be quiet. The clock on the wall showed it was nearing the top of the hour. Sammy gave a short mention about her before heading into national news. They sat through the top stories and commercials quietly, smiling at each other without speaking. Then, on schedule, a red light above the door that said "On Air" lit up, and it was show time.

SS: I've got a real live Barbie doll here. What else do I need? Well, Caresse, you look normal. (laughs) Good morning.

CR: Good morning.

SS: We're saying good morning to Caresse Redd. Am I getting this right?

CR: Yep, you're pronouncing it right.

SS: I mean, it couldn't possibly be Ca-*reese*. Go ahead and describe yourself.

CR: Describe myself?

SS: Yeah. This Barbie doll thing.

CR: This Barbie doll thing?

SS: Are you a collector? Are you an aficionado?

CR: I'm primarily a collector but also a Barbie doll writer, insofar as I'm a staff writer for *Barbie International* magazine. You wouldn't believe how many people out there are collecting Barbie dolls. There are thousands and thousands of adults as crazy about her as I am.

SS: Fiftieth anniversary, I understand, of Barbie doll in 2009.

CR: Right.

SS: And let me remind my listeners, Caresse here, she's no slouch. I mean, this woman has a B.A. in Journalism, a master's degree from USC. Why don't you slip on your headphones there? My guest is Caresse Redd, and we're talking about Barbie dolls. She is a Barbie doll collector, a writer. She knows her Barbie dolls. And I'm Sammy Stoudt. And sure, we'll open up our phone lines. We have some people that want to join us. Call 1-800-555-KVEC if you want to talk about Barbie dolls with Caresse. Let's go out to San Luis, and we have Della on the line. Good morning.

D: Good morning.

SS: Are you a Barbie doll collector?

D: No, I'm not. I had Barbie dolls when I was younger. I'm forty-two now, so when she was first coming out, I really enjoyed just putting the clothes and the accessories together. I didn't really make up stories or worry about what the doll itself was. But I just loved all the outfits. You would buy a whole outfit that had every little accessory and thing with it. But what I really called about was, of course, G.I. Joe has a very similar thing to Barbie doll. My brother played with G.I. Joe and had dozens of them, and of course, G.I. Joe doesn't necessarily look like your average man, and he had all the outfits and played with them for quite a while. And I know that there are people still out there, trying to collect G.I. Joes, the original twelve-inch size.

CR: Definitely.

SS: So it's not just a female weird thing. It's a guy weird thing too.

CR: It's true, and you see little boys today who are so into action figures and all the things that are attached to them—their guns, their shields, their environments. And you're absolutely right about Barbie doll and her accessories and all the great outfits. Mattel was smart in doing such a quality job with all the little things they made for her. I mean, you could just stare for hours at the little pieces that went with everything.

D: And the cases and things they came in that opened out, the houses. And all the outfits weren't released at once, of course. You would hear that there's this new outfit out, this new situation that Barbie doll was in, so you would really look forward to it and tell your grandparents that's what you wanted for Christmas, and when it came, it would just be thrilling to put it on her.

CR: Absolutely.

D: Yeah. You had this whole little world there with the cases and the places where Barbie doll was. It was kind of like again, now you have the *Star Wars* sets or the *Jurassic Park* kind of thing where you collect the different dinosaurs. I mean, the kids now, they collect all these—

SS: But it's just not the same as collecting Barbie dolls to collect dinosaurs.

D: No, I'm talking about a specific—like, Batman and Robin and—

SS: Oh, yeah.

D: People will collect the Batman action figures or *Jurassic Park* as an action figure kind of situation, where you're collecting all the accessories and the doohickeys that go with them. What made playing with Barbie doll so interesting? All the things she had—not just the doll and the figure and everything.

CR: Absolutely, but you know what bothers me? In going back to the catalogs from the Sixties now, because they've been reprinted, I can't believe how much there was that I didn't know about. It's like, oh, they had so much more than the average girl can even dream was out there.

D: My grandmother used to make clothes for me as well as my Barbie doll—and you can imagine those itty-bitty little outfits that she had to sew--so it gave people around you something to give you to help you out with your collection.

CR: Very, very hard to make clothes for her.

D: Yes.

SS: Interesting. Della, thanks for calling in. I appreciate it.

D: Bye-bye.

SS: What I'm curious about, Caresse, as we go to the break here, is that you're a writer. You're a very creative person. And I'm wondering if you see any connection between your childhood experiences with Barbie dolls and the stories and having that as a child and what you have become now as an adult.

CR: There's a definite connection, and I think you see it in a lot of girls. What they gravitate toward in a Barbie doll collection may definitely spell out where they're headed. My love of staging doll dramas has obviously shown up in my love of writing stories. My childhood friend Mary loved to give her Barbie dolls haircuts. None of them had the same hair they came with within weeks of her receiving them as gifts. Needless to say, she works as a stylist in a salon now.

SS: (laughs) It's twelve forty-three here. Hey, this is great. I'm glad you're here. This is why I love this job. Every day, somebody new comes through this door. In the first hour, George and Tom were talking about Alaska. And now here's Caresse, talking about Barbie dolls. I love this job. I *love* this job. I'm Sammy Stoudt. Stick around, everybody.

32

With great disinclination, P.J. went with Darby to a party in Venice Beach for their Aunt Liz and Uncle Stuart's fortieth wedding anniversary.

They lived in the 600 block of Boccaccio Avenue, a healthy hike inland from the ocean, but to P.J., they were so far from the Pacific, they might as well have lived in the San Fernando Valley.

That most Venice bungalows cost more than a million dollars seemed wrong. She would put that down for a home in the Burbank Hills anytime—and in fact, she and her husband had.

Images of charming little homes overlooking the canals, tourists thronging Ocean Front Walk to peruse assortments of five-dollar sunglasses and shirts while listening to guitarists, couples strolling along the fishing pier at the end of Washington Boulevard—the appeal of this was lost on P.J., and she would never get it. Darby, on the other hand, reveled in the fact that so many Beat Generation artists from this laid-back surfers' paradise sent out ripples that influenced the world. He swore their spirits remained and invigorated the entire area, spilling into Santa Monica and beyond like vibrant paint bleeding off the edge of a weather-beaten canvas.

P.J. was in the driver's seat, gunning her white four-speed Miata roadster around every curve on the freeway. Darby relaxed on the passenger side, reveling in the knowledge that he now had a bigger and better collection of firearms than possibly anyone else in Glendale, thanks to his half-sister.

His eyes had been bigger than Jupiter when she brought the gun bag into his apartment and unzipped it, presenting each gun as though she had fashioned it herself in a tiny Arsenal By Elves workshop.

Despite the wind and the noise of the traffic, Darby shut his eyes and rambled about how cool the guns were, how truly *special* the collection was, and how truly great she was to think of him.

Somewhere in the midst of his babble on Mossberg hammerless, pump action repeaters, P.J. recounted what had happened the night of her escape from Vegas.

The red Mercedes had pulled into the driveway and the huge man at the wheel had shouted, "Hey," but it wasn't because he'd seen her. He was talking animatedly with the man who sat beside him, taking no notice of P.J.

"Hey! You tell that bitch what you think?"

"Sure did. Soon as she get back."

"How you find out?"

They got out of the car and both car doors slammed simultaneously.

"Big Joe. He say she outta town "

"And she borrow money from you for a what?"

"Say she need an operation."

The muscular men were on their way up the impossibly long driveway, their backs turned toward P.J. as they made the trek.

"So she don't need no operation?"

"Say she ain't got no medical insurance, but Big Joe say she do."

"She tell you she need money for an operation and she in Reno?"

"Gambling, dawg. All of it gone."

"Sheeee-it."

Their voices were fading and P.J. took a tentative step out of the shadows. It was now or never.

Picking up the duffels, she walked as briskly as she could, considering the weight she carried, past the cherry-tomato sports car. At the bottom of the driveway, she dared to glance back. The men were at the door, talking, when one of them turned and looked down the driveway.

He stopped and squinted, putting his hand over his eyes to cut the glare from the porch light.

P.J. momentarily froze and then came alive. She turned on her heel and ran down the street to her car.

Fumbling with the rental's keys, she finally opened the driver's side, threw the duffel bags in the back seat, and started the engine. A quick look into the rear view mirror told her no one was following her.

She was certain they hadn't known what they'd seen. She was certain they did not suspect anything was wrong inside the house. She was certain they could barely see her, standing there in the dark, so many yards away.

But she had made one terrible mistake. Although she had one bag filled with cash and guns, and two more filled with bling and dolls, she had left the other two Army bags packed with dolls upstairs in Zivia's doll room.

At least I got the doll I wanted most, P.J. thought, as she unpacked Zivia's prized Japanese side-part Barbie doll with silvery brunette hair in Darby's storage space.

The Miata careened off Venice Boulevard onto Oakwood Terrace. She made a quick right onto Boccaccio and zoomed down the street.

"You know whose house that was?" Darby asked, after they passed it.

"Whose?" P.J. was distracted.

"Back there on the corner," he said, pointing back over the seat toward Oakwood.

"No."

"Used to belong to Barbara Avedon. She wrote for really cool shows like *Bewitched* and *Gidget*, and she co-created *Cagney & Lacey*."

"How do you know that?"

"Got a friend who lives in an apartment across the street from her. Well, where she used to live. She died in '94. But he remembers her. She had great parties and everyone in the neighborhood was invited."

P.J. pulled up in front of her aunt and uncle's home, best described as a bungalow times two, expanded into a decent-sized showcase of glass and chrome thanks to the purchase of neighboring property.

She wondered if she might have the opportunity to see her aunt's Barbie doll collection today, but she seriously doubted it. The last time she was there, it had been boxed up and moved to a spare bedroom. Every time she excused herself to the bathroom, she stole a look at the boxed treasures, marked with intriguing identifiers like "mod," "Francie," "900," and "Suzy Goose."

Her cousin Lynne, three years older, had been standing in the room when P.J. passed by on her third excuse to pee. Lynne had glared at her as if to say, "Fat chance you'll ever get your hands on this," and P.J. felt a chill. When she was done combing and re-fastening the clasp on her blond ponytail, she emerged from the bathroom with a forced smile on her face, looking as if the non-verbal face-off had never occurred.

Lynne was Liz and Stuart's only child, and P.J. had her pegged as insufferable the first time they'd played dolls together as young girls. The Madison home had been smaller then—they hadn't had the money to expand in grand fashion until Stuart's years at Boeing began to add up and he landed a prized promotion. Lynne and P.J. had been playing in Lynne's bedroom, with vintage Barbie dolls Aunt Liz had supplied in two vinyl cases, one yellow and one black. Lynne had the sunshine-colored one, which featured graphics of Barbie doll and Skipper dressed in red on the front. P.J. was handed a Barbie doll, Francie, and Skipper doll trunk that featured graphics of a Tudor structure in the background, with Barbie doll, her sister, and her cousin standing in the foreground. Inside each case, there was a Barbie doll and a Skipper. Lynne had matching brunettes and P.J. had matching blonds. Their first argument erupted as to what P.J. would name her Skipper, because after all, it was Lynne's house, and if her Skipper was Skipper, then P.J. had to think of a new name.

"How about Poopy Pie Pants?" P.J. asked.

Lynne would have giggled, but being seriously depressed and anxious even at the tender age of five, she didn't.

Instead, she said, "That's not a name."

P.J. had felt sorry for her cousin even then. She had inherited the least complementary features of both parents; Stuart's jug ears and Liz's beaked nose. In years to come, she would gain weight and kids at school would avoid her. She would pull inward and study subjects relegated to hardcore academics—Latin, Anthropology, Genetics, Medieval History, and Physics. She would worship her mother, who was every bit as sophisticated as P.J.'s mom Angela, wishing (as P.J. did) that she had inherited the truly white blond hair both mothers had. Only Liz's harsh nose ruined the overall effect, but she had since taken care of the problem, getting a nose job in Beverly Hills as soon as she could afford it.

Lynne would never get a nose job or worry about her ears. She lived alone in a loft downtown and worked for a genetic research firm, seldom seeing others outside her job. She didn't trust others and didn't even seem to like people, but P.J. suspected her attitude had been built up from years of being treated poorly by a society that judges you on what you look like and how you dress before they stop to consider what you have to say and think.

Two roads diverged in the woods, as the poem went, and P.J., blessed with natural beauty, always knew she could do anything she wanted, have anything she wanted, take anything she wanted—except for Aunt Liz's dolls, because they were her repugnant cousin's birthright.

P.J. scrutinized her aunt that Friday and wondered if she would ever kill her to get her dolls. Looking at how her pretty blond hair fell on her shoulders as she bent to cut the designer anniversary cake that day, she knew she couldn't, knew she wouldn't. There were too many things about her that reminded her of her own beloved mother— her throaty voice, the way she flicked her ashes into an ashtray with two taps, the way she scratched her head right above her left ear when she was thinking. She was family, and she had never pissed P.J. off.

The question to follow, then, would be, would she ever kill Lynne for the dolls once the brat had inherited them? No. As annoying as Lynne was, she had never done anything to insult or hurt P.J. In fact, when Liz had given P.J. the freckle-less Midge doll years earlier, Lynne had done nothing but stand back as if to say, "It's just another Midge. I'll have hundreds of Mommy's dolls someday.

I'm sure one won't hurt."

She had smirked as though her mom had ripped off a genuinely insignificant piece of her doll empire and thrown it to P.J. like a bone.

Just a taste, Lynne's eyes seemed to say.

Lynne was due to get her bounty of dolls, but she had so little else going for her, it was impossible for P.J. to feel anything but pity for her.

33

The receptionist brought Caresse water in a paper cup during the commercial break, and then she and Sammy were back on the air. Instead of looking bored, Sammy seemed captivated, his beard visibly quivering from the exhilaration of great talk radio.

SS: I'm Sammy Stoudt. We're joined this morning by Caresse Redd. Interesting. Like I said at the top of the hour, I just started collecting political campaign buttons, but I'm not that serious a collector yet, and now here's a woman, she's really into this Barbie doll stuff, and it sounds like a lot of people out there are. So tell me, Caresse, why did Barbie doll become such a huge success?

CR: She symbolized the times back then. At least her earlier image did. She was just that well made and aesthetically pleasant. I'm sure a lot of moms did *not* want to buy her for their child because she was a sexy-looking doll. But she took. Girls wanted her. They wanted to be all grown up and have the breasts and the boyfriend. You know how really small girls play with baby dolls? It's fantasy. They are getting to be something they're not, but may someday be. Same with Barbie. Young girls get to imagine being beautiful, popular in school, married, having any career they want, buying their own home, wearing fabulous clothes, being independently wealthy, living on their own. What could be more liberating for a second grader?

SS: Any of the accessories, any of the things like the dollhouse or the cars that completely bombed because the marketing didn't work?

CR: I can't really think of anything that did bomb. She had a boat I don't think many people were aware of. I guess you could use a boat, but it just wasn't popular. She also had an airplane early on that never really took off— excuse the pun.

SS: And this may sound like a silly question, but I'm really curious about this. When you look at accessories or pieces of clothing, how do you authenticate them?

CR: This is where research comes in handy. Within the past fifteen years, close to a dozen good research books have been released by places like Collector Books and Hobby House Press. You get the identification guides and study. If you like it, you learn it, and then you can tell what's fake from what's real, meaning what's fake from what's Mattel.

SS: Give me something you might look for to authenticate a Barbie doll or an accessory.

CR: Okay, well, let's take clothing. In all of Barbie doll's vintage clothes, there should be a black and white Mattel tag. Most of what she wore had labels throughout the early years. But to identify a piece of clothing without a label, most of the early outfits were sewn in Japan and the craftsmanship is just astounding. The buttons are maybe one-sixteenth of an inch in diameter, and they're sewn on perfectly. The snaps are tiny, sturdy, and sewn on just as well. Then there are the tiny little loops and closures, attached flawlessly.

SS: When did Ken come along?

CR: Ken came along in '61.

SS: All right, so she started out in '59, and Ken came along in '61. Why did they feel the need for Ken? What's the story behind that?

CR: In many girls' fantasies, a girl needs a boyfriend. I mean, you know, it's just natural. It's the dating thing. And for young girls to pretend that their doll is going out on a date is fun. What's interesting, though, is that through the years, Barbie doll's had a lot of careers. Ken has never done anything.

SS: (laughs) That's a great quote, yeah.

CR: Why does she keep him around? I mean, think about it. She's been everywhere and done everything. She's hanging onto someone who's nothing.

SS: Although we are talking about dolls that reflect real life, aren't we?

CR: (laughs) Okay, okay. Well, he's there for her.

SS: Where do the names Barbie and Ken come from, by the way?

CR: Ruth Handler's children were named Barbie and Ken. Ironically, Barbie Handler, the real Barbie that Barbie doll was named after, could care less about her.

SS: Yeah. I mean, can you imagine what that's like, having that hang over your head? Oh, here's Barbie.

CR: Yeah, yeah. Well, Ken's not too happy about it either. He—you know, he gets approached. He said the best thing about it was that, over the years, he's met women who are Barbie doll collectors, and it's so easy to start conversation with them because of who he is, but—

SS: Yeah, they can always ask him if he's got a job yet.

CR: Yeah. (laughs) But you know, he is kind of taking it better than his sister.

D: All right. We're talking about Barbie doll with Caresse Redd. We welcome your calls this morning. 1-800-555-KVEC. Let's go down to Oceano, and we're joined by Herbie.

H: Good morning, everybody.

SS: Hi, Herbie.

H: Hey, this is fun to listen to. I'm a collector of a lot of different aspects of our American culture, and Barbie doll is sure, I think, maybe the major influence to what the planet is today. I think really, if you think about it, most of the Barbie dolls and Kens have probably risen up to anchor spots on television news now.

CR: There you go.

H: That's all I wanted to say.

SS: All right, Herbie, thanks for calling in.

CR: I do want to point out that the Barbie doll we think of as the stereotypical Barbie doll is not the only

Barbie doll that's out there. She comes in many nationalities, many colors. The body is the same, I'll grant you that. But she comes in many faces and guises nowadays.

SS: Hey, when did that change?

CR: The first African-American friend for Barbie doll, Christie, came out in 1968. And do you remember *Julia*, by any chance?

SS: The TV show with Diahann Carroll? Yeah.

CR: After Christie came out, Mattel issued a Julia doll in, like, '69, and from then on, there were some African-American friends, and then we got into Japanese dolls and Chinese dolls, and now probably twenty different countries and ethnic groups are represented.

SS: Caresse, I know she's just a doll, but if Barbie doll were sitting over here, what kind of woman would she be?

CR: Her personality is supposed to just be helpful, kind, friendly—the ultimate Girl Scout.

SS: Sort of like Brooke Shields.

CR: Yeah. And she's supposed to always be politically correct in everything she does. She's dead set against fur.

SS: And how do we know that?

CR: Actually, an event came up a while back where some real fur was being used in her outfits, and a statement came out that Barbie doll is against the use of fur.

SS: Does she have any faults?

CR: I don't think so.

SS: Is there the fever for Ken? Is he worth anything to a collector?

CR: Much less. Again, I'm sorry, I feel like I'm down on the poor guy. Not really fair, is it? Barbie doll has always stolen his thunder and there's nothing we can do about it now. The porcelains were issued years ago where early Barbie dolls were done in porcelain for a few hundred dollars each. And when the thirtieth anniversary Ken came out in porcelain, nobody really wanted him either. I don't get it.

SS: But it's fair to say that without Barbie doll, there'd be no Ken. I mean, he's like the sidekick.

CR: Oh, yeah, yeah.

SS: So, on his own, he just doesn't stand, no pun intended.

CR: Absolutely. You know, maybe it's that he kind of looks like Dobie Gillis or something. He just doesn't look— you know, I would rather see Barbie doll date G.I. Joe. I mean, at least he's got some muscle to him.

SS: Let's go out to San Luis, and we have Pat on the line. Pat, good morning.

P: Good morning. Hey, what an interesting show.

SS: Thank you. Yeah, kind of different.

P: Yeah. I've got a daughter six years old, and she has more Barbie dolls than I can count. My wife goes to garage sales and one day she picked up a box, probably a three-foot-long box, full of absolutely everything for, like, five dollars. Totally amazing the things that they can get— the intricate little shoes and furniture and all kinds of things.

CR: Mm-hmm.

P: I understand that they've got Barbie dolls from everywhere, all over the world, Australia, and it kind of made me think about all the mothers out there who try to slip another Barbie on the shrimp. (chuckles) I just had to say that.

SS: I knew he was leading up to something. I knew it was a setup. Another Barbie on the shrimp. That's funny, though. Barbie doll fever. A lot of different people collect her. Is there a profile for collectors? Like, for example, people who collect Barbie dolls, is that the only thing that they collect or do they collect other things as well?

CR: Most people who collect Barbie dolls, they can be into other dolls, but as a general rule, they're not. Barbie doll is their first love. I know one woman who collects trolls and Barbie dolls, another woman who collects rocks and Barbie dolls, so yeah, you can spread out from there, but Barbie doll generally comes first.

SS: I'm afraid to ask this, but are we gonna find ourselves in a whole wave of Cabbage Patch doll fever? I mean, are people gonna be pursuing Cabbage Patch dolls like they do Barbie dolls?

CR: Never.

SS: Man, I wish you could see the look on her face when I mentioned Cabbage—it's sacrilegious. Boy, Caresse, the hour has gone by far too quickly. I want to thank you for coming by. To me, the sign of a good show is when I learn something.

CR: Uh-huh.

SS: And I know I've been giving you a rough time about this, but I've actually learned a lot, not just about collecting but a little bit about our culture as well. So I thank you, and maybe you can come back sometime and talk about Barbie doll and talk about your years in Los Angeles, too, 'cause you've got that experience as well. Is there part of the Barbie doll collection, a doll or an accessory, that you would give your left arm for, something you've been searching for but you haven't been able to find?

CR: No.

SS: You've been able to get what you want?

CR: I basically have. I like the new repros. I like Francie, and I like old talkers. You know, the dolls that say phrases when you pull their strings.

SS: But with the talkers, doesn't that remove some of the mystique?

CR: Well, you know, I don't think so. I mean, the typical talker's gonna be saying, "Let's go get a cheeseburger."

SS: Or "Let's go get some tofu," 'cause it's California. "Let's get some tofu."

CR: That's right. But yeah, when you only have three or four words to get out in a phrase, it can't mean that much.

SS: Fifty years from now, when we're listening to the Sammy Stoudt Jr. Show, are we still going to be talking about Barbie doll? Is she going to be that big that far in the future?

CR: Absolutely. Her popularity is growing every year. There's no stopping her. And I predict the one-hundredth anniversary that'll come up in 2059, even though we'll be gone, is just gonna be outrageous.

SS: And unfortunately, Ken still won't have a job. He just won't have a job. What does your group, the Central Coast one, do when you get together?

CR: We talk about Barbie doll, just like you and I have been.

SS: Yeah. So it's just like an information exchange?

CR: Yeah, and if people have gone to doll shows—because there are doll shows, you know, at different places, like ballrooms at Holiday Inns and Embassy Suites and whatever—and if they've found good deals, they share that. Some members actually sell at shows. So we've done road trips.

SS: When's the next big one coming up?

CR: Oh, gosh, probably the next big one would be up in Foster City on March 30th, which seems pretty far off. I don't think anything else is happening sooner than that.

And if you want to go to the National Convention in Kansas City, Missouri, you can do that in June, but--

SS: Oh, I'm tempted. Missouri. I'm tempted.

CR: (laughs) I don't see too many people looking forward to Missouri.

SS: I've got about a minute left. Caresse, thanks for coming by. Final thoughts? How about the rumor there's a serial killer on the loose in America, killing collectors for their dolls? Think that's possible?

CR: I do. And it's very frightening.

SS: There have been two murders in Oswego and another in Tucson that I've heard of. This killer shows no sign of slowing down, true?

CR: True.

SS: Do you think you're gonna help them catch the person who's doing this?

CR: Me? I'm not sure I'm smart enough.

SS: I'd disagree with that. Okay, parting thoughts from Barbie doll.

CR: Oh, well, let me just tap into her consciousness here and see what she says. (pause) "Thanks for loving me."

SS: (laughs) Why not? Caresse, thank you. Hope you come back. Well, where else could you go to learn about Alaska and Barbie doll in the same day? My thanks to Caresse, George, and Tom. Have a good day. Have a safe day. I'm gonna go see a doctor, and we'll see you here tomorrow with a new show. I'm Sammy Stoudt. Terri, put the soup on; I'm heading home.

34

The anniversary party was winding down. The guests had come and gone, most leaving behind gifts that ranged from bottles of wine and flowers to framed photos to add to the gallery of prints lining the living room walls.

When Darby saw that Liz was ready to kick off her shoes and sit a while with her niece and nephew, he pulled out his pack of Kent Golden Lights and lit a cigarette. Liz had been smoking all day, so it was clear no one was going to ask him to step outside.

P.J. couldn't have been happier. She rose from the black leather couch she'd settled into and moved to Darby's couch to catch the second-hand drift.

Lynne spoke up from a chair in the corner, where she had been watching everyone since noon, not saying much aside from the fact that if someone might bring her a second slice of cake, she would very much appreciate it.

Stuart took off his jacket and tie and slung them onto an empty chair. He sat down beside Liz and held her left hand while she smoked with her right.

"Feels like a wake," Lynne commented.

Her parents exchanged a quick glance.

"How so, honey?" Liz asked.

"I mean, all these people, all this food." She darted a quick glance at Darby and P.J. "And relatives."

"So, Sierra, how's the magazine doing?"

Darby grinned. Only relatives and people at work called P.J. by her given name, and Darby knew how much she hated it. Even fewer people knew P.J.'s maiden name was Croesus because, like Madonna, she'd fancied herself a one-name wonder since high school.

"P.J., please, Aunt Liz," P.J. said. "And the magazine's doing great, thank you. I hired three more people to help me in our home office because I've been doing a lot of traveling lately."

Stuart perked up. "Anyplace interesting?"

"What's the circulation up to now?" Liz asked.

"Half a million," P.J. said, glad her aunt had buried her uncle's question.

"That's good," Stuart said.

Liz smiled. "You happy with your staff of writers and photographers?"

"Getting better all the time. We've got some good people on board."

P.J. took off her shoes and crossed her legs Indian-style.

"You should know, Aunt Liz," Darby said, grabbing his wineglass off the coffee table. "You subscribe, don't you?"

"Yes, I do," Liz said, "but I like to hear it from the horse's mouth. It's nice having a niece who's done so well in publishing. Putting out a monthly periodical is tough."

"I swear, it runs itself now, really," P.J. said. "I've got twenty people, half of whom are always dealing with subscribers and shipments, five who do the layout and graphics, and five more who do whatever else I need them to. All I have to do is come up with my editorial column each month and sign off on content before it goes to press."

"Do your writers come up with ideas or do you?"

"It's kind of a mix."

Lynne spoke up from her corner, distressed that her mother was showing her cousin so much attention.

"I've been busy trying to identify the gene responsible for various neurogenetic disorders like paroxysmal chorea, myokymia, and spastic paraparesis. Our research—"

Stuart let go of his wife's hand and faced his daughter squarely. "That's nice, Lynne, but we haven't seen your cousins in a few years, and we're trying to catch up."

Darby lit a second cigarette from his first and smiled uncomfortably, touching the top of his head self-consciously and wishing he had his Lakers cap on.

"You heard from Mom?" he asked.

Liz smiled at her nephew. "We spoke last week. She was thrilled to hear you were coming to the party."

Lynne was ready to share again. "Your mom's in France," she said to Darby and P.J. "My mom's right here."

P.J. attempted to sound cheerful. "Yes, and aren't you lucky? All you have to do is get in the car, and you're here in less than an hour."

P.J. stole a quick glance at Darby. Had something happened to their cousin's mind? She had to be brilliant to be doing genetic research, but she was so socially awkward, she was an embarrassment.

Lynne wasn't finished. "They have different dads," she told her parents. "Sierra's dad is Steve and Darby's dad is Dirk. Aunt Angela is married to Dirk the jerk. No one knows where Steve is, but he's probably dead. Only don't call Sierra by her right name. Call her by her wrong name, P.J., because she always used to wear pajamas, even on Saturdays when the sun was shining."

No one said a word for one distressing moment. Then Liz bit her lip, got up, and left the room.

Another beat, and Stuart was up, heading out of the living room after her.

Darby looked at P.J., who was staring at their cousin. How could she be a research savant, yet be so unaware of what she was doing and saying?

When he couldn't catch his half-sister's eye, Darby looked at Lynne too.

The room buzzed with absolute silence.

Lynne had her back to the front picture window, and dust motes floated around her head in the filtered brightness like corpses of fireflies.

Across the street, a man walked a black Newfoundland and a woman pushed a baby stroller.

Lynne yanked up the sleeve of her peach eyelet blouse and rubbed the inside of her left arm. A series of small, horizontal, healed cuts started near her wrist and ticked their way up her forearm.

The man with the Newfoundland disappeared from view and the woman with the stroller began crossing the street.

Finally, Lynne looked up at her cousins and gave them a ghoulish smile.

"I didn't take my meds today."

35

Caresse took her jacket off and smiled at Anjo, who was on the phone.

She stared at her own phone, willing Todd to call her. It was all up to him. She had given him her direct line. Maybe he'd call, maybe he wouldn't. All she knew was that if she stopped waiting, he would call sooner than he would if he sensed she was pining away.

After entering a handful of engagements and wedding announcements into the system, Anjo was finally off the phone.

"That was a long call. What's up?"

"Let me ask you something," she said.

"Okay. Shoot."

"If an armed robber entered your home around nine and you had already fallen asleep for the night, and—you're married right?"

"I'm with you so far."

"Your husband sees the guy enter, but he doesn't wake you up, right? He slips out the back and runs over to the neighbor's house to call the police. Do you keep sleeping?"

"The question is, what's wrong with the husband, not waking his wife up and getting her out of there?"

"He can't. The bedroom is upstairs, and he and the robber are both downstairs. The guy thinks he should just get out of there and notify someone. So would you just keep sleeping?"

"Sure, if the robber was quiet."

"Well, the wife wears earplugs when she sleeps, but I'm sorry, I just think she would have known something and woken up."

Anjo elaborated that a pizzeria in Paso Robles had been robbed and the suspect decided to enter the home to hide from the police, who had been called to the scene.

"How far from the pizza joint did they live?"

"About a block. County SWAT and the Paso police showed up and tried to get him to surrender."

"Well, I'll bet she woke up by the time SWAT was on the scene. Did he take the lady hostage?"

Anjo was laughing. "I don't even think the robber knew she was upstairs!"

She logged on to her computer and started typing furiously. Now that she was in story mode, Caresse knew there would be no breaking through. From out of left field, Todd crept into her mind again. She wanted to ask Anjo about him to see if she could find out more. Anjo knew Todd and might have a clue what was up, and Caresse was all for filling in the blanks at this point. Sighing, she decided to tackle the pile of community releases stacked in one of her trays. The fliers and notices would be turned into tiny blurbs regarding upcoming events that required no special fanfare. Factual and dry, the notices were easy to write. It took no special effort to cull the "who, what, where, and when" out of them.

SAN LUIS OBISPO – Two new courses are being offered at Unity Christ Church, the first on the "Metaphysical Interpretation of the Old Testament" and the second on "Earthquakes and Godquakes: Making the Shifts On All Levels."

The metaphysical class will be held at the church from ten-thirty a.m. to noon and again from seven to nine p.m. each Wednesday for six weeks beginning March 5 and ending—

Caresse caught movement in her peripheral vision, so she stopped typing and looked up. Rhea and Nibbles from Culture, Lifestyles, and Entertainment approached her desk with purpose written on their faces. They had obviously taken a before-work fashion conference, because they wore complementary pieces from the same Liz Claiborne mix-and-match coordinate set. Rhea was garbed in a pastel blue and pink plaid jacket with a baby blue dress and Nibbles wore the same plaid in skirt form with a baby blue shell and cardigan.

"You guys still shopping together?" Caressed wondered.

"That's not why we're here," Nibbles announced.

"You're coming to The Graduate Sunday evening," Rhea informed her, as though she already knew Caresse was sans plans.

Caresse glanced over at Anjo to see if she was catching all this, but she was locked in a world where only County SWAT could get an alleged robber to surrender.

"I'm going to The Graduate Sunday evening?" It was always best to repeat what they said so they stayed on-topic.

"It's for Jenna's going away party, and you're invited," Nibbles sniffed, as if she would have preferred otherwise. Obviously, something was at play that put Caresse in the game.

"Okay," she said slowly, waiting for the other Yves Saint Laurent pump to drop.

"We've set you up on one more date for your Personal Ads Valentine Edition story," Rhea said, rolling out the title with emphasis on each word.

They had to know if she had a date Sunday, she would have to scramble to turn the story in and have it proofed by Tuesday.

"You've set me up on one more date?"

Rhea and Nibbles exchanged glances like Caresse was stupid.

"That's what Rhea said," Nibbles affirmed.

"His name is Nick and he's a friend of Bree's," Rhea said. "He's a stockbroker. Got wads of cash. You'll like him."

"If he's so great, why don't one of you hook up with him?"

"Oh, we've got dates, honey," Rhea laughed.

"So be there at eight," Nibbles said.

"Wait. If you're setting me up, this has nothing to do with answering personal ads."

The women glanced at each other.

Rhea was disdainful. "You can always pretend you met through the ads. You can pretend, can't you?"

"I'll bet she pretends all the time," Nibbles said in a stage whisper.

The brats ran away from her desk, satisfied that they had ruined her day. She glanced over at Anjo, who was still lost in conversation. It was time to log on to the Best Barbie Board to see what was up.

It was a good thing she did.

The Barbie doll killer had taken another victim—BBB member Zivia Uzamba from Las Vegas.

36

It was the weekend of February ninth, and P.J. was basking in the fact that her husband Heath was away on business. Tucked high up in the hills of Burbank, their home overlooked a city where entertainment industry professionals sped around in their BMWs, made deals, and went to various studios for tapings and recording sessions.

P.J. had married into money because she was pretty enough, smart enough, and thin enough. She'd met her husband in a bar when she was only twenty-two and he was forty-four. The age difference didn't matter a whit. What mattered was that she had a five-million-dollar home, the means to publish a monthly magazine and manage a staff, and total freedom from the time she got up in the morning until she went to bed at night.

Her little white cockapoo Chao sat at her feet as she studied her face in the upstairs bathroom vanity. The round bulbs bordering the mirror's frame cast her face and shoulders in a golden glow. Peering closer, she noticed a zit on her forehead and frowned. She didn't get it. Makeup caused zits, and she was quick to remove hers when she returned from the anniversary party. She bent down and searched the cabinet for her economy-size jar of Noxema. Taking a towel, she tossed her head forward and wrapped her hair in it. Then she thrust her head back to finish creating her terrycloth turban. The lid came off the dark blue jar easily, and she readily dug into the pungent goop with her fingers. She smeared patches of it across her forehead, nose, cheeks and chin. It stung, but she waited it out, sitting on the toilet seat while her pores opened up.

The smell of Noxema reminded her of Christmas pine, but she didn't want to think about the past holiday season. Heath had been gone most of December, handling matters regarding his food packaging business, making it home only on Christmas Day to give her what she told him she wanted—a series of Silkstone Barbie dolls for her lighted display cabinets downstairs. She'd also received something she could have cared less about—another diamond ring, this one commemorating ten years together.

She had never had a memorable Christmas growing up, and she hated those who had—the kids who got every toy on their list, the girls who got all the Barbie dolls they could ever play with without begging, whining, or cajoling their parents. She thought about her cousin Lynne and the conversation she'd had with Darby on the way home from Venice.

"You're always saying you can do whatever you put your mind to," he'd said quietly, after she'd parked her car *in front of his apartment. "But did you ever consider that*

maybe you go after doll collections because you can't have Lynne's inheritance? Kind of like eating, but never feeling full because of something else? Or eating to push down feelings that are too painful?"

"No," she said. "In the case of your stupid food metaphor, if you hadn't noticed, I don't have issues with what I eat. I kill the women I choose to kill for their dolls. I kill the bitches because they've been rude, and I hate them. I enjoy going in and taking what I like."

Darby's last words had stung. "And you call Lynne a brat."

The Noxema mask began to harden on P.J.'s face.

"I'm taking my childhood back," she said aloud, in a moment of clarity. "I get to redo it my way, and no one can stop me."

P.J. knew happiness meant having options, and she simply hadn't had any in her entire life before she met Heath. Then, when he finally arrived, she asked for the moon and he reached up, grabbed it for her, pulled it down and hung it in their backyard amidst the spans of Japanese party lanterns. What was missing? Nothing.

Those of you who think you have control over your lives, what you collect, what you do every day, have a lesson to learn, and it's coming from me, she thought.

She would continue to steal their best Barbie doll treasures and then take the ultimate valuable: their lives. Only then would she be better than they were. She would have the best doll collection in the world, and she wouldn't have any competition. She would be the Barbie doll goddess, the leviathan, the expert, and the one who not only knew it all but had it all.

"Just like Barbie doll," P.J. told Chao, heading out of the vanity.

Like Gloria Swanson in *Sunset Boulevard*, she swept down her staircase to her magazine office on the south side of the house. Heath would be coming home Monday for a week of rest and relaxation. She had just enough time for a weekend doll spree, but she had to find a victim who lived close enough so she could get there and back in less than forty-eight hours.

P.J.'s *Barbie International* offices consisted of four rooms, the best of which was a converted sun porch filled with lounge chairs and potted plants. It was here that staff meetings were held at the start of each new week. It was here that P.J. reviewed the upcoming issue on a large table in the center of the room. It was here that P.J. felt relaxed and strong, gazing at framed shots of the magazine's cover art lining the perimeter of the room, starting at the doorway and running from left to right. When one row was complete, another tier began.

She took the high stool near the large table now and studied the layouts for the eighty-page issue due to ship in two weeks. The March issue consisted of P.J.'s monthly editorial on all that was happening in the world of Barbie doll, a feature on pink dressed boxed dolls, an identification guide to the many different shades of Barbie doll's closed-toed pumps, an article on Bild Lilli, a review on a book about Barbie doll structures and furniture, a guide to hair colors for Twist 'N Turn Barbie doll, a look at Barbie doll bidding on eBay, and a feature on Barbie doll's vinyl cases by Caresse Redd.

Darby had checked P.J.'s subscription database and determined why the surname Krieger had sounded familiar to her. In Redd's earliest articles, she used her maiden name as a middle name. The byline Caresse Krieger Redd from P.J.'s back issues had stuck in her mind and

Darby, as usual, was able to help his half-sister make the connection.

So I probably met Caresse's brother, P.J. mused, glancing through the six-page spread covering Nancy Roth's vinyl treasures.

P.J. walked over to her locked filing cabinet and took off the necklace she wore at home, which included a tiny key to access her drawers of paperwork.

She had had a run-in with Nancy Roth, aka NANCY_PANTS, about a year before when she had PayPaled her for a Swing-A-Ling Tutti Round Train Case and had not received it. She had filed for her money back from PayPal but Nancy had countered by providing a delivery confirmation receipt, reassuring them that the package had been delivered. What P.J. had received in the mail was a box with old, scrapped pieces of cardboard, newspaper, and Styrofoam peanuts. The case, which was small and would have weighed less than six ounces, was accounted for in weight by random packing materials.

P.J. reached for a folder in the bottom drawer, where she kept files on everyone she hated. She found the one marked ROTH, NANCY. Inside, there were notes covering the PayPal dispute, as well as private emails and board postings printed out to keep on hand.

PJ-RULEZ: No, I just suppose you listed it on eBay for shits and giggles, and when I won it, you had seller's remorse and changed your mind about parting with it. I don't know what it means when you "sell" something and send someone an empty box instead, but I call it theft.

NANCY_PANTS: You're a liar, P.J. Ask anyone else here on the board if I've ever sent them an empty box. As if!

Several Best Barbie Board members had leapt to Nancy's defense. P.J.'s protests were steamrolled off into a corner, doubted and dismissed.

P.J. let her full anger rise. What did she want that Nancy had? Well, she was partial to her smaller vinyl pieces—the train cases, the wallets, the pencil cases, and the smallest doll cases for Tutti and Todd and their friends. Tutti and Todd were pretty much neglected as Barbie doll's siblings, having enjoyed only the shortest of runs in America from the mid-Sixties to the early Seventies, but P.J. knew Nancy had branched out from gathering only vinyl to include the actual dolls in her collecting plan.

There was much to be said in moving the smaller vinyl pieces and dolls too.

It certainly shouldn't prove as cumbersome as the Vegas haul, she thought.

P.J. walked over to the layout table and looked at Caresse's article again. There were at least two dozen pictures included in the feature, and one showed a black patent 1962 Mattel wallet. There were graphics of a blond bubble cut dressed in Enchanted Evening on the right, a sweep of stardust across the center, and then another blond bubble wearing a red version of Friday Night Date on the left.

Want that.

Another photo of a wallet, this one in light blue vinyl, showed graphics of a blond bubble's face on the left and a body shot of a brunette bubble wearing Dinner at Eight on the right.

Want that.

There were photos of Ponytail pencil cases, including one in black vinyl with 1961 graphics. A blond bubble cut dressed in pink and a pink ponytail wearing turquoise were positioned alongside the words "Barbie Pencil Case," with graphics of a pencil and a pad of paper in the center. A fabulous blond ponytail profile sketch covered the right-hand side.

Want that.

Next came photos of the small Tutti play cases. P.J. particularly liked the ones that had transparent windows so you could see the dolls when they were packed away. There was an orange one covered with daisies, a pink one with beach graphics, a rose one with winter and summer scenes, and a yellow one with Tutti and her gal pal Chris on the front.

Want them.

P.J. backed away from the layout table and started to pace the room. Caresse had written that Nancy lived in Walnut Creek, California.

Walking over to her computer and taking a seat in her black leather office chair, P.J. called up the *Barbie International* subscriber database and got Nancy's address. She entered it in MapQuest and arrived at the route, an approximate drive time of five hours and twenty-seven minutes, and an estimated distance of 353.62 miles.

She glanced at the Fossil Barbie doll watch she wore at home and decided to take it off. She put it in her top desk drawer.

Next, she took off her Barbie doll necklace, which included tiny keys and actual Barbie doll accessories, and put it with the watch.

Lastly, she took off her Barbie doll bracelet, the one Caresse's brother had noticed—if he had been Caresse's brother.

She had argued with Darby.

"Krieger isn't a very common name," she said.

"How many men named Krieger have sisters who are so into Barbie doll they wear Barbie doll bracelets as adults?" Darby retorted.

"I don't even know if Caresse wears a Barbie doll bracelet," P.J. said.

Darby thought about it. "You identified yourself as Devvon. How would anyone be able to associate a Devvon West taking a Greyhound to Las Vegas with a Barbie doll theft and double homicide taking place that weekend in Vegas?"

"It's just a creepy coincidence," P.J. concluded.

Darby agreed. "No doubt."

"But it doesn't mean she's not on my radar now," P.J. added.

"You've always been a bit paranoid," Darby laughed.

They had left it at that.

Today, P.J. was feeling brazen. Fuck Amtrak. Fuck Greyhound. Neither of them would get her up to Walnut Creek much before midnight, and then she'd have to struggle to coordinate things to get herself back to Burbank tomorrow.

I'm taking the Miata, she thought. *I'll be there in five and a half hours, and it'll still be daylight.*

Caresse's article had mentioned that Nancy's husband Ward sold used cars and that Nancy's paralegal work kept her knee-deep in files each weekend.

Weekend sales were notoriously critical for used car salesmen. Ward would be at work, and Nancy would be at home.

P.J. questioned how many breaks Nancy needed to take from proofing legalese, because it seemed like she compulsively popped up to post comments on the Best

Barbie Board every hour on the hour from sun-up to sun-down every Saturday and Sunday. P.J. pictured Nancy reading boring casework for an hour, breaking to log on to the BBB to chat, and then logging off so she could return to reading briefs.

Something interesting to keep her awake, P.J. thought.

She had read media coverage of the homicides in Oswego, most of it involving Gayle's loudmouthed sister-in-law Megan, but if anything had been mentioned in the national news about the murders in Tucson, Oak Harbor, or Vegas, she had missed it.

Lurking on the Best Barbie Board had brought only a few things to light.

Megan Dailon posted a list of Gayle's dolls and asked collectors to be on the lookout for them on the secondary market. So far, no one had seen any of them, and it amused P.J. to imagine them scouring eBay listings in vain.

Even though theft hadn't been ruled out as a motive thanks to Beth's assessment of Hailey's room, the Raphael homicide case might be motivationally muddied if law enforcement officers were focusing attention on the young schoolteacher's boyfriends.

Another case two degrees shy of cold was the Time Taylor murder investigation. Since cash and drugs had been on the scene before Time's father went to jail, detectives were undoubtedly following up leads involving revenge or the quest for hidden money or illegal substances Time's father had bragged the cops hadn't found at the time of his arrest.

Lastly, there was the Vegas murder, the one P.J. had botched. No one had said boo about it yet, even though she had left dolls behind, packed to go. Intuition told her the police would pin it on some kind of Lil Beef drama and that a rival music group would be blamed. To P.J.'s way of thinking, rappers and hip-hop artists were nothing more than thugs who created music. If someone wanted to kill Lil Beef's bodyguard and his wife at home, there were at least a dozen rival recording artists and their entourages eager to see it happen.

Six murders, and the K9s were quiet. Could she risk driving her own car up north for the next kill?

The way she felt today, she was certain she could.

37

At seven p.m. Sunday, Caresse was on her way to The Graduate restaurant and nightclub in San Luis Obispo for Jenna's going-away party. It was windy outside, and she was dressed in powder pink from head to toe, from the peak of her hooded sweatshirt to the tips of her pink vintage Pappagallo flats.

In addition to celebrating Jenna's departure from the *County Times*, she was ready to commemorate being done with the personal ads dating scene with one tall, tart drink. The article would be done in thirty-six hours, and then she could get some much-needed rest. Prepared for another disaster, she had packed a legal pad and a few Sharpies in her oversized pink bag in case her arranged date with Nick was a bust.

Sunday evening was the right time to hold a gathering at The Grad. It was a huge establishment typically packed with Cal Poly kids moshing in the center of the planked, wooden football field-sized dance floor. A bank of flat screen TVs, a bar (complete with boisterous bartenders), and food service windows lent a college rathskeller appeal. The lighting, as always, was low. Tonight, in honor of Jenna, they were playing her favorite movie, *Legally Blonde,* on the big screen.

The bar area was packed when Caresse walked in, so she headed in that direction. She stopped beside Seth, who was rubbing his round-lensed glasses with a napkin while arguing with Pressroom Skip.

"Listen," Seth was saying, "You can't denigrate AT&T for laying off 40,000 employees. There's nothing wrong with streamlining a corporation to make it more efficient and competitive."

"You're an idiot, Tanner!" Skip exploded, sloshing beer in Caresse's direction. He noticed her and his mood changed. "Oh, hi, Todd magnet."

Caresse was ready to open her mouth, but Skip flip-flopped back to being angry with Seth. "Think it's efficient when one man ends up doing four men's work and two-thirds of it doesn't get done?"

Caresse leaned between them and called to the bartender. "Tom Collins."

Seth was smug. "Hire the right person who can do four men's work. That's the answer."

Skip was sarcastic. "Right."

They had agreed to disagree. Seth turned his back, and they watched as he wove through the throng in the direction of the men's room.

Skip moved up to the bar with Caresse and put his beer down. The bartender hadn't asked for money, but she threw a few bucks down on the glossy bar anyway. Her drink had arrived, complete with cherry, and Skip smiled at it. He was old school all the way, in his late fifties, and everyone's favorite cigarette-break sage. Tonight he wore a green plaid flannel shirt he'd made an effort to iron. It rose over his belly and hung down past his belt.

Caresse checked out his cowboy boots, which had been buffed to a shine.

She was feeling brave. "So tell me everything you know about Todd."

Skip smiled mischievously and sipped his beer. Women on fishing expeditions always amused him. "He's married. I know that much."

Oh, God, she thought.

"Well, he's married, but he's *not* married."

"What's that supposed to mean?"

"Well, he has his own place and is legally separated, but the divorce hasn't been finalized. He might call her an ex already because, I mean, who doesn't? What are your options? My separated-from-but-not-ex-yet-wife/husband?"

Caresse had the sinking feeling Todd's separation wouldn't stick. She decided to take another blind stab. "And the kids?"

"Well, they've got the one boy who's about your son's age, but here's where it gets complicated." Skip ran his worn hands over his balding dome, smoothing back what little hair he had left.

Anjo nudged in. "I can take it from here, Skip. I should have told her about Todd a few days ago."

"The day it happened, how about?" Skip was accusatory. He took no delight in discussing personal matters. This was women's work.

"The day *what* happened?" Anjo shrieked. "The second immaculate conception?"

Caresse thought about tall, handsome, blond, bearded Todd and sighed audibly. *Mmm, Todd babies.*

Anjo jerked in Caresse's direction. "You're not."

"No," Skip interjected. "From what I heard, they might have made out in his car after lunch, but there wasn't any sex. Not even the Bill Clinton kind."

Anjo was surprised. "Todd talked to you about her?"

"Look, I saw the whole thing come down firsthand," Skip said. "They met, started to talk, and the pressroom erupted in a blaze of testrogen."

Anjo was nearly shouting. "Testrogen?"

"That's my combo word for testosterone and estrogen. Love it or hate it."

"We've got to tell her," Anjo told Skip. "She's our friend."

Skip shrugged and sipped his beer. "I'm *her* friend, I'm *your* friend, and I'm *his* friend. Sounds like lose-lose-lose."

Anjo gave him her I-smell-something-disgusting face. "Truth triumphs, even if it hurts."

"Amen, sister," Caresse said, bracing herself for the bad news by biting the tip of her straw.

Anjo was ready to lay bare the facts. "Todd and his wife Fianna had their baby boy Harley four years ago. Same age as Chazzie-Wazzie. Then, last year, Fianna had an affair with a guy in Skip's garage band."

Skip looked ready to volunteer a name and then stopped himself.

Anjo continued, "Fianna got pregnant and moved out with Harley, leaving Todd the house they'd lived in. Fianna moved in with buddy-boy and had the baby. Then Fianna and buddy-boy started to fight. Fianna kicked buddy-boy out and started calling Todd, wanting to reconcile. Todd is trying to decide whether or not he still loves his cheating wife—"

"Separated-from-but-not-ex-yet-cheating-wife," Skip clarified.

"Who now not only wants to bring Harley back home but a newborn daughter as well. So, she's changed her mind, and he still loves her, but he's mad at her for cheating and leaving. They have a child together, but in accepting them back, he'll have to raise another child who will remind him of buddy-boy forever."

"It's difficult," Skip surmised.

Caresse's eyes filled with tears. "Too messy for me."

Anjo put her arm around her and then came in for a full body press.

The waterworks began.

Skip tried to hand Caresse her drink, but she pushed it away.

Nibbles and Rhea approached, flanking a kid who had to be ten years Caresse's junior. He was smooth-faced and bright-eyed, with tousled hair the shade of almonds.

Rhea touched Caresse's shoulder, nudging Nick forward at the same time. "Caresse, this is Nick. Nick, Caresse."

Nick looked frightened.

"Her crumpled look," Anjo joked, and everyone laughed.

Caresse grabbed her drink from Skip, downed it, wiped her eyes with the damp napkin stuck to the bottom of the glass, and laughed weakly.

"Excuse me, Nick. I'll be right back."

38

While one of the Las Vegas investigators dabbed Rick Uzamba's neck with a clean cotton swab moistened with distilled water where the hypodermic needle had left a dot of dried blood, another technician was upstairs, dabbing Zivia's upper arm for the same reason. Both samples were then air-dried and packed in envelopes with sealed corners.

If the killer had touched Rick, it was necessary to test his clothing, so it was cut from his body and bagged in paper, along with his shoes. The fact he wasn't wearing any of the jewelry he generally never removed was duly noted.

No one seemed daunted by the fact they had to scour not only the outside of the residence and garage, but nine bedrooms, six bathrooms, the kitchen, the living room, the screening room, the bowling alley, the music room, the doll room, and the den.

Everywhere in the home where the floor was not carpeted, one team of investigators culled footprints from dust using an electrostatic lifting device while a second team used lifting film, taking care to preserve and store film containing impressions by taping the edges securely in shallow photographic paper boxes. When they ran out of the boxes, they utilized the alternate procedure of taping an edge of each piece of film securely in clean, smooth, high-grade paper file folders.

The backyard was examined exhaustively, from its tiered Cocobolo decks, umbrellaed tables, and lounge chairs to the hot tub, lampposts, and pool. The shrubs, hedges, and garden beds were searched for anything out of the ordinary as well.

Footprints across the perimeter of the backyard, leading to the point of entry were photographed, including an object for scale, with particular attention paid to those in the softer soil.

"Large feet," an investigation named Lou Gersikoff commented. "Looks like the imprint of a male sports shoe."

"Basketball, football, running?" his friend Uri James asked.

"The tread looks familiar," Lou replied. "But we'll know for sure soon enough."

Latent prints on the sliding glass door leading into the home were dusted with black powder and photographed before they were removed with rubber lifts.

Russ Alexander stared at the linoleum at the edge of the carpeted room. The small square, which would serve as a space for a mud mat, was bare, save for a tiny, yellow-tinged dried liquid splotch slightly smaller than the head of a tack.

"What have we here?" he asked rhetorically. Treating the scabbed mark with the same methodology he'd use for dried blood, he lifted it with a clean cotton swab moistened with distilled water, air-dried it, and placed it in an envelope.

Upstairs, in Zivia's doll room, the smashed cabinets were photographed, left to right, floor to ceiling, so that the eight-by-ten prints could be fit together to create a panoramic shot of the entire room. Wearing cotton gloves, technicians collected the Lexan fragments from the cabinets. Each piece was then marked and packed in a labeled container.

Investigators combed the $8.5 million Las Vegas residence for more than thirty-six hours. Due to the high-profile nature of the Lil Beef case, FBI entered the picture about ten hours into the evidence collection process. Weapons and ammunition remaining downstairs in the secret room were confiscated.

The FBI was purportedly there to draw an association between rival hip-hop artists, but they were forced to reconsider motive when they spotted the two Army duffel bags stuffed with Barbie dolls lying on the floor in the doll room.

39

After Caresse finished washing her face in the restroom at The Grad, she emerged and looked around. The place was as wide and tall as a raftered barn, made homey with wood paneling, picnic tables, and sawdust scattered liberally on the floor. She found Nick in a dark corner with his back to *Legally Blonde.* He had gotten her a fresh Tom Collins, which sat on a fresh napkin beside a half-pound Gradburger and a full-pound Supergrad. He was drinking dark beer, waiting for her.

"Didn't know which one you'd want."

"Oh." She was a week away from being hungry now, so she looked at him forlornly.

"More for me," he laughed, pulling both burgers closer to his brew.

She sat down slowly. "Thanks for the drink."

"Sure."

Caresse was used to talkative guys, so she didn't know quite what to do with the ensuing silence. Normally, she would jump to fill any conversational voids, but she wasn't feeling it tonight. She waited. She watched him eat. His dark, bright eyes focused on the food like a squirrel inspecting the perfect pile of nuts.

It took a full fifteen minutes for Nick to grow uncomfortable.

He cleared his throat. "So, you live around here?"

"Yeah, a couple miles from work."

"I work in Pismo," he said. "I'm a—"

"Stockbroker," they said in unison and laughed.

"How does someone in his twenties get started in that?" she asked.

Nick took a deep breath and was preparing to launch into his personal history when he caught the subtle change in her expression.

"You don't really want to know, do you?"

Caresse thought for a moment. This was her chance to be brutally honest. But was there a way to minimize it with humor? She thought about Bree and Nibbles and Rhea and sighed. There was nothing to laugh about. "This is absolutely my last date for my article. I'm ready to write it, and I'm kind of worn out."

Nick stood up and pointed in the direction of some offices. "Grab your drink and a burger and come with me."

Caresse tottered behind him, struggling with her purse, the plate, and her drink.

He led her to a closed office and knocked on the door before opening it.

He snapped on the overhead lights. The cozy cubbyhole was empty.

He turned toward her. "I know the guy who works in here. He's gonna be busy in the restaurant tonight, so I'm sure he won't mind. I'll tell him you're borrowing his space, anyway. This way, you can start writing your piece."

"What's his name, in case anyone asks?"

"Gavin," Nick said.

She put her drink, the burger, and her purse on the desk.

Gavin had a quality leather office chair. She sank into it, putting her arms on the rests. Nick came toward her and, gentlemen that he had been so far, she expected nothing more than a quick hug or a kiss on the cheek.

Instead, he zeroed in on her neck and gave her a tiny, twisted little bite. A hickey.

She yelped and Nick backed away, grinning. "Sorry."

Her jaw was still on the floor as he left, closing the door gently behind him.

She stared at the *300* poster plastered mid-center on the wall above Gavin's desk and then looked around at his other posters and knickknacks while rubbing her neck. She didn't have a mirror, but as long as Nick didn't have rabies, she would be fine.

She opened her purse. Out came the yellow legal pad. Out came a stack of random notes, held together in the corner by a navy, coated paperclip. Out came a green Sharpie.

The desk was fairly clean, so she spread out her notes. Todd would go last, serving as the poignant capper to her Internet search for love.

She re-read what she had written, but didn't know if it was any good.

"Having been divorced since the fall of 2007, first thoughts of re-entering the world of dating filled me with trepidation. After meeting more than a few men through personal ads recently, however, I've become a dating veteran.

"When playing the personal ads game, you've got two choices: respond to ads or run your own. Some people, like me, do both. If you're like me when you're responding, you look for a few different things in a person's greeting. What do they sound like? If the timbre of their voice grates on your nerves after only a minute, it's likely that an hour or two of chatting will give you a migraine. Another factor to consider is speech patterns. Are they articulate and socially adept? Lastly, what the heck are they telling you? They've got a minute or so to reveal themselves, and what they choose to say in such a short span of time is often insightful. Listen and take heed.

"When you're on your first date, do they discuss children or ex-spouses? Remember, what you're getting is someone with a history, and, above all, issues regarding offspring are critical. If you have a child and he has a child and you fall into a relationship, the kids fall into it too. Attitudes toward exes are also crucial. What went wrong in the past may be part of a pattern you won't want to repeat.

"What personal ads do is open doors between people who are admitting to wanting to meet someone who might become special to them. I'm thankful for them. They are a bold advancement on the hit-and-miss chances you take in bars, grocery stores, or anyplace public, for that matter.

"Dating is not for the faint of heart. If you're not ready to embrace the cold, cruel world of dating, which requires having the hide of an armadillo, confidence in yourself and your looks, and curiosity when it comes to meeting intriguing members of the opposite sex, forgo it. There are far less painful things to do with your time.

"While not into pain, I, however, am hooked on the quest to find a good man to enhance my world and imbue it with all the good things a great love has to offer. Sure, I can stand on my own two feet. I do it all the time. But the intimacy to be had with someone you love, on a regular if not daily basis, is a dessert I prefer not to forgo."

She stopped reading and picked up the burger near her unfinished drink. It was cold, but it was delicious. She wiped her hands, picked up her green Sharpie, and began to write. "Feel the same but not ready to pick up the phone yet? Sharing some of these personal ad dates I've been on may be just what you need to get going.

"The Bridge Player. Went well, as far as first meetings go. He kept turning to watch the football game on Brubeck's TV. Talk revolved around lingerie, old people, death and dying, and kids. Stats: Tall, forties, dark-haired, with Tommy Lee Jones eyes and a gaunt frame. Scorecard: Dinner, wine, jazz, walk back to my car, free book, no kiss, no second date."

She chewed on the barrel of the Sharpie while she thought about her Starbucks date with Jerry. Someone knocked on the closed door, and she gave a jolt. She glanced over and braced herself, not knowing what to expect.

Anjo stuck her head in. "Hi, Mop Top."

Caresse relaxed immediately. "How'd you find me?"

Anjo shrugged. "When it's important to find someone, you usually can. How are you feeling?"

"Crappy. But my article's going well."

"Ready for some big news?" She sat on the edge of the desk and looked at the burger, drink, purse, and paperwork.

"Todd's pregnant?"

Anjo smiled. "The police want to talk to you."

"The—what?"

"A woman up in Walnut Creek was found murdered. Your name and email address were on a slip of paper, in her handwriting, on her desk."

"How—what?" She was in full-sputter now, springing away from the desk, into the center of the room.

"Relax. I found out through John, who was talking to friends up there. All they're gonna do is take a drive down here, interview you, see what your relationship to the vic is, and find out if you might know who wanted her dead."

Caresse was incredulous. "Wanted *who* dead?"

"John said her name was Nancy. Nancy Roth."

40

Before dawn on Monday, P.J. stowed her packed doll duffels and the compact .380 Makarov Darby loaned her from the stash she'd given him upon returning from Vegas.

The ever-handy Darby had known just what to use from the hardware store to devise a slip-on silencer. This was the first time P.J. had used a gun to kill someone, and everything she'd learned from days spent at the Glendale Firing Range with Darby had come back to her like a long-lost lover when she was face to face with Nancy.

P.J. stood in the exercise room adjacent to her home office and smiled with satisfaction. This was one room Heath never came in, and when he visited her here, he never stayed more than a few minutes. There was nowhere to sit, other than on the Precor 846i-R recumbent cycle, and he had always been a sit-down kind of guy.

She had closets, cubbies, and an entire downstairs shower and vanity area. The duffels and gun went into a cabinet near the bank of windows facing her garden. She took off her necklace and locked the cabinet door just before Katia entered the back entrance to the office and snapped on the lights.

P.J. watched her through the glass door across the hallway.

Katia was a hard worker, terminally cheerful. She was in love with the color yellow, which contrasted nicely with her black-highlighted dark brown hair and sepia eyes. She was in charge of handling matters pertaining to the latest issue of *Barbie International,* which would now be in the mail and on newsstands. P.J. liked to call her the Queen of Fallout.

Katia put down her purse and bagged lunch before heading over to start the morning pot of coffee for the gang.

P.J. walked across the hallway and tapped twice on the glass so Katia wouldn't be startled.

Katia swiveled and gave P.J. a wave before turning back to measure scoops of Maxwell House into the filter.

"Good morning," P.J. said, breezing in and heading over to her desk near the layout table.

"Morning," Katia chirped. "I'm down to the last few retailers who say they didn't get the February issue, so I thought I'd come in and get a head start."

P.J. looked at the bank of windows facing the garden and decided to open them. The windows were large and heavy and lifted from the bottom, much like classroom windows that needed to be propped to stay up. The fragrance from sweet-smelling Sampaguita and Plumeria shrubs melded to create a jasmine-heavy scent that was so heady it begged analysis by Ulric de Varens.

The office was without cubicles, with most desks paired up and facing each other. P.J.'s desk and the layout table served as the room's focal center.

Every desk had its own Zinnwaldite-colored AT&T phone; P.J. had bought them in bulk from a local company that went out of business. Every desk also had a Dell computer, a *Barbie International* coffee mug or three, and a bouquet of fresh-cut flowers from the garden. Today, Sharidan would run out back and clip new bouquets so Friday's wilted blossoms could be replaced.

Dressed in navy sweats, Kumi showed up next, opening her Hello Kitty backpack before she even made it to her desk.

"Lottery tickets for everyone!" she cried.

P.J. stared at her. "Kumi, there are only two of us here."

"That's okay. She can pass them out and everyone will be surprised when they get here," Katia said, clapping her hands together and jumping up to help.

P.J. rolled her eyes and retrieved her mug from her desk so she could grab a cup of coffee.

The phone rang, and Katia dashed to answer it.

As she listened, her smile sagged. It had to be a complaint call. While Katia was the Queen of Fallout, she had a hard time dealing with negative people.

P.J. walked over, set her mug on Katia's desk, and took the receiver from her.

"This is Sierra Walsh," she said.

Katia gave P.J. a grateful smile and ran back to help Kumi pass out tickets, making sure she saved the three-dollar Double Bingo for her boss.

P.J. laughed. "No, I don't find anything suggestive with the cover art at all. What? Are you kidding? He's holding her in his palm. No, she's fully dressed!"

Kumi and Katia listened as they finished passing out the lottery tickets. It took about five minutes for P.J. to get

176

the caller off the phone, and when she hung up, she was laughing.

"A subscriber thought the shot of King Kong holding a Barbie doll was inappropriate." P.J. was incredulous.

Both women nodded as if to say, *what else is new?*

P.J. went back to her desk and fired up her computer, and Katia and Kumi followed suit. Nona and Tess, the Adobe InDesign professionals, entered through the back door next. After greetings all around, they settled in at their desks. The sun was coming up and the day was off to a promising start.

While Tess was whining about inferior graphics submitted by a small Mattel dealer for his ad and Nona was complaining about the lack of photos for a last-minute report on newly released repros, Katia was reassuring mom-and-pop shops that their shipments would arrive soon, and Kumi was busy Googling Silkstones.

"Oh, my God," Kumi sighed. "I would kill to have the Dahlia Silkstone Barbie."

Tess and Nona stopped kvetching long enough to address their friend.

"She is awesome," Tess agreed. "Love her red hair."

"Love her black gown," Nona added.

"And it's great she's limited to 999," Tess noted.

"Too bad she's not cheaper," Kumi lamented.

P.J. stifled her laughter. Was the $400 asking rate really too high?

Kumi seemed to read P.J.'s thoughts. "Maybe if she goes down to $250 and I put aside $10 a week, I can have her in time for my birthday this summer."

Pathetic, P.J. thought. She knew she didn't pay her staff well. They were here because they loved Barbie, not because they wanted to get rich, but having to save up to buy a doll was really sad.

Barbie International's proofreader, Lilani, came through the back door slowly. Her light brown hair was windblown, and she struggled with the Yummy Cupcakes box she carried.

"Hey, welcome back!" Katia called out.

Lilani had been out for the past ten days, recovering from a bad bout of sciatica and back pain. They had all had a good laugh about the fact she would never seem to learn *not* to wait till the cat litter waste bucket weighed fifty pounds before lugging it out to the trash.

"I'm done," Lilani announced to the room. "When I scoop poop from now on, I am sticking to taking out little bags every three days instead of waiting a month and trying to lug out a barrel-full."

"You need fewer cats," Nona suggested.

"Do cats really poop that much?" Kumi wrinkled her nose.

"Three cats," Lilani replied, hobbling half-erect over to the coffee pot and setting down the box, which proved to be filled with everyone's favorite selections from Burbank's best cupcake shop.

Tess rushed over to grab a Black Out, which had a pure chocolate ganache center and fudge-like ganache frosting. "Oh, Lilani, you should be out more often if it means you're gonna come back with these!"

P.J. stayed at her desk, sipping coffee. She could live without cupcakes. Each one of those women could afford to lose at least twenty pounds, and skipping decadent treats like those Fluffernutter peanut butter cupcakes topped with marshmallow buttercream would be a great start.

"So did you get any rest?" Katia asked, joining the rapidly forming cupcake camarilla.

"I'll tell you what," Lilani said, rubbing her hip joints frenetically. "Taking time off should be about stopping to smell the roses. I feel like I've had my head shoved in a rose bush. Even with painkillers, I've been anguished. Did you know that when you have sciatic nerve pain, you move your leg even a little, and this bolt of pain goes shooting right through you? And if you sneeze, you jolt in torment from head to foot? And when you try to get to the bathroom, you're just about crawling because you can't stand upright?"

Lilani's friends selected their cupcakes and moved back to their desks. They didn't want to hear about physical distress any more than they had to.

"Well, I'm glad you're better," Katia offered, biting into a coconut-filled Almond Joy cupcake, trailing crumbs all the way back to her post.

The phone rang again, and P.J. picked it up.

"*Barbie International.* Sierra Walsh speaking."

The crew of edacious cupcake fans watched P.J. talk on the phone, straightening the coiled cord as she spoke. They should get back to work, but they loved to watch their boss in action.

"Okay, give me an address," she said.

She listened further.

"If it's what you say it is, I'm sure there's a story in it," she agreed.

With the business formalities addressed, P.J. hung up and turned to Katia.

"Katia, where's Pismo Beach?"

Katia worked with MapQuest on her Dell and replied, "Central Coast."

"How far is it from San Luis Obispo?"

"About ten miles."

"Great." P.J. got up and walked a slip of paper over to her. "Email Caresse Redd and have her call these folks. They've moved here from Germany and claim to have the best European Barbie collection ever. They want to be featured in the magazine."

"Who are they?" Nona piped up.

P.J. stared at the slip. "Bronauer. Arnolt and Vala."

"Yeah, Vala's on the Best Barbie Board," Nona said. "I've seen her mod era stuff. Anyone would trade their soul for it."

P.J. raised an eyebrow. "Tell Caresse if there's a story to write it for the April issue. And tell her if she goes over there to take her camera and email me some pictures to whet my appetite."

Heath gave three short raps on the glass hallway door before pushing it open. He carried a large, wrapped gift tied with a floppy cream bow into the office and placed it on a chair near the door. Then, rushing across the room, he caught P.J. in a bear hug near Katia's desk. "Sweetie!"

P.J. struggled a bit, embarrassed by the PDA. She extricated herself from his arms and kissed him chastely on the cheek. The office girls exchanged glances, rolling their eyes.

Seen more affection doled out by stewardesses greeting you preflight, Kumi thought.

Heath hammed it up, bowing to the ladies present.

"And all of you are well?" he asked.

"All except for Lilani," Tess said.

"I hurt my back," Lilani shared.

"Have a cupcake," Katia offered.

The women liked Heath and couldn't understand what he saw in P.J. One might think it would be the other way around—that any man in his fifties would be lucky to have a trophy wife twenty years his junior—but this trophy wife was only painted 24K, and it was she who was lucky to have him.

"I think I will," Heath said, heading over to the counter.

P.J. ran and grabbed his arm, refusing to let go. "What about your cholesterol?"

Her voice was shrill, and Heath gave a mock shudder.

The ladies laughed. They could relate to being berated by the boss.

"Maybe next time," he said, nodding at the women as he gently released P.J.'s grasp and put his arm around her. "I've been gone a while, and I need to borrow this beauty for a bit."

The women watched as Heath led P.J. to the door and scooped up the present he had set down on the way in. Allowing her to pass first, he followed her out, turning to wink at the ladies before the door closed behind them.

The women were quiet until they were certain the lovebirds were well on their way upstairs.

"What does he see in her?" Nona asked.

"He's so cool," Tess enthused.

"I'd marry him," Kumi volunteered.

"He's probably the type of guy who likes a demanding woman," Katia said.

"They make those?" Nona asked.

"Some guys like a challenge," Katia replied.

"And some guys like to be dominated," Tess reflected.

"Bet he likes to be tied up and whipped and beaten," Kumi said, her eyes huge. "You know, like S&M? Bondage?"

The woman laughed in surprise.

"Kumi!" Katia cried. "You're so bad."

"Oh, beat me harder, Sierra," Kumi cried, playing it up. "Make it hurt so good!"

The others decided to jump in, wailing and moaning and crying until they got so carried away, they dissolved into tears of mirth.

"Oh, wait, I think I hear her coming back," Tess announced loudly, with a straight face.

The women stopped their silliness immediately, until they realized Tess was kidding.

Then they were off again, kidding and joking in a way they never could when P.J. was around.

41

Caresse was home alone Monday morning, excused from work because she was expecting a visit from the Walnut Creek investigators in charge of the Nancy Roth murder.

The upcoming days were going to be interesting. She had gotten an email from Katia at *Barbie International* mentioning that Sierra wanted her to interview Arnolt and Vala Bronauer in Pismo Beach for the April issue, and plans were set for them to meet. Meanwhile, to tide her over, she was due to get her March issue of *Barbie International* in the mail any day.

Putting her time to good use, she made a strong cup of coffee, scrambled a few eggs, and sat down at her computer to finish her Personal Ads Valentine assignment. Working off the nervousness she felt about her impending visit from law enforcement, she channeled her energy into writing. She was dressed for a day at home, in gray sweats that felt flannel-soft and cozy. Her bare feet danced on the computer cords tangled on the rug. It was going to be great to wrap this up. She had Brubeck's Bill out of the way, and it was time to move on.

"Number Two. Mr. Environmental Science and I went to Starbucks for some java. He was nice enough, but doesn't seem to have the intensity I like. After he gets his degree at Cuesta, he wants to work in a park. Stats: Tall, auburn hair, blue eyes, thirty-seven, divorced, no kids. Scorecard: Good talker, cousin-appeal, some laughter, friendship, no second date.

"Number Three. The Guitar Picker/Real Estate Appraiser and I met on a spontaneous whim at seven p.m. at Applebee's, and we had no problem connecting emotionally and intellectually, mostly because he asked me questions about my favorite hobby, Barbie dolls. There was just, alas, no physical chemistry. Stats: Six feet tall, dark hair, mustache, brown eyes, forty-five years old. Scorecard: Great talk, awesome appetizers and Shrimp Alfredo, more of a business meeting than a romantic encounter.

"Number Four. The Realtor. Ooh-hoo-hoo. Well, I learned a few things this time out—specifically, what I don't like in a date. First, don't drive a car that's older than I am. Don't have cigar butts overflowing in the ashtray. Above all, don't cram your glove compartment full of White Owl Cigars and Irish folk tapes. All that would be fine if I dug that stuff, which I don't, so the date was pretty much over before it began. Lunch at Fat Cats was pleasant, but the onion rings gave me indigestion. Also—and I'm just learning this—I don't think I have much in common with most men born in the fifties. Stats: Gray hair, mustache, fifty-five years old, divorced, two kids. Scorecard: Dead air, no laughter, no common points of reference, no second date.

"Number Five. The Electrical Contractor. Sunshine Doughnuts at eight a.m. in San Luis Obispo? Color me crazy. Met an absolute sweetheart of a man who treated me to buttermilk and lemon doughnuts. We talked easily and laughed a lot. He's hardworking, non-commitment-phobic, and warm. If I can yak a blue streak at the crack of dawn and he can stand the sight of me this early in the morning, more power to us. Stats: Graying brown hair, hazel eyes, thirty-seven, boyishly good-looking, not too tall, two kids. Scorecard: Great talk, coffee, doughnuts.

"Number Six. The Stockbroker. Every woman should date a man who is twelve years younger who *prefers older women*. If he's attracted to you, it is nothing so much as like going out with a playful puppy. The question is, do you like playful puppies? We met at The Graduate, where an office party was in progress and *Legally Blonde* was showing on the big screen. I have no idea what happened after Warner asked Elle to dinner at their special place. Stats: Brown hair, brown eyes, twenty-five, 5'9", fully loaded with muscles and money. Scorecard: No sweet talk, one hell of a hickey, great Gradburgers, and too much eagerness.

"Number Seven. The One That Got Away. Wow. I took the big fall over this guy. Lunch at Outlaw's in Atascadero, our first date, lasted hours. The physical chemistry between us wouldn't quit. He has an offbeat, unusual sense of humor and is musically gifted, artistically balancing out my love of writing. We are both goal-oriented and have specific things we want to accomplish in this lifetime. Comfortable around each other, we were a comfort to each other. Neither of us has chosen a conventional route through life, and we both have roughly equal amounts of baggage.

"Unfortunately, it is some of his baggage that was left unfinished which he needs to deal with now, nixing any happy ending for us. One thing is certain—I think things would have worked, and I would have liked them to. Stats: Tall, hunky, fun, sexy, blond-haired, bearded, forty-one, with sweet blue eyes and a to-die-for voice. Scorecard: One afternoon together, one massive make-out session, one broken heart. But hey, who's counting?"

Caresse gazed at a favorite Barbie she kept on a stand atop her tiny bookcase next to her printer. *No wonder I love dolls so much,* she thought. *They never disappoint me.*

She smiled and did a file/save as a word doc. Then she opened her Gmail and sent the article to Jenna, who would be at the *County Times* till the end of the week, training her replacement. She'd heard the paper was bringing in an outsider, someone from New York City, and that *that* person was a "he."

Someone knocked loudly on her door and she smiled at the timing. The feature was done and her schedule was clear. Should she be nervous about talking to the Walnut Creek police? Too late to worry about that now.

She answered the door.

A huge African-American guy who looked like the bailiff Renard from *Cristina's Court* and a small blond guy who resembled Andrew Daly from *Mad TV* filled her front doorway. She ushered them in and shook their hands when they introduced themselves. The big guy was Ince Rowell, and his sidekick was August Carter.

Caresse pointed toward the couch facing the window and chose the one across from them for herself. She had opened the drapes behind her so the men might be distracted into focusing on the outdoors rather than her. Chances of that were slim, though. The street was quiet at this time of day, and looking at the trees got way old real fast.

She sat down carefully. The couch beneath the window offered a better vantage point for viewing TV shows. The sound was muted, but she had left *All My Children* on. Even though she hadn't seen the show in ages, she noticed Erica was still throwing tantrums. She frowned. The fleeting images weren't going to distract her. Nothing would. She worried she'd be in handcuffs and on her way to jail within twenty minutes even though she hadn't done anything. The men were dressed in dark suits, without ties. Both their dress shirts were open at the collar. She imagined this was to create a more relaxed vibe, but she wasn't feeling it.

"So, Ms. Redd," Rowell began.

The phone rang once, twice, thrice. They all stared at the desk, where the tiny Southwestern Bell Freedom phone was trilling on its pod.

"Don't worry," she said. She raised her bare feet up onto the couch and grabbed the nearby hand-knit blanket to cover them. She was shivering inside her sweats.

"The answering machine will—" she started.

Vonage kicked in and they listened.

42

On Sunday afternoon, February 17, Heath Walsh got up early for a game of golf with a few pals at the Lakeside Golf Course in Burbank.

P.J. slept in, but once she was up, she was all business. After reminding the weekend maid Vicky that Chao could use a morning walk, she made sure her personal assistant Wendy had scheduled to pick up Heath's suits for dry cleaning, checked on the delivery time of a living room sofa she was having reupholstered, and talked to the landscaper about trimming the shrubs that lined her front walk. Finally she enjoyed a breakfast of waffles and fresh strawberries prepared by her weekend chef Michel out in the back garden before heading to her exercise room to pack up her recent hauls to move to Darby's garage in Glendale.

She discarded the notion of keeping a low profile and dressed for the day in a sequined top, tight black leather jeans, and spiked heels. She tied her long blond hair back with a chiffon ribbon and took extra care with her makeup. While she had missed seeing *Dateline: Crime* when it aired, she caught excerpts in numbered installments posted on YouTube by someone named danno5145. The composite drawing that supposedly captured what Rick's friends saw of her from the doorstep of Rick and Zivia Uzamba's home was completely off base. They had recalled her blond hair correctly, but it had been tied back, so there was nothing to indicate how long it was. Facial features themselves were vague. The drawing almost resembled Heidi Klum, with dark eyes and lean, hollow cheeks. In fact, P.J. had apple cheeks and blue eyes, and looked more like a living Barbie doll than Heidi Klum ever would.

When she arrived at Darby's apartment building in Glendale, she parked her car out front and went to his unit with one box-load strapped to her luggage cart. When she rang the bell and got no answer, she used her key and let herself in. Standing there in the center of his living room, she listened to the silence, punctuated by soft moaning and rustling upstairs, followed by a musical giggle. There was an ashtray filled with two different brands of cigarette butts on the table, Kent Golden Lights and Virginia Slims. A matchbook from The Blue Moon Lounge in Montrose was open next to the ashtray, and there were three matches left. Smoke lingered in the air.

Glancing over at the couch she had grown fond of napping on these past few years, she saw a woman's cheap handbag and a cotton jacket.

The girlfriend.

P.J. went over to the fridge and looked inside. It had been wiped down with cleanser. Everything rotten and moldy had been discarded. A box of baking soda stood open on the bottom shelf. Cheese, fruit, chicken, milk, eggs, bread, pickles, mayo, and veggies filled the shelves. She sighed, closed the fridge, and went to the front door. Pulling on the cart to give it a jump over a snag in Darby's worn carpet, she left his unit and went down to the parking garage.

The sheet covering the front of Darby's storage unit had been removed from the inside, exposing the area to onlookers.

P.J. frowned. Popping the lock with the tiny key on her necklace, she pulled her cart through the gate and released the elastic cords that held the boxes on the small metal base.

An entire wall of storage drawers was three-quarters full, largely thanks to her Vegas hit. Now it was time to unload her Walnut Creek belongings. Pacing the length of the stall, the translucent drawer second from the top in the third unit from the chain link gate caught her eye. The feet of nine dolls should have aligned with the feet of the nine dolls in the drawers above and below. But there were only eight. She pulled out the drawer. Her blond American Girl dressed in Senior Prom was missing.

P.J. felt blood rush to her face. She opened the drawers above and below and then went through every single drawer she had filled.

188

The gate P.J. had left closed but unlocked creaked open. She looked up. A diminutive young blond smoking a Virginia Slim walked toward her.

"Darby thought he heard you," Jordanne said cheerfully, extending her right hand in greeting. "I'm his girlfriend."

Darby appeared next, wearing a Lakers t-shirt and faded jeans. He was barefoot, smoking a Kent Golden Light.

"Darby," P.J. said, ignoring Jordanne's extended hand. "I seem to be missing a doll. Might you know something about that?"

Jordanne lit up, her smile broadening to show perfect teeth. "Oh, is that what's kept in here?" She turned to Darby. "Is that why you gave me a Barbie, honey?"

P.J.'s attention swung fully to Jordanne. "What Barbie did he give you?"

"Oh, a real pretty blond one in a green and blue tulle gown."

Standing behind Jordanne now, Darby tried to hide his alarm.

P.J. spoke slowly, trying to contain her anger. "That wasn't his to give," she said.

Jordanne's mouth fell open. Flooded with uncertainty, she looked from P.J. to Darby.

P.J. approached Jordanne and put both hands on the young woman's slender shoulders. "I want her back."

Darby pushed P.J. away. He grabbed Jordanne's arm and pulled her toward the chain link gate.

"What happened to the sheet I had up, Darby?" P.J. screamed.

"You took it from my room!" Darby screamed back. "I wanted it back!"

"I bought you a new set of sheets!"

"Too bad. You had no right to do that!"

"You had no right to give this skank one of my dolls!"

Jordanne cringed and buried her face in Darby's shoulder.

Gently, Darby led Jordanne back to his apartment.

As always, P.J. had gotten the last word. She lifted the lid of the first box she had intended to unload. The black patent 1962 Mattel wallet featuring blond bubble cuts in Enchanted Evening and Friday Night Date and a second wallet in light blue with the brunette bubble cut wearing Dinner at Eight were placed carefully alongside the Swing-A-Ling Tutti Round Train Case P.J. had paid Nancy for but had never received. She slammed the lid back on the box and reattached the bungee cord back to the handle.

Heading back to her Miata, she reloaded the boxes into her car. Then she returned to the garage and loaded a set of drawers onto her cart. She returned to her car, unloaded the drawers, and went back to the garage. Giving Jordanne one of her dolls was an unforgivable breach on Darby's part.

I will never, ever talk to Darby again, she vowed, kicking the gate hard.

She took another set of drawers, locked up the storage area, and left.

Heath would be heading out of town for work in the morning, and her schedule would be clear. She could come back for the rest of her belongings and be done with her half-brother once and for all.

43

"Hi, Caresse, it's Marilyn. We're missing you this morning. I know you hate the phone, so you won't pick up. Just wanted to wish you well with the investigators this morning. Make sure you hide the bloody knife before they get there. Oh, by the way, you're going to love Jenna's replacement. His name is Anthony Price, and he's hilarious! He and the brats are like oil and water, and Jenna is looking like she can't wait for training to end so she can get the blank out of here Friday. Well, your machine's going to cut me off, so I've got to go. Love ya. Bye."

The investigators from Walnut Creek exchanged glances.

"Bloody knife?" Carter asked.

Rowell smiled grimly. "A joke, I'm sure."

Caresse's throat was dry. "Yeah. She was joking."

Rowell straightened up on the couch, casting a shadow clear across the room. He looked down at the notes he'd pulled out of his pocket.

"So the reason Nancy Roth had your name and number—" he began.

Nervous, she cut Rowell off. "She had it so she could do an interview with me. I called her and left my number. Then she called me, and I called her back. I do interviews for *Barbie International.*"

"We know," Carter spoke up. He removed his glasses. Digging a tissue out of his pocket, he rubbed the lenses before putting them back on. They were the more modern, rectangular-framed specs, making him look more like a college professor than a street-smart cop.

"You know?" she asked.

"We already talked to her husband, obviously," Rowell said. "He told us about the magazine story."

Caresse felt an adrenalin rush from head to toe. She knew it didn't really mean anything. It just connected her to the victim, and that's what they were concerned with.

"Do you want a drink? Coffee, maybe? No problem making a pot. I can drink most of one myself in a matter of hours. Sometimes I'm up all night long."

Rowell was curious. "For a good reason, I hope?"

She didn't answer. Even though they didn't say yes to the java offer, she threw off the blanket and stood up.

She was heading toward the kitchen when they stood as well.

"Mind if we look around?" Rowell asked.

And what, see if I have any of Nancy's doll cases?

"No problem."

She had nothing to worry about. She didn't collect cases. Most of them were big, bulky, and basically not her thing. And it was a good thing Nancy hadn't sent her any to photograph. Like Lucy, she would have had a lot of 'splaining to do.

She went and started a fresh pot of coffee made with a combination of Colombian and vanilla coffee beans she'd ground up earlier, listening as the men were bumped around in her tiny bedroom. One of them knocked a box down from the shelf in her closet, and she heard it thud on the hardwood floor. She was ready to call out and tell them to stay out of her underwear drawer, but these weren't friends she could joke with. This was serious.

When the coffee began filtering into the pot, she left the kitchen and returned to her place on the couch by the window.

The men came back and sat down in the exact same spots they'd been in earlier.

"It'll be ready in a minute," she said.

They stared at her.

"The coffee," she added needlessly.

The phone rang again, and the machine picked it up.

"Hi, Care. Long time no talk. It's Craig. I know you're probably at work, but I didn't count on talking to you in person anyway since you never answer the phone, so a message is just as good now as later. Did you catch *Dateline: Crime* last night on TV? The reason I ask is because there was a double homicide in Vegas, and the killer supposedly had to leave in a hurry when some friends of the victims showed up, so the murderer left behind some stuff they'd planned on taking. Namely—drum roll, please—two duffel bags full of Barbie dolls. Someone out there is stealing Barbie dolls and killing people. What is the doll world coming to? Oh, by the way, I've been running around Los Angeles and Vegas this past month, going back and forth, and I sat next to a Barbie collector on one of my trips. She was wearing a Barbie bracelet, so I asked if she was a collector. She said her name was Devvon West. I figured you probably know her. She was really pretty, with long blond hair. Kind of even looked like a Barbie doll. Anyway, I can't believe your machine hasn't cut me off yet. I'll talk to you before too long. How about you promise to answer all calls on, say, Memorial Day? Will you do that for me? Loads of love. Bye."

The room was silent for a moment.

"Who's Craig?" Rowell wanted to know.

"My brother."

"Do you always get this many calls?" Carter asked.

"No, I—" She stopped, reconsidered. "I guess I have

a few messages to listen to when I get home every evening, so I guess this is when people leave them."

The men were still silent.

"That's weird, about the Vegas thing," she said.

Rowell and Carter exchanged glances.

She was certain they were going to let her babble to death.

"How long have you lived here?" Carter asked.

"Less than a year."

Rowell looked at his notes. "And you've been writing for *Barbie International* for—"

"Oh, God, for years. As soon as I discovered the magazine, I was all over it. Write about what you know, right?"

The men exchanged glances.

She jumped up. "Let me get that coffee."

She left the room, and this time, the men stayed put on the couch.

"Milk? Sugar?" she called.

"Black," Carter said.

"Got Sweet 'N Low?" Rowell asked.

"Equal."

"That'll do," he said.

She brought them two of her Gary Larson mugs, hoping to lighten things up. One of them featured a moose holding a gun on a hunter, and the other featured a bunch of ghost children floating around two ghost moms with the caption, "It's hard raising the dead."

She ran to get hers last. Her mug was a plain white Starbucks cup with tasteful black lettering and the company logo. She sat back down on the couch opposite them, pulling her legs up into a pretzel and covering her lap with the blanket.

"So, Barbie dolls," Rowell began.

The phone rang again.

"Hi, Caresse. Hope I have the right number. I'm looking for Caresse. Caresse, my name is Rob Weber. You answered my personal ad. Sorry it took so long to get back to you. I've been out of town with my stepfather. I'm back now, and I'd love to meet you. So, anyway, here's where you can reach me."

Rob left his number and said good-bye before disconnecting.

The investigators were tired of the calls.

"Can you unplug that thing or—"

"Sure." She jumped up, ran to the phone, and turned off the ringer. Then she returned to the couch and sat down again.

"So, Barbie dolls," Rowell said. "Why Barbie?"

Ah, the psychology of doll collecting. She was on familiar ground, finally.

"Well, until lately, I didn't know owning them posed a danger," she said. "Except maybe for Dave Barry, who's always experimenting with them in conjunction with Pop Tarts and toasters. If you saw how many adults are into Barbie doll collecting, you probably wouldn't believe it."

"You're right," Rowell said. "We probably wouldn't."

Carter took a sip from the Larson ghost mug, looked at it and almost cracked a smile. "Where were you on Saturday?" he asked.

"At Laguna Lake with my son Chaz."

"And he can verify that?"

"Well, he's only four. I don't think he'd lie. It was his friend Tessa's birthday, and there was a party for her at the playground there."

Finally, she'd said something right. She could see it on their faces.

"You wouldn't happen to have notes from your interview with Nancy about her doll case collection, would you?" Rowell asked.

She couldn't jump up fast enough. Her elbow slid off her thigh and her cup jerked. Some hot coffee splashed out, but the thick blanket absorbed it quickly. She held it out for a moment and then dropped it on the floor. "I can do better than notes." She ran over to her computer desk and opened the top drawer. She retrieved her micro-cassette recorder and popped a tiny tape out. "I record everyone I talk to so I can capture quotes verbatim."

She took the tape over to Rowell and handed it to him. He looked at it as if he'd never seen one before.

A bag materialized in Carter's hands, and Rowell dropped it into the clear sleeve. Carter marked and sealed it before handing it back to Rowell so he could put it in his briefcase.

"And Nancy's husband took pictures for the story, which she emailed to you. Might you have those?"

"I sure do." She ran back to her computer and loaded her photo folder named NANCY, all caps, onto a USB flash drive. The folder contained not only the photos Nancy had emailed her, but a copy of her finished story for *Barbie International* as well. The Seagate drive had cost her fifty bucks new, but she was ready to surrender anything in lieu of being sent up the river as a murderess.

"Nice flash drive," Rowell noted as she handed it to Carter. "Looks like a doughnut."

At least he knew a flash drive when he saw one.

"You can have it," she told them.

Carter went through his baggie routine, and the USB flash drive was sealed and marked. "Oh, no," he assured her. "We'll get it back to you once we have the pictures on our hard drive."

"We have your address," Rowell added.

"Indeed you do." She remained standing. She had nothing more to give them and she wanted them to leave. When they didn't budge, she returned to the couch across from them and sat back down.

"So you know a lot about Barbie," Carter said.

"Maybe more than the average Joe. I've been on the Sammy Stoudt Show on KVEC Radio. And I've appraised dolls at public events."

"That call you got from your brother about the double homicide in Vegas," Rowell said. "We believe someone's stealing dolls and killing the women who owned them."

A chill ran down her spine. They wouldn't tell her that unless they were fairly certain. "How creepy is that?"

"So we might need someone who's considered an expert to talk to," Carter said.

She thought—briefly—about steering them in the direction of Sierra or any of the employees at *Barbie International*. They would be able to do as well as she could. But it was so cool they were actually asking her for help, she couldn't say no. Anjo was going to love this. "Sure. Call me anytime. Or better yet, email me. Do you have my email address?"

Rowell looked at his notes. "It's caresseredd, all one word, at gmail.com."

"Right."

At last they stood up, prompting her to rise and walk them to the door.

Carter handed one of his cards to Rowell, and Rowell combined it with one of his before handing both to her.

"We want you to think about why someone would be doing this," Rowell said.

"Sure."

She had mistaken their reserved professionalism as judgmental and cold. Now she suspected they might even respect her.

The door was open.

"Any chance you taped the radio show you were on?" Carter asked.

She grinned. "I've got it here somewhere, and I'll send you a copy."

44

The next morning, P.J. returned to Darby's apartment in Glendale. She was driving a U-Haul she rented on South Flower Street in Burbank, and she dressed for the part in Liz Claiborne overalls and a plain blue ball cap. As she pulled into the parking garage and parked the U-Haul as close as she could to the storage unit, she debated whether or not she should go knock on Darby's door.

Ultimately, she voted against it. His scooter rested neatly against the garage wall, and the world was quiet save for the sound of birds singing their Monday blues away. As she loaded each set of drawers into the truck, she flashed on the Nancy Roth murder.

She had arrived at Nancy's condo at four p.m. Saturday, pressing two hours too close to the time she felt Nancy's husband might return from his job in sales at the used car lot a few miles away. Northbound traffic had been a bitch, and she was feeling frazzled.

Dressed in dark jeans and an x-large black leather motorcycle jacket, she had covered her head with a red wig she pulled from her extensive Halloween costume stash. She fancied she looked a bit like Ginger *on Gilligan's Island*, complete with facial mole and pouty lips. Anyone after the beautiful blond killer depicted in the Vegas police sketch wouldn't find her in the face of the ravishing red-head she'd temporarily become.

The .380 Makarov pistol with the Darby-devised slip-on silencer rested in a deep-pocketed vest she wore inside her jacket. With one hand inside her coat, she released the safety and rang the doorbell. The empty duffel bags were jammed inside the back of her jacket, strapped to her vest with electrical tape.

A hoarse voice called, "It's open! Come on in!"

P.J. pushed the door open slowly and looked around, taking an instant mental snapshot. Nancy was at her desk, sitting in front of her Apple. Her dark hair was highlighted burgundy, and she appeared to be somewhat short and heavy. The computer desk was adjacent to the kitchen table, where four laminated chairs were pulled in tight. The place was Country Kitchen cute, decorated with ducks and hearts, bunnies and whimsy.

It was a straight shot from the front door to Nancy. Nothing stood in the way.

P.J. stepped in and closed the door behind her.

With a smile on her face, Nancy turned to see who it was. She was the kind of woman who knew her neighbors, the kind of friend who had an open door policy and made sure she made baskets of muffins and cookies for parties and potlucks.

Moving her feet a few spaces apart, P.J. took her stance, pulled the gun and fired at Nancy point-blank.

Pfft!

One shot hit the chair Nancy sat in and blew it to shreds.

Pfft!

The second shot nailed Nancy in the forehead. She flew back toward the desk and then forward onto the carpet.

P.J. approached and stood over her.

Nancy was face down in the Delft blue carpeting, her right arm outstretched, her left arm toward her side.

Pfft!

Pfft!

Pfft!

P.J. fired shots into Nancy's head and torso at close range, watching the blood pool out and turn the carpet a sticky grape.

Glancing at the ducky wall clock in the kitchen, she realized it had all gone down in a matter of a minute. Without a window facing the street and only small ones in the kitchen and dining room facing out back, she was confident no one had seen her. Nevertheless, she went to lower the Levelors on both the small windows, singing the *Gilligan's Island* theme song as she crossed the room.

Just sit right back and you'll hear a tale, a tale of a fateful trip that started from this tropic port aboard this tiny ship.

Crossing back toward the door, she stepped over the body to lock the front entrance lest any cheerful neighbors pop in.

Wouldn't they be surprised? P.J. thought, stifling a short laugh.

Upstairs, next to the master bedroom, a bland beige room was crammed floor to ceiling with goodies. She stopped to remove her jacket and put the safety back on the gun before tucking it into her vest pocket. Next, she stripped off the tape around her body and removed the duffel bags at her back, unfolding them and snapping them flat like bed sheets.

The mate was a mighty sailing man, the skipper brave and sure, five passengers set sail that day for a three-hour tour, a three-hour tour.

In went the Mattel wallets, in went the Ponytail pencil cases, in went the Tutti play cases. In went Tutti, Carla, Chris, and Todd. In went Sundae Treat, never removed from the box. In went Buffy and her little doll Mrs. Beasley. In went Lori and her little bear Rori, Angie and her little doll Tangie, and Fran and her little doll Nan. In went the white, red, and black versions of the Barbie and Midge Travel Pals, and a Lunch Kit for good measure. In went the Tutti suitcase featuring graphics of Tutti standing on a stone pathway in front of a wooden door. And then P.J. saw it on the shelf. She blinked once, then twice. It was the Swing-A-Ling Tutti Round Train Case she had paid Nancy for but never received. Nancy had kept it, choosing to send P.J. an empty package instead.

Red swam in P.J.'s line of vision, and she had to hold onto the shelf to steady herself. The notes on the Best Barbie Board stung anew.

PJ-RULEZ: No, I just suppose you listed it on eBay for shits and giggles, and when I won it, you had seller's remorse and changed your mind about parting with it. I don't know what it means when you "sell" something and send someone an empty box instead, but I call it theft.

NANCY_PANTS: You're a liar, P.J. Ask anyone else here on the board if I've ever sent them an empty box. As if!

P.J. could barely see straight as she zipped the duffel bags, retrieved her jacket, and marched downstairs. She stepped over Nancy and stomped over to the computer, dropping the bags and kicking the shattered chair out of the way.

Nancy was still logged on to the Best Barbie Board, her legal paperwork stacked next to the keyboard. P.J. squatted down and began to type in the blank message window in the center of the screen.

NANCY_PANTS: Hey, guys, I forgot to tell you something. Remember when P.J. and I had that run-in about the Tutti train case? I know, it was a long time ago, so a lot of you probably won't remember it, but I still do! Turns out I didn't send it to her! I still have it! Think she will forgive me if I send it to her now? Gulp! LOL!

P.J. hit send and stepped back from the monitor, watching as the message posted itself at the end of the long stream of endless chatter.

Gilligan's Island was far from her thoughts now. The Skipper would never be rescued and the Professor would never consummate his relationship with Mary Ann.

With full force, she lunged at the monitor and knocked it a good six feet off the desk

She stepped back twelve paces and aimed her gun at the computer itself.

Pfft!

Pfft!

Pfft!

The tower disintegrated.

P.J. approached the desk. The motherboard was still intact.

Pfft!

It flew off the desk and clattered on the kitchen floor.

Composing herself, P.J. put the gun back in her vest. Then she grabbed her duffel bags, stepped over Nancy, and made her way toward the front door.

She opened the door and looked outside. She had no idea how long she had been inside Nancy's condo, but the street was quiet. She was ready to head to her car. With a moderately quick step, she made it to the Miata and threw the duffel bags in back. She was parked in front a single-story home. Curtains on the picture window parted momentarily, and a bald man peered out and squinted.

P.J. smiled at him, jumped in her car, and pulled away from the curb.

In short order, she was back on the freeway, and the cooler evening air began to clear her mind.

The sun was setting and noctilucent clouds painted the horizon.

She would sleep better that night than she had in weeks.

45

Valentine's Day had come and gone. Caresse's story ran in the weekend edition, and by Friday afternoon, she had received plenty of compliments. Her story was up for best feature of the month, and she was glad she'd made an impression.

At work, Anthony had assumed Jenna's job with aplomb, but he had taken a definite disliking to Jenna's entourage, which Anjo had recently dubbed "the enter-tainted."

When he came over to Caresse's desk and noticed the Ken Cop near Anjo's phone, talk turned to, of all things, Barbie.

Anthony was metrosexual, and the women at work agreed there was nothing quite as wonderful as a man who cleaned his apartment and smelled good every day. He wore clear gloss on his nails and had impeccable taste in clothes. His hair was cropped short in a highlighted blond crew cut style, and his Italian loafers were buffed to a high shine. But the best thing about him? His eyes. They literally sparkled when he talked to you, and it was hard not to be cheered up by his broad, silly grin.

"I like Ken myself," Anthony said one afternoon, holding Anjo's cop in his hands as if the doll were fragile or expensive. "Do you go to any shows?"

"I make it to the ones in Anaheim sometimes," Caresse told him. "I write show reviews for *Barbie International*."

"The last time I went to a show with Matthias—we're in a committed relationship, just so you know I'm taken—we saw a Shimmering Magic ensemble a dealer had on her table, and Matthias said, 'That's a mint Shimmering Magic,' and I looked real close and saw a slight stain on the bodice of the dress and said, 'No, it's not, it's got a stain on the bodice.' And he said, not missing a beat, 'Well, it's a *mint* stain.' Wait! Did you just say you write for *Barbie International*?"

He didn't leave her desk for forty-five minutes. It was friends at first sight for both of them. Anjo, meanwhile, was mulling over the fact that Rowell and Carter from Walnut Creek had asked for Caresse's input on the Nancy Roth murder investigation.

"Are they going to send you photos of the crime scene?" she asked.

"Why would they?"

Anjo was exasperated but looked too beautiful for work. She had taken time to curl her dark hair so it framed her face perfectly and barely touched her shoulders. Her dark green blouse had an embroidered breast pocket with a swirl of tiny flowers on it. She had definitely lunched with her SLOPD pals.

"Look at it this way," Anjo said. "They have everything you got—all the pictures you were sent by Nancy—as well as your story. You've only got one-half the puzzle. If you saw what they had, maybe something would come to light. You would notice something and—"

"I get it," Caresse said. "But I don't feel comfortable asking them for anything that's in their files. I'm new to this, you know?"

"Leave it to me then," Anjo said. She stopped for a moment, looked thoughtful, and then dove beneath her desk to retrieve her purse.

"You're seeing Chazzie today, right?"

"You bet," Caresse said. "Leaving right now to go pick him up from preschool."

Anjo pulled a small blue box out of her purse and handed it to her. "For his ever-growing Lego City collection," she said.

Caresse smiled and was filled with warmth. What a pal she was.

Outside the *County Times'* huge glass windows, it was raining steadily.

"What are you guys gonna do?"

"We love it when it rains," Caresse assured her. "We've got umbrellas and raincoats. We're gonna walk around downtown and then go home and take really hot baths, make cocoa, and have a really healthy dinner."

"You're a good mom," Anjo said.

"Thanks," Caresse said. "I try, but you never know."

46

P.J. was exhausted by the time she drove the U-Haul into the Burbank Hills and pulled into her driveway. She had already thought about asking the staff to come out and help her bring everything inside, but that would raise too many questions. They were busy making sure deliveries of the March issue of *Barbie International* were reaching their destinations, so she decided it would be best to just unload everything into the ample, three-car garage and then move everything into the exercise room when they were not around.

Into the garage the storage units went, one after the other, until the space next to her Miata was filled. While she was re-stacking the drawers in the order she wanted them in, she heard someone rolling the trash barrels up the driveway. She assumed it was Bob the gardener and that she would have to offer him some kind of excuse regarding the U-Haul and all the dolls.

But it was Darby.

He was sporting a periwinkle Izod shirt, which was as out of character for him as the Dockers and RayBans he wore. He had forsaken his Lakers cap and had his hair combed neatly, parted on the left side. He had bothered to shave and smelled like Old Spice. He entered the garage and stood about twelve feet away.

P.J. tried to pick up a vibe from him. She didn't know if she should be afraid. She knew he wasn't as crazy as their cousin Lynne, but he was certainly as capable of violence as she was.

He had only been to her house a few times, while Heath was away. Heath imagined P.J. disowned him because of his poor choices and lifestyle. All the photos they had of him with P.J. that were previously arranged atop the grand piano in the living room had long since been wrapped in tissue and packed away.

"Hi," Darby said.

P.J. had vowed not to talk to him, so she glared at him and continued rearranging her storage drawers.

"I wanted to apologize for giving Jordanne one of your dolls."

P.J. scowled. *Where is it then? If you're really sorry, you would have gotten it and brought it with you.*

"I know you don't want to talk to me anymore or have anything to do with me."

You got that right.

Darby's rage at P.J. for treating Jordanne poorly was barely contained. Until P.J. was genuinely sorry and apologized to Jordanne, she would not be getting her missing doll back.

He approached his half-sister and stood an arm's length away. "I just wanted to say something that I think is important. At least for me, it is. There was a time I thought you cared, but it was more about what I could do for you than anything else. Now that I've become too much trouble for you, you have no problem putting me out of your mind. One of these days, you're gonna wake up and realize something. You're gonna realize that the only way to be happy is to open up, be real, look someone in the eye, love them, talk to them, and share what you're feeling. Even the stuff that isn't so wonderful."

P.J. was angry. The tiny Jordanne had accomplished the impossible. She had opened Darby's eyes to his own worth and potential. The tiny brat had changed him; he was a man in love.

Darby continued, "You have to commit to the closeness. Not be afraid to let someone in, even if they might not be around tomorrow. Not be afraid to love, lose, pick yourself up, and try again. You're gonna have to learn how to need someone, want someone in your life, and not just because they pay the bills. It's not about dolls. They're plastic. They can fill your shelves and you can adore them, but they can't fill the place in your heart another human being can when you're open, vulnerable, and truly intimate."

Shut up, P.J. thought. *Just shut up.*

"You run around doing whatever you want, but you're lacking something critical in your life, and that's why you're empty. Feeling entitled is deeming yourself more important than those around you. Until you realize that you're no better or worse than anyone else and that we're all in this together, until you open up and start to care, really care about someone, your life is worthless."

P.J. stepped back.

Darby stuck his hands in his pockets and stared at his feet. "That's all I wanted to say."

P.J. hated him now, absolutely and unequivocally. Who did he think he was, preaching to her? He had fucked up his life beyond belief and lived in a crappy apartment. He had nothing, not even a job. He might believe love had saved him and that love could change his life. He might even believe he could become the man Jordanne saw when she looked at him, a mate to be proud of, with a job, with a life.

She turned on her heel, walked to the U-Haul, and waited for him to exit the garage.

When he came out, she lowered the garage door, got into the U-Haul, and backed out of the driveway.

She glanced backward only once. He was getting on his scooter, preparing to leave.

I shouldn't have tried to be nice to him, she thought. *He was a complete waste of my time. Fuck him. Fuck Heath. Fuck everybody.*

47

An hour and a half later, Chaz and Caresse were marching through puddles on their way to Monya's Antiques.

Chaz had already opened his gift from Anjo, which turned out to be a hard-to-find Lego Street Sweeper, in charge of keeping the avenues of Lego City sparkling clean. The driver, who had a bit of a skeevy mustache, was a bit of a downer, but the street sweeper itself was extra cool because it had a lifting hatch so the driver could get in and tool around town. If they couldn't find anything at Monya's today, Chaz's street sweeper could motor up and down the aisles, dusting the floors.

The skinny guy with jet-black hair and *Blues Brothers* shades was skulking in the shadows, standing in front of the curtain that covered the entrance to the back room. Chaz and Caresse took off their raincoats and shook them, leaving them by the front door. Then they collapsed their umbrellas, shook them out, and placed them with their coats.

"Is Monya here today?" Caresse asked, approaching the counter.

Chaz zoomed off to the area of the shop where toys were piled high.

"She's in the—" he began.

A toilet flushed a room or two away, and they both smiled. No need to finish the sentence.

Monya entered the room and filled it with her presence. She wore a Bird of Paradise print muumuu today, and her lips were pumpkin to complement her safety-orange nails. Her copper red hair was dazzling. Caresse wondered if there was a posse that showed up regularly just to check out what plumage she might wear next.

She approached the main counter, smiling. "Remember me?"

Monya extended both her hands, taking both of Caresse's smaller, plainer hands in hers and holding them for a prolonged moment.

Finally Caresse broke the ice bluntly. "Did you know Nancy Roth?"

Monya looked blank for a moment and then said no.

"She collected mostly vinyl Barbie cases, and she lived up in Walnut Creek. Someone killed her and raided her Barbie collection. It's just like what happened to Gayle."

Monya paled visibly, and her hand went to her throat, where an elaborate tourmaline and pearl choker was wrapped loosely around her wattle. "Gayle and Mike Grace in upstate New York, Zivia and Rick Uzamba in Vegas, Time Taylor in Washington, that poor little schoolteacher what's-her-name in Tucson, and now another one?"

"I've only heard a little about the Vegas murder," Caresse said. "What happened there?"

Monya led her to a set of upholstered chairs and plopped down in the larger one. Caresse removed boxes from the one next to it and sat beside her.

"Killer came in, murdered the husband by injecting him with some kind of drug, and then went upstairs and did the same thing to Zivia." She paused for dramatic effect. "She was in the shower."

Caresse shivered. "Did she have a lot of dolls?"

"So many that the killer was going to make two trips, but she was spotted by someone, so she never returned for the other bags she packed. *Dateline: Crime* walked viewers through the whole house. Even after it was trashed, that doll room was to die for."

"Literally," Caresse said, thinking hard. "You say *she* was spotted?"

"Two friends came to visit when the husband didn't answer his pager. They were on the porch, ringing the doorbell and getting no answer, when they spotted a blond woman holding duffel bags, standing at the foot of the driveway. There were two duffel bags left upstairs packed with dolls she was gonna come back for. But after they saw her, she split."

"Do they have a sketch of this woman?"

"The Vegas PD does. They showed it on the program. Google *"Dateline: Crime"* plus "Vegas murder at home." They should have a picture of her online. How did the woman in Walnut Creek die?"

"She was shot."

"Might be a whole 'nother deal going on there. None of the others died from gunshot wounds, right?"

"I don't think so," Caresse said. "But I think stealing the dolls ties them all together. I'll bet the killer is just varying her m.o. to throw them off."

"That's smart," Monya said.

Chaz approached their chairs, holding a Z-Bot.

"What is this?" Caresse asked when he handed it to her for inspection.

"It's a Z-Bot," Monya answered for him. "They were

invented by a group of scientists to protect the world from evil. They were popular in the early Nineties."

Caresse studied the little yellow and blue guy as she was informed he was a Robochamp named Zentor.

"They're pretty small," Caresse said.

Chaz nodded eagerly. "There's a whole box full of them."

"Where's your street sweeper?"

Chaz pointed to the deep front pocket of his jeans.

"Let me see the box."

Chaz ran off, and Monya and Caresse exchanged smiles.

"So the police want me to help out with the Nancy Roth murder investigation. Meaning, they want me to try and figure out why someone would be doing this and maybe put out feelers inside the collecting community to see what's up."

"The Best Barbie Board is the right place," Monya said. "Maybe I can join you in reading through the chat threads and pick up on something. You never know."

"Thanks," Caresse said, and meant it.

Chaz returned and nearly stumbled over the corner of an Oriental runner. The box of Z-Bots landed in Monya's lap, and she laughed.

Chaz looked embarrassed but recovered quickly.

"How much for the whole box?" Caresse asked Monya.

"The whole box, twenty bucks."

Caresse stood up. "You drive a hard bargain," she said, giving her a warm smile.

The box was no bigger than a shoebox, but it was crammed full.

Caresse slid Monya a twenty-dollar bill and gave her a hearty hug.

"You don't have a valuable collection the killer might want, do you?" Monya asked, as though the thought had just occurred to her.

"No. My doll collection is small, mostly repros," Caresse assured her. "And I guess I should be glad."

Monya looked relieved. She watched as Chaz and Caresse donned their raincoats and started to open their umbrellas.

"Don't open them in here," she admonished. "It's bad luck."

Chaz looked up at his mother, questioningly.

"She's kind of right, Chaz," Caresse said, stepping outside, giving Monya a wave before the door closed.

Once they were outside, she clarified it for him. "If you're superstitious, there are certain things you do or don't do to make sure luck stays with you."

"I'm very lucky," Chaz assured her.

She rubbed his raincoat-hooded head. "You sure are. You've got a mom who loves toys."

He hugged his shoebox as they walked toward Mitchell Park. "And you know what?"

"What?"

"I think I might like these as much as you like Barbie dolls."

48

P.J. parked in the lot next to the Glendale Market on Sunday, March 2, close to two p.m., and watched for signs of Darby's girlfriend Jordanne.

If she worked the six a.m. to two p.m. shift, she would be leaving soon.

P.J. waited until two-thirty, grew impatient, and then realized she should call Darby's apartment and find out if Jordanne was even working that day. If she wasn't, she would likely be with him. The phone rang eight times before the call kicked over to the answering machine. P.J. hung up without leaving a message.

Restless, she got out of her car and went into the market, making a beeline toward the back of the store to avoid scrutiny by management up front. She poked around in the frozen food section for a while and finally decided to buy a pint of frozen raspberry yogurt.

There were eight checkout stands flanked by magazine racks and the usual impulse-buy assortment of gum and candy. The first checkout was being handled by a dark-haired man, the second by a middle-aged woman wearing glasses, and the third by a blond-haired woman who looked like a taller version of Jordanne sans her annoyingly cute snub nose.

Checkouts four, five, six, and eight were vacant. At the seventh checkout, an authoritative-looking man in his mid-forties was sorting through slips of paper.

P.J. approached checkout seven.

"Hi," she said, reading the man's tag. He was "William, Day Manager."

"Hi," he said, looking P.J. in the eye before his gaze slid to her breasts.

She couldn't fault him. She was wearing a sexy, skin-tight paisley top with a tiny bow at the neckline.

William turned red and forced himself to face her squarely, refusing to allow his gaze to drift downward. "What can I do for you?"

"Jordanne's not in today?" she asked.

"Monday through Friday," he said. "Two to ten."

Second shift.

"That's right," P.J. said. "She has weekends off. How'd she swing that, by the way?"

The manager turned red again. "We rotate quarterly."

P.J. smiled benignly. "I'll bet you do."

"Is there anything else?" he asked.

She relished his discomfort.

"No," she dismissed him, setting the frozen yogurt on the counter. "Just this."

The manager rang her up, and she paid cash.

It was only on the way out that she realized she needed a plastic spoon.

49

Vala Bronauer met her at the door. "You're Caresse Redd, right?"

Vala seemed as small and fragile as the dolls she collected. Her dark hair, approximately the same shade as Caresse's, was worn short.

"Absolutely," Caresse told her.

A tall man appeared at her side. "Arnolt Bronauer," he said, introducing himself. He was dressed casually but smartly in a striped dress shirt and V-neck sweater. Like his wife, he exuded extreme intelligence and charm.

Vala was dressed in white, like an angel, wearing white linen pants, a white cotton sweater, and a white scarf that kept her dark bangs off her forehead. She belonged on a greeting card where everything is black and white except spot color, which in this case would be the subject's cheeks and lips, blushed a warm rose.

"You're here to interview us?" She sounded neutral on the subject, but not bored by the prospect. It was as if she had never initiated the idea of being the focus of a feature for *Barbie International.*

Arnolt interrupted his wife gently. "Not us, dear heart. I need to go down to the office for a few hours."

Vala looked alarmed. She was obviously dependent on him and wanted him around for emotional support.

"All right." She sounded reluctant.

"This doll stuff," he said, throwing up his hands in a helpless gesture. "It's really your thing anyway."

"Well, come in then," Vala told her, and Arnolt and Caresse both crossed the threshold simultaneously, going opposite directions.

"Wait," Caresse said, remembering the camera and tripod still in her trusty Honda. "I need to get my Olympus. I'll be right back."

She ran to her car and glanced back at the house. It was a fabulous Pismo Beach estate, set close to other homes in prime real estate two blocks from the ocean.

Arnolt startled her by appearing at her side.

"One moment of your time, if I may," he said, lowering his voice lest it carry toward the house.

"Yes?"

"She doesn't like me to worry," he said in a low voice, taking her elbow and walking her farther away from his residence.

Arnolt's demeanor suggested he didn't have an ounce of worry in him. He had stepped from the pages of an executive issue of *GQ* and exuded as much confidence and presence as Wayne Dyer. Caresse tried not to look at the somewhat rough toupee covering his dome, focusing instead on his twilight-blue eyes.

"These women who are collectors, they're getting killed and their dolls are being taken," he said. "You saw *Dateline: Crime*, right?"

"About the Vegas murders, yes—I mean, no, but I know what you're talking about."

"Maybe you can talk to her," he said, glancing back toward the house quickly as though he'd suddenly noticed Vala in his peripheral vision.

Caresse was puzzled. "About what?"

"Convince her not to be so quick to open the door when the doorbell rings. Suggest we get a security guard or even a large dog. You would think she would listen to me after all these years, but my voice has become like constant, running water to her. She tunes me out." He grabbed her sleeve. "But she listens to strangers, new acquaintances, and friends. She takes everything they have to say very seriously."

"What do her friends say?"

"These Barbie people, they're obsessive. They don't forgive or forget any opposition or contrary opinion. Vala's got a collection of dolls that must be worth a half a mil by now. They're jealous."

"And you think one of them might be jealous enough to kill her and steal her dolls?"

"I'm sure more than a few wouldn't hesitate to hurt her and take her prized possessions."

Caresse sighed. "Then what the heck are you doing, having an interviewer from *Barbie International* here, doing a story on what she owns? It'll be a six page advertisement inviting trouble, like a banner over your house saying, 'Vala lives here, so come on in!'"

Arnolt's mouth formed a tight, impenetrable line. His eyes glinted with anger.

Caresse waited him out.

Finally, he spoke. "The story will serve to foster interest in the sale of the collection. Once the dolls are gone, she'll be safe. If I can keep her alive the next eight weeks, we can put to rest that she might ever become a target."

It all made sense now. "So you're looking for the story to whet the appetite of interested buyers. Sell the dolls, and you don't have to worry about anyone coming to get them *or* your wife."

Sadness flashed across his face. "I'm sorry she has to give them up, but it's the only way to keep her safe. She's the only thing that's important to me. She is the love of my life."

Caresse touched his arm. "Don't worry. I'll make it a great feature."

"Thank you," he said. "And now I must go, because she's going to wonder what took you so long to get your gear."

He looked down at Caresse's camera and tripod and smiled before turning on his heel and heading toward his garage. The wind rustled through the trees as she watched him go. She didn't know what to make of the man. He seemed to genuinely love Vala, but she didn't see why getting a pack of Dobermans *and* keeping the dolls wouldn't solve the problem.

Caresse met Vala again at her open doorway and struggled to manage her purse, tripod, and camera without dropping anything.

"Can I help you?" Vala asked, making no move to do so.

"No, I've got it," she said, following her inside.

Vala's home was the most beautiful residence she had ever seen in San Luis Obispo County. It was a virtual museum, with glass-fronted cabinets stretching the entire length of several rooms. But the most magnificent thing of all was that the rooms formed a box around an indoor pool that sat square in the home's center, almost out of view beyond the hallway they now stood in.

Caresse exhaled audibly.

Vala's smile was glorious, her teeth as white as her sweater. "You like it?"

Caresse was drawn to the center of the house, where turquoise water beckoned. All four sides of the pool were screened but there were wide entrances. She walked in and took a lounge chair without being asked. She needed to put her things down and couldn't wait for the invitation. "This is breathtaking."

Vala pressed a button beneath the patio table and took the opposite lounge chair, kicking off her sandals, flexing her bare toes on the Mediterranean tiles.

When a young woman appeared, she waited to be introduced.

Vala smiled warmly. "Caresse, meet Becca."

Becca nodded hello. Despite her golden tresses, she was much plainer than one might suspect at a distance.

"Diet Pepsis," Vala told Becca, electing not to offer a selection of beverages to her guest.

When Becca left, Vala spoke again. "She goes to Cuesta College. Needs extra money, and we need the help. It works out fine."

Caresse nodded, noticing a bracelet on Vala's left wrist as it slid out from underneath the cuff of her sweater. Charms encased in Plexiglas cubes caught her eye, and she recalled her brother mentioning having met a brace-leted woman named Devvon on the Greyhound to Vegas. Vala's bracelet consisted of charms that seemed to be small doll accessories. The links and clasps appeared to be solid gold.

Vala noticed her interest and extended her wrist in her direction. The car keys to Ken's Rally Day, a gold cork wedge sandal, a princess telephone, a lei, the crystal snake bracelet to Commuter Set, the gold-tone charm bracelet to Resort Set, the wax fish belonging to Picnic Set, a brass alarm clock, the scissors to Sweater Girl, and the hot water bottle for Registered Nurse floated before her eyes.

"All of these Barbie accessories are prototypes," she explained.

Caresse turned the circle around and examined the encased sixth-scale items. Each one was similar to those she had seen or owned, but each bore distinct differences. The car keys were double in number, the wedge sandal had a scalloped strap, the princess telephone had a different dial, the snake bracelet had more coils, the charm bracelet had additional charms, the fish was more orange than bluish-gray, the time on the alarm clock read eight instead of ten, the scissors had black handles, and the hot water bottle was corked.

"Prototypes?"

"Different than what the items turned out to be when they were mass-manufactured," Vala confirmed. "First attempts, as it were."

Caresse struggled to comprehend Vala could have something so rare.

"This bracelet is virtually priceless to a true Barbie collector."

Indeed, she thought.

"Want to see the coup de grace?" She didn't wait for an answer. She reached down into the v-neckline of her snow-white sweater and pulled out a long gold chain strung with real, sixth-scale brass Barbie compacts, each as small as a baby's thumbnail.

"These are the first thirty compacts from a trial batch Mattel ran back in 1959 before producing Roman Holiday, one of Barbie's earliest outfits."

Caresse knew Roman Holiday. It had always reminded her of an outfit Barbie might wear to an upscale Fourth of July party.

"The reason these thirty are rare is because Mattel actually engraved all three of Barbie's initials, bRm, on them before considering that they were too small to read clearly. Ultimately, they went with only the letter B."

Caresse smiled, remembering how difficult it was to pry the compact open when she was little.

"The one on my bracelet, though, is actually rarer," Vala continued, extending her left hand again, this time with her wrist up.

There was a charm Caresse hadn't noticed because it was smaller and placed close to the clasp.

"It's engraved bRm on the outside, has a real mirror on the inside, and beneath the powder puff, it's engraved XO, KC."

Kiss, hug, Ken Carson, Barbie's boyfriend. Holy guacamole and a basketful of chips.

Vala withdrew her hand and tucked her necklace back down the front of her sweater.

"Why use Plexiglas? Doesn't that ruin the items?"

"Each of the items needs to be preserved, and this seemed to be the best way to do it," Vala said. "My jewelry's not for sale anyway. Just the other things I'll be showing you today. No true collector would ever sell a prototype."

"The other things you'll be showing me. Your collection at large."

"Yes."

"When are you planning to sell?"

"In May at the latest. Arnolt needs to infuse the money back into his business to open a second office. I reluctantly agreed. He is, after all, the breadwinner here."

Caresse smiled. So he gave her the story he needed the money. With the story running in the April issue of *Barbie International,* the collection would be out of the house before Mother's Day, and Arnolt would be able to rest easy, knowing his wife wouldn't be murdered for her dolls.

Vala fetched the necklace from her cleavage again, as gracefully as anyone might manage it, and actually took it off. Caresse watched as she slid a single compact off the chain.

Vala extended it toward Caresse, who accepted and examined it. The compacts on the necklace were not encased in Plexiglas but were instead coated with some indelible, clear substance that preserved them.

"Look at the detail that went into that," Vala whispered in a tone bordering on reverence.

After examining the compact, Caresse closed her hand, savoring the warmth of the brass as though it were a precious pebble in her palm.

She finally laid it on the table, and Vala took it, clasped it back onto the necklace, and refastened the chain around her neck. She was clearly proud of what she had, and she had every right to be.

Becca returned with the Diet Pepsis, placing them on the patio table and vanishing as quietly as she'd arrived. Vala took a small sip of her drink, watching the dark liquid travel up the clear straw in her glass. Caresse took a sip of hers and a faint whiff of chlorine hit her nostrils.

She turned to stare into the placid expanse of crystal-clear water that filled the pool. It was mesmerizing.

"You're welcome to come swim anytime," Vala said.

"I couldn't just drop by," Caresse protested.

"You could call and invite yourself over, and if we weren't busy, I would like nothing better than to have you come for a swim."

"Thank you." She believed Vala was sincere in her offer, and she felt honored. She pictured how much fun Chaz might have in the heated pool in the dead of winter.

"So, grab that camera of yours and let me show you what I've got."

Caresse stood up.

"And bring your drink," Vala advised. "Once you see how large my mod collection is, you're gonna wish Becca spiked it."

50

P.J. was back at the Glendale Market at a quarter till ten on Monday evening. She waited for Jordanne to finish her shift and then watched as the petite blond exited, removing her red apron as she walked.

Parked in an adjacent lot, P.J. had a good enough vantage point to see the young woman get in an older Mustang, throw her apron and small purse on the passenger side, and start her engine. Keeping a safe distance behind, P.J. followed her to Concord Street, where she made a left-hand turn followed by a right onto Arden Avenue.

Jordanne crossed the intersection at Estelle and pulled over to the curb in the 800-block of Arden. P.J.

drove past and parked farther up the street, getting out of her Miata so she could watch Jordanne get out of her car and enter a four-plex.

Walking back up the block, P.J. stopped in front of Jordanne's residence. A light went on in the upstairs unit on the left. Inside, Jordanne went over to her front window and opened the drapes. She looked out, onto the street below, and saw P.J. standing there.

As quickly as she'd opened the drapes, she shut them.

P.J. laughed, a low, guttural chuckle.

Jordanne ran across the small living room to her phone and dialed Darby's number. He picked up on the second ring.

"Your sister's outside," Jordanne whispered.

"What? Jordanne, is that you?"

Jordanne cleared her throat and tried to speak louder, but her vocal chords were constricted. "Your sister is here."

"Here? What do you mean, here?"

"She's outside my apartment."

Darby struggled to understand. "Outside?"

"I saw her from my window, standing on the sidewalk, looking up at me."

There was a loud rap on Jordanne's apartment door.

"Oh, my God, Darby," Jordanne said. "I think she's here."

51

Caresse knew something was up with Anjo before she even made it to her desk first thing Monday morning.

"The FBI is all over it!" Only a notch below a shout, others in the newsroom turned to stare.

"What?"

"The Barbie doll murder cases are all connected," she said, lowering her voice. "So the FBI is treating it as the work of a serial killer-slash-killers, and—"

"And?"

Anjo flipped back her hair with a flourish and presented Caresse with a fat manila envelope. "Open it."

Caresse's hands shook as she undid the clasp on the back. The front of the envelope was marked "WCPD," which meant the Walnut Creek Police Department had come through with photos from Nancy's file.

She was unprepared to see the photos. Even though they were black and white, the amount of blood pooled beneath Nancy seemed excessive. The gunshot wounds gaped wide like open mouths, and she thanked God she could not see the victim's face, which was buried in the carpet.

There was a shot of Nancy's shattered chair, pushed away from the computer desk. It looked like it had been hit at close range by a cannon. Another shot showed Nancy's computer monitor, lying on its side on the kitchen floor where it was thrown, several feet from the desk. Close-ups of Nancy's computer showed it had been riddled with gunfire, rendered as useless as a bookend on an empty bookcase.

The next shots were of Nancy's doll room, shelf by shelf, starting at the top and traveling left to right along each one. While some collectibles remained, there were spaces where missing items had been. Since Nancy's entire collection was kept on open shelves, it would be possible to determine everything taken after assessing what remained.

She took a deep breath. The next few pictures seemed insignificant. They were photographs of the floor in the doll room. The first showed bits of gray electrical tape stuck to the rug. Another showed a clear shoe imprint in the carpeting at the top of the stairs. Still another showed an extreme close-up of a red hair found on the staircase landing.

"This is awesome," she told Anjo.

"I took notes. You want to hear?"

She looked around the newsroom. Seth wasn't in yet, so now was as good a time as any. "Game on."

Anjo smoothed out her shirt and forced herself to sit, facing her computer. "I typed as I talked to them," she said. "Time of death, approximately four p.m. on Saturday, so Nancy's husband was at work. The killer must have known that.

"Neighbor reported seeing a redheaded female who was a stranger in the neighborhood get into a white four-speed Miata roadster in front of his house sometime after five p.m. She was wearing an over-sized black leather jacket.

"Victim died of six gunshot wounds to the head and torso. Weapon was a .380 Makarov pistol, likely used with a silencer, as no shots were heard in the neighborhood around the time of the murder.

"No sign of forced entry. Victim either knew the killer or the door was open.

"Blinds lowered on both small windows. Husband says blinds were always kept raised to let light in since the condo was generally so dark.

"Items missing from doll room to be determined. No list available at this time."

Caresse exhaled. That was a lot to take in.

"Okay, you got that so far?" Anjo asked.

"Yeah."

"Okay. So let's start at the beginning. The first murder was in Oswego, New York. The husband and wife were murdered in a car explosion at SUNY Oswego, but dolls were taken from the home. A list is available of the missing dolls.

"An eyewitness who was in Sheldon Hall, the building which overlooks the parking lot, came forward two weeks ago and said he saw a blond woman in white spike-heeled boots hanging near the Grace vehicle for a while before getting into an Altima which bore an Enterprise rental sticker.

"The Oswego police took impressions of the spiked-heel boots and tire impressions. The Altima was rented from the East Avenue Enterprise dealership in Oswego to a Devvon West, residence: 1275 W. 29th Street, Los Angeles, California 90007. That address, as you might have expected, isn't a residential address. It belongs to the Terrace Apartments, built in the early Eighties exclusively for USC student housing."

Caresse was familiar with the building. It stood where Terrace Avenue met 29th Street. She was beginning to feel cold, even though she was wearing a heavy sweater. She didn't like the coincidence that the address the killer used had a connection to her alma mater.

Up front, the lobby doors opened and Caresse saw Monya from the antiques store enter. The skinny guy with jet-black hair and *Blues Brothers* shades from her shop was there to help her along, and his gentle patience warmed Caresse's heart.

Already at her post up front, Laura was in full gossip mode on the phone, but she stopped when she saw Caresse's flamboyant friend. "Some dress!" she exclaimed at the sight of Monya's muumuu de jour, a green and gold affair that glinted like a money tray in the morning light streaming through the lobby windows.

"Thank you, darling," Monya said.

Skinny guy was holding a manila envelope thicker than the one Anjo had already handed Caresse.

"I'm looking for Ms. Redd," she announced.

"Hold on, Anjo," Caresse said, rushing up front.

Monya had brought her a stack of pictures sent to her by her sister Annie, who had gotten them from Gayle Grace's sister, Megan.

"Everyone knows Megan and Gayle inventoried Gayle's dolls, but not everyone knows Megan photographed them for insurance purposes."

For the second time that morning, Caresse's hands shook as she undid an envelope clasp. Inside were photos—good, clear photos—of every 1600-series outfit shown in Eames modeled by a near-flawless array of American Girls.

"We're thinking that if you have photos of the actual dolls and you see any of them during the course of your professional investigation, you can be certain they belonged to Gayle," Monya said, sounding grave.

Caresse looked her flashy friend, whom she had already grown so fond of, squarely in the eye.

Professional investigation. Monya was taking her seriously, and Caresse loved her for it. She would not let her down. She reached for Monya's hand and saw that her nails were burnished saffron. Despite the wrinkles and liver spots, there was strength in her grasp that belied her years.

"Thank you for these," she said. "I'll take good care of them."

She returned to her desk and watched Monya leave like Elvis after a concert.

"Was that for an obit?" Anjo asked.

"No, it's about this," she said, holding up one of the full-color eight-by-tens. "Pictures of what's missing from Gayle's collection."

Anjo was impressed. "You're really working this."

"You've already told me so much, my head is ready to explode."

"Great. Then I'll just keep talking."

"I knew you would."

52

"Oh, my God, Darby," Jordanne said. "I think she's here."

The pounding on the door continued.

"Don't let her in, whatever you do," Darby advised. "I'll be right over."

"Okay," Jordanne said, ending the call.

Staying a safe distance from the door, Jordanne walked in circles before heading to her couch. She buried her face in a pillow, trying not to scream.

Across the hallway, a door opened.

"What the hell is going on?"

Jordanne had never been so happy to hear her neighbor Neil's voice. He might not be able to take P.J. down, but his ability to be loud, particularly when disturbed by noise, was considerable. P.J. responded in a low voice. Jordanne couldn't catch what she said.

"If she's not home, she's not home. Come back tomorrow!" Neil shouted.

Again, P.J. responded quietly.

"Then she's home and she doesn't want to see you! I don't blame her!"

Jordanne listened as P.J. clattered down the staircase.

Once out on the street, she stood there, looking up at Jordanne's closed curtains. Her rage burned white-hot. She assumed Jordanne called Darby, and she had no wish to deal with him. Their cousin Lynne was insane, and she herself was homicidal. There was no question Darby was cut from the same crazy-quilt cloth.

P.J. jumped into her Miata, gunning it down Arden to Concord to Glenoaks, heading back home to the safety of Burbank.

53

Chaz wanted to go to Taco Bell that night for dinner, so Caresse drove them to the Madonna Plaza, where they got enough food for a Quinceaños. After they settled themselves at a table near the soda dispenser, she spread out the notes she received from Anjo and re-read them.

"Murders one and two, Gayle and Mike Grace, Oswego, New York, car explosion. List available of dolls taken. Eyewitness noticed blond female near Grace vehicle. Drove Altima rented from Enterprise. Used Devvon West I.D. with L.A. address. Wore white spike-heeled boots."

She added, "Photos of dolls taken available through Monya, who got them from Annie, who got them from Megan, Gayle's sister. Write to Craig and confirm the woman on the bus to Vegas told him her name was Devvon West.

"Murder three, Hailey Raphael, Tucson, Arizona, tack hammer. Complete (?) list available of dolls taken. No eyewitnesses. Blond hair recovered from scene.

"Murder four, Time Taylor, Oak Harbor, Washington, chemical explosion. Complete (?) list available of dolls taken. No eyewitnesses. Fingerprints on battery. Footprint impressions in carpet.

"Murders five and six, Zivia and Rick Uzamba, Las Vegas, Nevada, lethal injection. Complete (?) list available of dolls taken. Eyewitnesses saw blond woman near bottom of driveway. Police sketch available. Numerous footprints determined to be from Nike Huaraches, size nine, blond hair, spot of serum (?) near back entrance."

She added the note, "Borrow videotape of *Dateline: Crime* from Anjo." Anjo recorded every episode religiously and was coming through for her once again.

"Murder seven, Nancy Roth, Walnut Creek, California, shot (.380 Makarov pistol with silencer). Bullets recovered. Time of death obtained: approximately four p.m. Man living nearby reported seeing woman (described as having red hair, wearing an over-sized black leather jacket, driving a white four-speed Miata roadster) in front of his house sometime after five p.m. No sign of forced entry. Victim either knew killer or the door was unlocked/open. Blinds lowered on both small windows (atypical, according to husband). Husband not considered suspect—present and accounted for at work at victim's time of death." Lastly she added, "Photos of doll room supplied by Walnut Creek PD to be compared to photos sent by Nancy for *Barbie International* feature."

She had the most to go on with murders one/two and seven, but that didn't mean she couldn't try to garner more information on the others. She put her head in her hands and sighed.

"Mama." Chaz climbed off his seat and went over to her, giving her a bear hug around the waist. She looked down at his little taco face and picked a crumb off his cheek.

"You know this isn't a very healthy dinner," she told him.

"Yeah, but it's fun," he grinned, reprising his first hug with one more fierce.

The leftovers were bagged and taken back to Caresse's apartment, where she discovered the March issue of *Barbie International* wedged inside her mailbox.

54

At three p.m. Tuesday, March 4, P.J. returned to Jordanne's apartment. She had spent most of Monday night worrying that Darby would storm over and attack her for bothering his girlfriend. Nothing played out.

Now Jordanne was at work and the unit across from hers, occupied by Jordanne's confrontational neighbor Neil was quiet.

P.J. carded the door and let herself in.

She was there to find her blond American Girl dressed in Senior Prom, and she wasn't going to leave until she'd gotten her back.

The apartment stank of stale cigarette smoke and sweet perfume.

Her first move, once inside, was to close Jordanne's slightly parted drapes, covering the window that over-looked the street.

She looked around the boxy abode, with its front living room, back kitchenette, tiny bathroom, and single bedroom. Furnishings were spare, and there were few places to hide treasures. P.J. went into the kitchen and pulled out every drawer, rummaging through bills and silverware, paper clips and pens. She systematically checked each cupboard, sneering at the cheesy Corelle dinnerware and cheap pots and pans. Spices were non-existent, as were condiments. The refrigerator/freezer yielded nothing aside from salad fixings, Diet Dr. Pepper, and Chunky Monkey ice cream.

Leaving the cabinets and the drawers open, she went into the living room and looked under the sofa and matching chairs by tipping them back on their rear legs. On a corner lamp table, an overflowing ashtray filled with both Darby's and Jordanne's cigarette butts demanded emptying. She grabbed it and took it to the kitchen trash, dumping the pile of ashes and butts onto trashed papers and discarded cans.

In the bathroom, P.J. followed the routine she'd set forth in the kitchen. First, she opened every drawer, rifling through hair clips, brushes, bobby pins, tweezers, and makeup. Then she opened the cabinets, which yielded nothing but shampoo, conditioners, cleansers, a crusty bottle of Drano, sponges, and a toilet brush.

The first place P.J. looked in Jordanne's bedroom was beneath her queen-sized bed. The bedspread, either left over from the Peter Max era or purchased from an overpriced retro shop, was a garish mix of pop art flowers. The floor beneath the bed was clear with the exception of one sneaker, a single sandal, and a pair of navy knees socks that were balled up and dusty.

The nightstand had one narrow drawer that was empty except for some Kleenex, a pen, and a Timex wristwatch. P.J. sighed. She had left the most obvious place one might stash a doll from prying eyes for last: the closet.

Trendy tops and tiny skirts were interspersed with ratty jeans, over-sized shirts, and conservative dresses. The closet floor was scattered liberally with shoes. P.J. compulsively paired the shoes and lined them up beneath the hanging clothes. When she was done, she counted twenty-two pairs and two odd ones, a considerable number of shoes for a recent high school graduate with a crappy job.

Returning to the bed, P.J. reached underneath and retrieved the sneaker and sandal. She took them to the closet and placed them with the odd ones, bringing the total up to twenty-four pairs. Now they lined up perfectly in two rows of twelve.

The high closet shelf was packed with bulky sweaters. P.J. knocked them all to the floor, hoping to jar a hidden doll loose from a chunky cable or a double-knit cardigan.

Nothing. The AG dressed in Senior Prom was not in Jordanne's apartment.

P.J. closed her eyes. The young woman either had the doll with her or had given it to someone for safekeeping.

She would have to confront Jordanne in person.

55

After Brian picked up Chaz that night, Caresse decided to put on flannel jammies and spend some time on the computer. She hadn't visited the Best Barbie Board or surfed in more than forty-eight hours, which had to be some kind of personal record.

Armed with a cup of coffee, she had the packet of photos Monya had given her at the *County Times* as well as the photos Anjo had given her from the Walnut Creek

PD handy. She pulled the notes she'd reviewed at Taco Bell out of her purse and laid them alongside the latest *Barbie International*, fully prepared to do some ruminating before she hit the sack. She faced the screen and realized something was missing. Ah, music!

With the radio on, the night was perfect. After logging in at Gmail, she deleted a personal horoscope email for Capricorns, a Hallmark e-card notification from Hoops & YoYo, Urban Dictionary's word of the day (grandboss), and a notice about Jo-Ann Stores' Final Two Days! Moonlight Madness Sale. She was about to read an email from her brother Craig with the subject line *"What? I was really sure you'd call back!"* when she was IMed by Sierra Walsh.

SW: Haven't heard from you. How'd the interview go?

Caresse was glad she was online. She had a lot to share.

CR: Gonna be a kick-ass feature. Forget the mod. That's just the tip of the iceberg. Vala's got Sorbonne, TantCaresse Pois, Atelier Fest, Ganz Festlich, Kindergeburtstag, Sonntagskleid, Huebsch Und Praktisch, and a huge array of Bild Lilli dolls...

Caresse paused and decided to hit "send." She'd already given Sierra a lot to digest.

SW: Wow!

CR: No guarantees the spellings are correct off the top of my head ;-)

SW: LOL!

CR: Her husband wants her to sell everything, so the article will run to promote the fact she's going to auction everything off in early May.

SW: Damn!

Caresse took a deep breath. She was ready to spill the big beans.

CR: I don't think she'll be selling her prototype accessories, though.

Sierra's reply came in less than a heartbeat.

SW: Prototype accessories?

Caresse smiled. Sierra was going to faint when she told her what she'd seen.

CR: She's got prototype versions of the car keys to Ken's Rally Day, the fish belonging to Picnic Set, the scissors to Sweater Girl, the hot water bottle for Registered Nurse, the snake bracelet to Commuter Set, and the charm bracelet to Resort Set. There are a few more, but I can't picture them off the top of my head. She let me take photos, but I don't think the photos of her prototypes are for publication.

SW: Ooh, share, share!

CR: That's not all. She got thirty compacts from a trial batch Mattel ran before producing Roman Holiday. Mattel engraved all three of Barbie's initials on them before deciding they were nearly indecipherable. She keeps those on a necklace. The one on her bracelet is even more special. Inside, it has a real mirror, and it's engraved XO, KC underneath the powder puff.

The IM window was blank for a full minute after Caresse hit send. She pictured Sierra on the floor of her office, in need of smelling salts.

Finally, she got a response.

SW: Got pictures to share of the compacts?

CR: You bet, but she doesn't want them in the feature. I don't think she's told too many peo-

ple about them. I mean, aside from friends and acquaintances. Which could be kind of a lot of people, but not the whole subscriber list to *BI*.

SW: That's a bummer. Readers would love to see that stuff.

CR: Well, we've got enough cool stuff for pix. And I can describe the accessory prototypes in text, so not to worry.

SW: Okay, thanks. Email your story with the pix you want to use when you're done.

CR: Will do. I aim to have it done in less than two weeks.

SW: Okay, well, when you're ready, I'm all eyes 8-)

Caresse smiled.

CR: Okay, CU.

The IM box blinked out, and Caresse was looking once again at her regular Gmail in-box. Craig's email, *"What? I was really sure you'd call back!"* warranted a look.

She opened his note.

Caresse, whatcha been up to? All is well here. Busy, busy. San Diego is beautiful, as always. Carol wants to take a trip this summer up the coast, maybe all the way up to Washington State (where her folks are). Would have to drop in on Cami and see how she's doing, but first, the motorhome needs a few things done to it before we embark on a thousand-plus mile trip. Cherry says hi, says you don't keep in touch. What else can we pick on you about? Oh, Mom and Dad said please call or they are threatening to visit one of these days.

She leaned back in her chair and smiled. Whenever she got her parents on the phone, her mom would be on one receiver at their home in Bethany and her dad on the other, but her dad never got a chance to say boo. Her mom was the official chatterbox, a former Chi Omega gal, president of her sorority in college, born to socialize. Basically, all Caresse had to do was listen, but making the call in the first place drove her to distraction.

Anyway, did you catch the *Dateline: Crime* about the Barbie doll theft and murders? Write when you get a chance so I know you're okay. Love, Craig

She hit reply. In the background, Nickelback was claiming a hero could save us.

Dear Craig, Sorry to be elusive, but what else is new? I have not seen the *Dateline: Crime* episode about Vegas yet, but my friend Anjo is loaning me the tape. She records all the heavy-duty true crime stuff. On that note, however, you mentioned meeting a Barbie collector named Devvon West on the Greyhound to Vegas. Turns out that a woman using I.D. in the name of Devvon West, with an untraceable downtown L.A. address, rented an Altima from Enterprise in Oswego, New York, the same day Gayle Grace and her husband were murdered, and her doll collection at home was pillaged. You said Devvon was blond and pretty (I think) on your voicemail. Anything else to add to that in light of this little "co-inky-dink"?

I think a trip up north to see Cami would be awesome. I should drop her a line. Strangely enough, she lives kinda near where another Barbie doll theft/murder took place. This has gotten way past creepy. Everyone, hide your dolls! Aah! ;-) Love you, Caresse

She closed out of Gmail and Googled "Dateline Crime Vegas Sketch." Three choices popped up. She went to the Las Vegas Now crime blotter blog, which offered a two by three inch reproduction of the penciled police sketch of the woman seen outside Zivia's home the night of the murders. She right-click/copied it as a jpg and wallpapered her desktop with it. In the background, Michael Bublé might have been surrounded by a million people but he still felt all alone.

The woman in the hooded sweatshirt looked vaguely familiar. Her hair had been sketched to suggest fair shading, and her eyes seemed dark, possibly hazel or brown. The shape of her mouth and possibly her nose gave her the idea she'd seen this woman, or someone similar, in the past.

She reached for her copy of *Barbie International* and flipped to the section that showed postage-stamp-sized head shots of the staff. Ruling out the guys who wrote regularly for the magazine, she focused on female staff writers. Strangely enough, all of the women had dark hair, so she ruled out all six and moved on to the in-house staff that controlled matters from the magazine's headquarters, including Sierra.

Sierra herself looked a little like the sketch, but her eyes were blue and her nose wasn't quite as pinched as the sketch suggested.

Caresse laughed out loud. The concept that the managing editor of *Barbie International* was committing homicides was ludicrous. She had heard Sierra got every doll she wanted and was constantly acquiring more. Yes, she could be a control freak, but wasn't that typical of bosses with stressful business demands?

In the background, Edwin McCain was singing about the gallows of heartache that hang from above. She looked at Katia, who handled distribution, and dismissed her upon noting her highlighted dark brown hair and sepia eyes. Sharidan was African-American and Kumi was Japanese, so she scratched them off the list next. Nona was a chubby redhead and Tess was dishwater blond with full cheeks, so they were crossed off as well. Lilani had light brown hair and a prominent overbite, so she was out. The rest were dismissed for other reasons, including a hooked nose, super curly hair, jug ears, and middle age. Among the *Barbie International* staffers, Sierra was the closest thing to a match with the sketch, so Caresse considered her match-the-face attempt a bust.

The Las Vegas Now blog dated March 2008 was still open on her screen, so she read the entry titled "No Beef With Lil Beef" while the band members of Seether were taking the light and undarkening everything around them.

Police say mitochondrial DNA evidence has now possibly linked the Vegas Barbie double homicide to another homicide earlier this year in Tucson, Arizona.

FBI investigator Vance Jacobi said, "While examinations can associate a hair to a person on the basis of microscopic characteristics, absolute personal identification cannot be ascertained. Nevertheless, due to similarities between the Tucson and Las Vegas murders—not regarding the MO but insofar as Barbie dolls were taken in bulk on both occasions—investigators consider this a meaningful break. The similarity between strands of blond hair found at both scenes is significant."

The composite sketch of the suspected Vegas killer was released for the first time last month when *Dateline: Crime* aired the story. Based on a

sighting by friends of the late Rick Uzamba, who had come to visit the bodyguard at his $8.5 million palatial estate, it was first assumed that the eyewitnesses, both roadies for Lil Beef, were offering up the idea of a mysterious blond woman holding duffel bags and standing at the foot of Uzamba's driveway as a red herring to cover animosity between Lil Beef and various rival hip-hop/rap artists such as Run DMC, Public Enemy, 2 Pac, Eric B. & Rakim, Jay Z, N.W.A., Notorious B.I.G., and LL Cool J.

Lil Beef has long been prominent on the hip-hop scene, receiving publicity at every turn for gimmicks including subsisting entirely on meat, labeling themselves "anti-vegetarians."

Uzamba was under house arrest at the time of his murder due to prosecution by federal authorities who charged him with possession of six unregistered machine guns. He was due to be released shortly before the third annual BET Hip-Hop Awards scheduled October 23, 2008.

Caresse closed the blog and thought for a moment. The killer had used different methods each time but hadn't used a gun until she went to Walnut Creek—after the murders in Vegas. If Rick kept guns, could she have picked one up while she was getting the dolls?

She reached for her Taco Bell notes and added "gun from Vegas?" under her scribbles about Nancy Roth.

Thinking about Nancy, she reached for the envelope of photos the Walnut Creek PD had supplied. She took a sip of coffee and leaned back in her chair, steeling herself for a reprise of the black and white carnage while Uncle Kracker was singing about how he'd lost what he'd found, but it would all turn around. She spread out the shots of Nancy's doll room and grabbed her issue of *Barbie International*, opening it to the feature on Nancy. Next, she opened the folder on her hard drive that contained all the pictures Ward had taken of his wife's collection.

Going left to right in each shot, she moved pictures from the NANCY folder to a new folder she'd created, which she'd named NOT_TAKEN. By the time an hour had passed, she was left with pictures in the NANCY folder of items that were missing.

She listened to Maroon 5 sing about a beauty queen of only eighteen as she studied what the killer had taken. Mattel wallets; Ponytail pencil cases; small Tutti Play Cases; a Tutti suitcase; a Swing-A-Ling Tutti Round Train Case; an assortment of NRFB Tutti and Todd sets including Sundae Treat; deboxed Tutti, Carla, Chris, Todd, Buffy and Mrs. Beasley, Lori and Rori, Angie and Tangie, Fran and Nan dolls; three different Barbie and Midge Travel Pals; and a lunch kit were absent from Nancy's shelves. The killer had selected smaller, choice items that, when gathered together, could be moved in one trip. She had obviously learned from her experience in Vegas not to take more than she could carry in a single haul. None of the items jumped out at her; they were all items any hard-core vinyl collector or Tutti fan would want. Nevertheless, Caresse now had a list of missing items for the Walnut Creek PD.

She stood up, straightened her twisted flannel pajama bottoms, and headed to the coffeemaker to refill her mug. She was finding excuses not to look at the more graphic photos in the packet, but she couldn't stall forever. Rushing through the photos of Nancy face down in the carpet and the close-ups of her wounds, she flipped to the shot of the shattered chair that had been pushed away from the computer desk. If Nancy had been seated at her computer when the first shots were fired, it would explain why the chair had been reduced to kindling.

It wouldn't explain, however, why Nancy's computer monitor was lying on its side on the kitchen floor several feet from the desk and the Princeton flat screen had been hurled as far as its cord could take it without becoming unplugged from the power strip. It also wouldn't explain why the computer tower had been decimated at close range.

She flashed on an old movie she couldn't name, where the main character didn't like what he was seeing on TV, so he pulled out a gun and blasted the screen to smithereens.

You would only shoot or throw a TV or monitor if you didn't like what you were seeing or reading, she thought. *You would only decimate a computer due to online angst.*

Nancy was a big fan of the Best Barbie Board, and she would logically log in to read messages and post her thoughts while at home.

Could the killer know her from the Best Barbie Board?

She opened Internet Explorer and logged in at the BBB. Doing a search for any threads containing Nancy's name called up discussions about her murder, but that wasn't what she was searching for at this point. She needed to take a look at the victim herself. Nancy's user name was NANCY_PANTS, so Caresse did a search for all of her posts from the most recent to those dating back as far as the archives would take her.

At four fifty-six p.m. on Saturday, February 9, Nancy had posted a message.

NANCY_PANTS: Hey, guys, I forgot to tell you something. Remember when P.J. and I had

that run-in about the Tutti train case? I know it was a long time ago, so a lot of you probably won't remember it, but I still do! Turns out I didn't send it to her! I still have it! Think she will forgive me if I send it to her now? Gulp! LOL!

Huh. At four fifty-six, Nancy was supposedly dead, so why would this post be showing up after the fact? Was P.J. the lead Caresse had been seeking? The "run-in" mentioned was something to pursue. She did a search for the phrase "train case" and struck gold with a patch of notes dating back to April 2007.

PJ-RULEZ: Just wanted everyone to know that NANCY ROTH is a liar and a thief! I PayPaled her for a Swing-A-Ling Tutti Round Train Case on March 15th and have NOT received it! I HAVE FILED for my MONEY BACK from PayPal but Nancy provided delivery confirmation to PayPal so I HAVE NOT BEEN reimbursed! Nancy DID send something, but it was a box filled with CARDBOARD and NEWSPAPER and STYROFOAM!

NANCY_PANTS: P.J., I never agreed to sell you my Swing-A-Ling Tutti train case, so I don't know what you're talking about.

PJ-RULEZ: No, I just suppose you listed it on eBay for shits and giggles, and when I won it, you had seller's remorse and changed your mind about parting with it. I don't know what it means when you "sell" something and send someone an empty box instead, but I call it theft.

NANCY_PANTS: You're a liar, P.J. Ask anyone here on the board if I've ever sent them an empty box. As if!

Memories of P.J. were vague. All Caresse knew about her was that she was a frequent poster who generally argued with everyone and criticized what many said and did. She checked her BBB profile, but it was devoid of data and photos, and her avatar was simply an orange frowny-face emoticon set against black. Her email address was not on file, and the only way to contact her was through the board.

While Tim McGraw was singing about dancing with the marionette, Caresse did a search for all of PJ-RULEZ' postings from the most recent to those dating back as far as the archives would take her. Her last notes, written January 5, involved a heated debate between herself and—holy Ken and Skipper—the late Gayle Grace.

GRACEFUL: P.J., thanks for posting the picture of your AG dressed in the Debutante Ball gown you won, but I think it has a replacement rosebud on it. Notice how it is off by just a shade? I mean, it was well-crafted and everything, don't get me wrong, and would pass inspection for all but the most discerning eye, but I really think the bud was replaced.

PJ-RULEZ: Hi, Gayle. Thanks for your comments, but you can take your "discerning eye" and shove it. I have the gown right here in front of me (you don't) and I know what I have, and the rosebud has NOT been replaced.

After that, P.J. was silent.

Keeping a low profile.

Now things were beginning to come together.

A thrill ran through her body. She needed the police to find out who P.J. was. There would be records at eBay and PayPal, including her home address.

She wasn't going to call Rowell and Carter, but she had to send them her audio cassette from KVEC anyway, so she had the novel idea of making a second cassette for them outlining what she had discovered. She retrieved the micro-cassette recorder from her desk drawer, popped in a fresh tape, sat back in her chair, and rambled for a good fifteen minutes. Then she ejected the tape, put it back in its tiny translucent case, and placed it alongside her KVEC interview tape.

Next, she wrote a short, friendly note on a piece of blank typing paper in blue ballpoint. She pulled out her wallet and retrieved the business card Rowell had given her. Grabbing a padded envelope from her bottom desk drawer, she slid both cassettes inside the mailer with her handwritten note.

The bigger tape is the interview I did at KVEC, which I promised I'd send along. The smaller tape contains some theories I've come up with. In other words, I think I have a lead on a potential suspect, but I would need you to agree enough to want to access some records if you think I'm onto something.

She smiled. The note was understated, as she'd wanted it to be. No amateur sleuth's over-the-top proclamations, exclaiming, "By gosh, I think I've got her!"

She signed it, **Best Regards, Caresse Redd.**

56

P.J had never been angrier.

She waited down the block from Jordanne's apartment Tuesday night, but Jordanne never arrived. At eleven p.m., she drove to Darby's apartment and saw Jordanne's beat-up Mustang parked on the street out front. So that was it, then. A stalemate.

As if Darby sensed his half-sister's presence, he appeared at his window, scanned the street, and spotted her. "Damn it! She's relentless!" He turned to look at Jordanne, who was resting on the aging brown couch. She was bundled in a plaid blanket and had a Care Bears pillow beneath her head. Darby ran his fingers through his hair and sat down in the overstuffed brown chair across from the couch. He was filled with love for his baby angel. He wanted to be with her. He wanted to care for her. He wanted to protect her.

"That was your sister?" Jordanne stared at him dully. The ordeal of being on P.J.'s bad side was taking its toll. "She's never gonna leave me alone."

"Then you should just move in with me," Darby suggested, temporarily brightening.

Jordanne's sour expression told him not to press it. "Darby, if we move in together, it shouldn't be because I'm hiding from your lunatic sister."

"Half-sister," Darby corrected her. "Our mother is sane. She's the one with a crazy father. Took off and never let anyone know where he went."

A tear slid down Jordanne's cheek and, embarrassed, she twisted in the blanket so she could bury her face in the pillow.

Darby got up and went over to the couch. He knelt down beside it and rested his head against her ribcage, listening to her heart.

"I love you, Jordanne," he said.

He heard a sharp intake of breath, and then the floodgates opened.

Darby knew that when it came to women, there was good crying and there was bad crying. He just didn't know which this was.

He got up, lit a cigarette, and paced.

He walked over to the window again and saw that P.J. had left.

He squinted at the moon, fat and glowering in the night sky. The moon blurred in his vision. Like Jordanne, he began to cry, but silently, wiping his eyes as soon as fresh tears leaked out.

You gotta go, P.J. Even if I've gotta make that happen.

57

Caresse got a call at the *County Times* from Rowell at four p.m. Friday, March 7.

"Let me ask you something," he began, without preface.

Her hand trembled like a leaf on the receiver. She held up her index finger to Anthony, who had come over to her desk to talk. She knew he was at odds with the trio of brats Jenna had left in his custody and that he was ready to give them their walking papers. She had overheard whispers all week that the fat needed to be cut from the budget and that they were candidates for trimming. Anthony stood there a moment, sipping coffee from his mug, grinning. He was wearing a dark purple shirt teamed with a perfectly matched plum and avocado patterned tie. She didn't know him very well yet, but he'd had her at Forzieri.

"Wha—what?" she asked Rowell. "I mean, sure, go ahead."

Rowell chuckled, deep and low. "How easy do you think it is for us to find a micro-cassette recorder in Walnut Creek?"

"Ve—ver—very hard?" She had wasted their time. She had sent them a tape they didn't have a recorder for, and they would have had to have found one in order to hear it. *And then, if they did, they probably thought what I had to say made no sense at all*, she thought.

Anthony motioned to her, still grinning like a cat eating crabmeat. He nodded, mouthed the word "later," and then raised his pinkie and thumb toward his ear in the universal "call me" gesture.

She nodded, waiting for Rowell to speak.

"It took a day, but we found one at Radio Shack."

So they *had* listened to the tape. "Listen," she began to apologize. "It was late. I was up and—"

"You're a brilliant woman," Rowell said.

The phone slipped a bit in her sweaty palm.

"I'm—"

"We got your letter on Wednesday and by this morning, after we worked with PayPal and eBay, everything was solid. You know her, by the way."

"Know who?"

"Someone who looks like a very promising suspect. Sierra Walsh."

Caresse was not only sweating, she was confused. "I thought the woman causing all the trouble on the Best Barbie Board was named P.J."

"That's Sierra's nickname. We called the number provided by eBay and one of Sierra's staff members at *Barbie International* answered. When she repeated, 'P.J.? I don't think we have a P.J. here,' Sierra took the phone from her and said, 'This is P.J.' Apparently it's a nickname only her immediate family uses, and she thought she was taking a call from someone close."

"She doesn't look exactly like the police sketch," Caresse said. "I mean, she's got the blond hair and everything, but—" The room started to tilt and she sat down hard.

"Close enough to question her and find out where she's been during the times of the murders. We've contacted the FBI and they're letting us do the honors of securing a hair sample. There's enough for probable cause, thanks to you. She should have known better than to write that note from Nancy's house. Oh, and guess what she drives?"

Caresse didn't know.

"A white four-speed Miata roadster."

"The same car Nancy's neighbor saw a redhead get into."

"The neighbor had additional details when we called him again yesterday. He mentioned she was carrying heavy bags that looked like Army duffels. He imagined maybe she was from out of town, visiting someone, and that it was just her luggage. But it struck him as strange that such a good-looking woman would be lugging Army gear."

Army duffels were missing from the Uzamba home in Vegas. "Wow."

"I know, huh? So we're gonna go talk to her on Monday, first thing."

"Wow," Caresse repeated, starting to feel foolish about her speechlessness.

"So that's it," Rowell said. "We'll let you know how it goes."

"Okay, thanks." She was stunned. She needed to process.

"Good work," he reiterated. "Oh, and by the way—"

"Yes?"

"You give a kick-ass interview on the radio. I'm gonna go get me a collector Barbie if all of this pans out."

58

It was Saturday, Heath was in Beijing, and P.J. was itching to move the Rubbermaid stacks from the garage into her exercise room. She longed to be alone in the house with her dolls, spreading them out on the carpet with room enough to see them all at once. It would be a magnificent assembly of goddesses, certain to lessen the sting of Darby's betrayal.

After breakfast, she told her maid Vicky, her personal assistant Wendy, and her weekend chef Michel that she had decided to surprise them with paid time off.

Delighted, Vicky parked the vacuum cleaner in the closet and gave P.J. a hearty hug. Michel asked if he needed to finish scrubbing the pans first, and P.J. told him no. Wendy threw her Day Planner, BlackBerry, and Kindle into her large bag, issued a terse, "Okay, see you next week," and hurried out before P.J. could change her mind.

P.J. sighed, went upstairs, and changed into denim shorts and a plain pink tee. She tied her hair back with a pink bandanna and slid on a pair of white Keds. She was going to work up a sweat, so she didn't want to overdress.

Once in the garage, she surveyed her storage bins. The stacked cubes with translucent drawers took the entire middle area meant for a third car. They were lined up in rows, positioned between her Miata and Heath's 1967 red Sunbeam Alpine. P.J. never drove Heath's car, and he never drove it to LAX or the Burbank Airport, preferring to take the shuttle or a cab there and back from his constant trips.

The concrete floor in P.J.'s garage was freshly swept, and sunlight poured in through the open garage door. There was no other way into the garage save for the way the cars entered. This was one drawback P.J. resented, because it meant she would have to carry the storage bins out through the front, around the corner, up the path, and into the house.

Carrying each set of drawers into the house and returning to the garage took ten minutes per trip. When she was done with eight rounds, she opened the driver's side of the Miata and sat on the edge of the seat.

I need something to drink, she realized, getting up and slamming the car door.

She grabbed one more set of drawers and went into the house just as Darby arrived and parked around the corner. Heading across the street to a fenced yard, he ducked behind a gnarled tree and looked toward P.J.'s home. Both the Sunbeam and the Miata were parked in the open garage, which meant Heath was out of town and P.J. was home. Knowing that she would never be gone long with her dolls in plain sight, he gathered she was moving them into the house. Quickly, he dashed across the street and into the open garage. The garage door opener lay on a shelf near the garbage cans, next to the Sunbeam. He grabbed it and darted back across the street, returning to his post behind the tree.

P.J. came down the path from the house, sipping a glass of iced lemonade. She was dressed for the chore of moving storage bins, and Darby knew he couldn't have picked a better time or place. Her assistant, chef, and maid would have parked on the street in front of the house, but their cars were gone. Darby intuited she had let them go home so she could move her dolls into the house without being questioned.

He waited for her to lift a storage bin and stand up before he stepped out from behind the tree and clicked the garage door opener.

Before she could react, the garage door descended.

P.J. was trapped inside.

59

Caresse regretted she hadn't found time to talk to Anthony before he left work for the day. She had seen Nibbles, Bree, and Rhea packing up their desks, so she knew big changes were at hand, but when she tried to talk to the trio, Nibbles gave her the finger and Rhea told her to fuck off.

Her mind wandered to Monya and how she'd told her that her sister Annie had started a Barbie magazine before Sierra had. If Sierra was the killer and she was taken out of the picture, Annie might consider filling the void left by Sierra's absence by getting back into the Barbie magazine scene. At the very least, she might take malicious delight in the fact that the woman who had trumped her in business so long ago was headed for a fall.

60

P.J. stood in the dark garage, holding the set of storage drawers in her chilly hands.

She didn't understand why the garage door had closed by itself. Had it malfunctioned? She put down the storage unit and stepped sideways, sending her glass of lemonade crashing from where she'd set it.

"Damn it!"

Slowly, she picked her way through the shadows, up to the front of the garage where the opener would be. She felt around on the shelf. It was bare.

She had a garage door opener on her key chain, but she'd left her keys on the kitchen counter, next to the juicer and nine squeezed lemons.

Kneeling down on the cold concrete, she searched the floor beneath the shelf. Nothing.

She moved the garbage cans and searched behind them.

The flap-style lids on the garbage cans were snapped shut, but she lifted the lids anyway and searched through the trash to see if the opener might be there.

Dumbfounded, she sat down on the garage floor.

Darby.

Across the street, Darby waited ten minutes, listening to the quiet neighborhood. The birds weren't singing. No dogs barked. The children all played elsewhere.

Nice to live in an exclusive neighborhood where the homes are an acre apart, Darby thought as he walked back to his car. *There's no one to bother you in your own precious, perfect world. But no one sticking his or her nose in your business might be a bad thing at this particular moment for one deeply troubled blond.*

He had it all worked out.

Since P.J. relied on him for computer assistance, he had access to all her log-ins and passwords. He had contact information for everyone she worked with, everyone she knew. He would call everyone scheduled to see P.J. in the coming days and relay the message that she had decided to go out of town and that they would not be needed in the coming days. She would get in touch when she returned.

Darby would also check to see how long Heath would be gone. It was not uncommon for him to be away for weeks at a time. With the staff out of the way as well, there would be no one to check on P.J.

No one would worry about her.

She had a glass of lemonade, so that would hold her for a day or two. But if a week to ten days passed and no one came to rescue her, she would expire from lack of food and water.

And he would be free.

61

On Monday at eight-ten a.m., the newsroom was empty. A note on Caresse's desk told her to come to the cafeteria for a staff meeting. She headed down the hallway, through the kitchen where everyone made their coffee, and into the cafeteria, where the staff had assembled.

Everyone she worked with every day was there, with the exception of Bree, Rhea, and Nibbles. Jenna's successor Anthony Price stood near the glass wall that overlooked the patio. Seth and Anjo sat at a lunchroom table in the center of the room. Marilyn from Classified sat beside Lobby Laura and Pressroom Skip at a table in the far right corner of the room. Managing editor Jeff sat alone, in back.

It seemed Caresse was late or at least the last one there. Ducking her head slightly, she made her way to Marilyn's table.

Seth stood up and moved to the window. He stood next to Anthony. His round-lensed glasses picked up reflections from the patio, which sparkled in the almost-springtime sunlight.

"Glad you all could make it," Seth said dryly.

Everyone turned in Caresse's direction and laughed.

"This meeting is being held to issue one award, one announcement, and two interoffice promotions. So we'll start with the award."

He cleared his throat and shuffled his feet. "The best feature award for February goes to someone who seldom gets the opportunity to express herself. Her days are typically spent dealing with funeral directors, brides-to-be, event planners, and church officials. She answers the phone—even though she hates to—" Seth paused and got the laugh he expected. "And she takes care of all of us, every day. Luckily for us, she also just happened to write the best online dating story this newspaper has ever printed. By now I imagine you all know I'm talking about Caresse, so without further ado, the best feature award for February for her Personal Ads Dating story in the Valentine's weekend supplement goes to Ms. Redd. Caresse, come on up."

She stood up and headed toward the windowed wall, where Seth gave her a quick handshake. Outdoing him, Anthony stepped forward and embraced her, refusing to let go, causing the room to erupt into gales of laughter. Finally, Anthony released her and they stood together, side by side, waiting for order to be restored.

Seth pulled an envelope from his suit pocket and handed it to her. She knew what it was—a check for $100, the standard compensation for best feature of the month. She thanked him and began to head back to her seat, but Anthony stopped her.

"If you could stay up here for a moment," he said, "And Marilyn, if you could come up and join us."

Marilyn looked flustered. She hadn't expected to be called upon. She rose and made her way up front to stand beside Caresse, impulsively grabbing her hand and not letting go.

"Marilyn, you've been doing such a great job in Classified, and we know you have your degree in English, which we think could be put to better use. We think you'd be having a lot more fun if you actually got a chance to write obituaries and datebook items, so we're moving you into Caresse's position."

The color in Marilyn's face rose and her smile grew as wide as Seth's outdated tie.

Anthony stepped forward a pace. "For those who don't know, we've been asked to trim the fat around here, so I let my staff go Friday—for good."

People throughout the cafeteria were nodding. There weren't many who would miss Nibbles and her gal pals.

"So that leaves me in need of someone to help me put together the entertainment supplement every week, and my choice for that is Ms. Redd."

Caresse gasped, and Anthony enveloped her in another hug. This time he released her, but he kept his arm around her shoulder as he continued. "I've been told she's been doing the work of three people around here anyway, so it looks like I've got an instant replacement for the three dearly departed ladies. And, my dear, Anjo has something to present to you, since we'll need to be in touch constantly."

A trickle of cold raced down Caresse's spine. She reminded herself that while surprises weren't always good, they weren't always bad, either. Anjo stood up, grinning, and approached her with a small, wrapped box. Typically the bearer of small gifts for Chaz, she unwrapped it, expecting to find a set of Legos.

It wasn't. It was a sleek black cell phone of her very own.

"We expect you never to turn it off and always answer it," Anthony warned. "In fact, your first assignment is to call every single person in the newsroom and give them your cell phone number. If your call goes to voicemail, you'll need to leave a message that you called and that you want them to call you back. I'll be getting reports from everyone to find out how it's going."

Everyone laughed. Caresse's phone avoidance was legendary.

"Thank you, all," she said. "I don't know what to say."

But she did know what she wanted to say. In fact, she knew what she wanted to scream. *I may have solved the Barbie murders! I may have played an instrumental role in the capture of one of FBI's most wanted!*

It was the biggest story ever, the story of a lifetime.

Going on dates for the newspaper and writing a story about it paled by comparison.

No story ever, anywhere, would eclipse her love for Barbie or anything connected with the doll, and if she had helped solve the most notorious case ever connected to Barbie, she would feel endlessly satisfied.

62

Ince Rowell and his sidekick August Carter arrived at P.J.'s home bright and early Monday morning.

P.J. had fallen asleep in the driver's seat of her Miata, but when she heard them, she scrambled out of the car and made her way to the garage door. She raised her fists and was ready to pound on the galvanized steel when she heard indistinct chatter filtering over a police radio. Lowering her arms, she listened.

Rowell came up to the garage door and bent down. He tried to lift the door, giving it two swift tugs. P.J. jumped away from it as though she had been scalded.

"Locked tight," she heard him say.

The men walked up the path toward the home, only to find the front door wide open and the screen door slightly ajar. Chao, who had been in the backyard since Saturday, began to bark.

"It's open," Carter said, smoothing back his blond hair and straightening his collar.

The detectives went inside.

Locked inside the garage, P.J. began to pace the aisle between the Miata and the remaining storage bins. The broken shards from her glass of lemonade had been kicked out of the way, beneath her car. In a desperate attempt to have something to drink, she had fumbled around on the garage floor until she found a few melting ice cubes no bigger than croutons. Blowing on them in case they were tainted with dirt or glass, she popped them in her mouth and savored them. Faster than LifeSavers, they melted into slivers and were gone.

It was Sunday, March 9, forty-nine years to the day Barbie doll was launched at the International Toy Fair. On a day typically spent celebrating by rearranging her dolls, P.J. spent interminable hours trying to cope with being locked in the dark, alone.

She felt around in the remaining storage bins, trying to identify her dolls and their outfits by touch. In the dimness of the garage, she could almost make out if they were blonds or brunettes. She could almost discern what they were wearing. Then she dropped one of their shoes and quit, frustrated by how long it might take to find it.

When Rowell and Carter came out of the house, they sounded excited. With their search warrant, they had it all: computer files, paperwork, dolls, hair samples, receipts, the white vinyl boots, the red wig, Dormicum tablets and vials, the Makarov pistol, empty Army duffel bags, and the customized bling that had belonged to Rick Uzamba.

"You got that bin, Carter?" Rowell asked.

P.J. heard the man referred to as Carter shuffle around a bit. She heard the bin hit the driveway, and she shuddered.

"I think we've got enough," Carter said.

"More than enough," Rowell said, "To have her put away for life."

"I wonder where she is?" Carter asked.

Rowell shrugged. "I don't know," he said, "but she can't hide forever."